PRONOUNCED PONCE

THE MIDTOWN MURDERS

RAY DAN PARKER

Black Rose Writing | Texas

©2020 by Ray Dan Parker
All rights reserved. No part of this book may be reproduced, stored in a retrieval system or transmitted in any form or by any means without the prior written permission of the publishers, except by a reviewer who may quote brief passages in a review to be printed in a newspaper, magazine or journal.

The author grants the final approval for this literary material.

First printing

This is a work of fiction. Names, characters, businesses, places, events, and incidents are either the products of the author's imagination or used in a fictitious manner. Any resemblance to actual persons, living or dead, or actual events is purely coincidental.

ISBN: 978-1-68433-585-5
PUBLISHED BY BLACK ROSE WRITING
www.blackrosewriting.com

Printed in the United States of America
Suggested Retail Price (SRP) $18.95

Pronounced Ponce is printed in Calluna

*As a planet-friendly publisher, Black Rose Writing does its best to eliminate unnecessary waste to reduce paper usage and energy costs, while never compromising the reading experience. As a result, the final word count vs. page count may not meet common expectations.

DEDICATION

From 1979 to 1981 *someone* murdered thirty of Atlanta's children and young adults. Some were male, some were female. All were African American. After many months, national media outlets noticed what became known as the Atlanta Child Murders.

On June 21, 1981, police arrested Wayne Williams for just two of those murders. To date, the rest remain unsolved. Their investigations remained closed until March 2019 when Atlanta Mayor Keisha Lance Bottoms ordered them reopened. To date, there have been no further arrests.

No one will ever know the impact these young people may have had on the world. They deserve to be remembered. To them I dedicate this book:

Edward Smith – 14
Milton Harvey – 14
Angel Lenair – 12
Eric Middlebrooks – 14
Latonya Wilson – 7
Anthony Carter – 9
Clifford Jones – 13
Charles Stephens – 12
Patrick Rogers – 16
Terry Pue – 15
Curtis Walker – 15
Timothy Hill – 13
Eddie Duncan – 21
Michael McIntosh – 20
John Porter – 28

Alfred Evans – 13
Yusef Bell – 9
Jeffrey Mathis – 10
Chris Richardson – 12
Aaron Wyche – 10
Earl Terrell – 11
Darron Glass – 10
Aaron Jackson – 9
Lubie Geter – 14
Patrick Baltazar – 11
Joseph Bell – 15
William Barrett – 17
Larry Rogers – 20
Jimmy Ray Payne – 21
Nathaniel Cater – 27

ACKNOWLEDGEMENTS

I would like to thank Jim McGaughy for his kind suggestions; Cole A. Scudder, retired Master Patrol Officer, Tampa Police Department, for his technical advice; and fellow authors Will Ottinger, Jerry Weiner, Julie Harper, David Kruglinski, and Mel Coe for their assistance in the editing process.

*To Jeff & Francy
Best wishes.
— Ray Van Parker*

PRONOUNCED PONCE

THE MIDTOWN MURDERS

To Jeff + Irene
Best wishes.
— John the Baker

CHAPTER 1
ALLISON EMBRY

Peachtree City, Georgia
Monday, August 6

Allison Embry sipped her coffee and gazed out the kitchen window at her well-tended garden. From the vase beside her wafted the fragrance of roses she'd cut just that morning. Early as it was, a neighbor was already mowing his lawn.

Allison would never get used to the new school calendar. It was barely August, and classes had already begun. The morning was bright and clear in the Peachtree City neighborhood of Orchard Springs and the temperature still mild from the rain that passed through overnight. That would change as soon as the sun rose above the trees.

Neither of Allison's children, Kyle nor Leslie, seemed to notice all this beauty as they grabbed their books. They were almost out the door when Allison yelled to them to remember their sack lunches. Leslie rolled her eyes. She was in the ninth grade now, a member of the freshman cheerleading squad, and none of her friends brought lunches anymore. Only losers brown bagged.

Leslie's eighteen-year-old brother picked his up without a word. It would be gone, Allison knew, long before the lunch hour arrived. Kyle would simply bum money from one of the pretty cheerleaders who were only too glad for the attention of the Starr's Mill High School quarterback.

Allison watched her children with pride as they hopped into Kyle's Jeep and backed down the driveway. Her husband, Rob, pecked her on the cheek on his way to the garage and his new white Lexus. She smiled and waved, though by now he no longer saw her. Rob had said he was leaving for work. He lied

Decked out in his pilot's uniform, Rob was every woman's dream. Allison figured it would take Wendy Miller about fifteen seconds to get him out of that uniform and into her bed. In her mind, Allison pictured the beautiful young ex-flight attendant sitting astride Rob in the full, upright, and locked position.

The mere thought of Rob and Wendy together enraged Allison. Wendy Miller could put on all the airs she wanted. She'd never be anything but cleaned-up trailer trash. She had managed to hook herself an aging, but successful, airline pilot and now she was looking for an upgrade.

Allison had known of their affair for months. So, it came as no surprise, last night, when Rob took a call in the middle of a wonderful supper she'd prepared. He had to fill in for another pilot who'd called in sick. Just to be sure, Allison contacted a friend who worked in the Delta office downtown, only to discover that it was, in fact, Lon Miller, Wendy's husband, who would be piloting that flight.

Had it not been for Kyle and Leslie, Allison would have left Rob long ago. She could rebuild her career, but it would take time, and she knew only too well the sacrifices newly divorced mothers make.

When Allison was eight years old, her father left his family for a younger woman. For years, Allison blamed herself. Her mother struggled to feed Allison and her younger brother, working two jobs and coming home late at night. By the time she remarried, Allison was in college on a National Merit scholarship. Allison worked damned hard building a new life for herself only to waste it on a man who couldn't keep his dick in his pants.

The one thought that brought a smile to her face was the image of her Walther PPK. It sat in the glove compartment of her aging Buick tucked inside a roll of maintenance receipts held together by a rubber band. No one would ever trace it. She'd bought the gun from a young man in College Park. He accepted cash and never asked for an ID.

The day would come, Allison told herself, when Rob and his little playmate would reap their rewards, but that day would have to wait. Allison was many things her relatives, friends, and neighbors would never suspect, but she assured herself, reckless was not one of them.

Today, she had a tight schedule. She changed out of her faded, baggy clothes into a stretch bra, shorts, and running shoes. She had a morning date with her new best friend, Denise Weathers.

Rob no longer noticed Allison when she was naked. Had he bothered, he'd have seen that she'd dropped twenty-five pounds and toned her every muscle to perfection, thanks to a daily regimen of five miles and P90X.

• • •

Ten years Allison's junior, Denise was already at the Clayton State University campus when she arrived. Today she wore her black hair pulled back in a ponytail with a sports bra and leggings that accentuated every detail of her taut frame. She leaned against the hood of her new, gray BMW. Divorced and childless, Denise could easily afford such luxuries on the commissions she earned as an AFLAC agent. The two women had met three months earlier and hit it off immediately.

Afterward, Allison followed Denise to a gym near her home in Stockbridge, where the two women continued their workout. From there she returned to her life as a suburban housewife. She stripped out of her sweat-soaked exercise clothes and showered. There was just enough time, before the kids got home, for her daily rendezvous with Jeremy Coleman.

Earlier in the summer, depressed and angry over her unhappy marriage, Allison sought out the eighteen-year-old drug dealer. Her first thought was to score a little something to help her through her day. The last time Allison smoked pot was right after college, while dating Rob. That was before the wedding, before the children, before the extra pounds, before she sacrificed her dreams as an advertising copywriter to become a stay-at-home mom.

At the first toke the old feeling returned. Allison was twenty years old again. Before she knew it, she was naked in bed with Jeremy in the basement of his parents' home, worried they might return at any moment. She tried to forget that Jeremy, before he went off to juvie, had been her son's classmate at Starr's Mill.

From then on, their preferred venue was a Motel 6 on Tara Boulevard. They met there every time Rob and the kids were away. It was far enough from Peachtree City that no one would recognize Allison, or so she thought.

Looking back now, she recalled the time Jeremy ordered a pizza to the room just before she arrived. Standing at the door, she turned to see the delivery boy sitting in his truck. He looked familiar but didn't seem to notice her. Allison told Jeremy she'd stop seeing him if he ever again pulled such a stupid stunt.

• • •

Allison was setting a sumptuous meal before her unappreciative brood when she heard her cell phone buzz in the next room. Picking it up, she checked the caller ID. It read "Dr. Cole." In the unlikely event anyone went through her contact list, they'd never give a second thought to what seemed like just another of Allison's many doctors.

As her family stuffed their faces, she ran to the master bath. "Hey, I told you never to call me at night," she whispered. What could possess Jeremy to contact her again so soon? Horny little bastard!

"We need to talk," he said. "I can't stop thinking about you."

"Jeremy, we've been through this a million times. This isn't that kind of relationship. Just think of me as another of your teenaged bimbos, except you can't go bragging to your friends about us."

"Allison, you don't understand. I want to be with you all the time. You're not like the other girls." He paused as though contemplating his next move. "If you won't leave your husband and run away with me, then my next call will be to your home phone." His tone changed. "Just imagine who might answer."

Now Allison was frantic. Her only thoughts were of her family, her friends, and her neighbors. "Look, I can't talk right now. My family's going to wonder what I'm doing. Where can we meet?"

"There's a place over near Fayetteville."

As he gave her the address, Allison typed it into her cell. She disconnected, dropped the phone into her pocket, and took a deep breath, flushing the toilet to provide cover.

"Oh, my God!" she said as she passed through the kitchen, gathering her purse. "I almost forgot. I have a church meeting tonight." Lame as it was, this was the best excuse she could devise for such an abrupt departure. She never looked back at the curious stares from her husband and children.

Ten minutes later she pulled into a potholed parking lot behind an abandoned distribution center. Jeremy was already there, standing beside his Toyota Matrix. He crushed out his cigarette and strolled toward to the Buick. Allison reached across and unlocked the passenger door.

Unseen by Jeremy, her hand went to the glove compartment and retrieved the Walther. Her plan was to scare some sense into him. She shifted the gun to her left hand, where she could hold it out of sight.

He slid into the passenger seat without closing the door and gave her a lascivious grin. "I'm glad you came, Allison… smart decision. You know we'll be happy together. We'll go somewhere no one can find us. I've saved up some serious stash…" His voice trailed off and his eyes widened as she brought up the gun.

"Jeremy, *we* aren't going anywhere. *You're* the one going away. You're going to disappear from my life and never return."

His expression morphed from bewilderment to rage as his hand went for the gun. Allison couldn't remember touching the trigger. But in the confines of her car, the explosion nearly deafened her.

Jeremy stopped as quickly as he had lunged. He gazed down in shock at the red blossom spreading across his shirt. He reached out to Allison as if in supplication. She flinched, squeezing the trigger again. The second round went through his forehead.

What followed was a blur. She would later recall dragging Jeremy's lifeless body across the pavement and laying it next to his car. With luck, days would pass before anyone ventured back here. By then, she prayed, any evidence of her involvement would be long gone. It was all she could do under the circumstances.

Jeremy's blood stains and DNA, Allison knew, would nail her as a suspect. She drove home, careful not to attract attention, glancing in the rear-view mirror every few seconds, expecting to see police lights.

Along the way, she stopped at a convenience store for a bottle of Clorox and some wipes. When her family asked about the smell, she could claim she'd spilled the bleach and use that as an excuse to replace the upholstery.

Pretending she didn't feel well, she climbed into bed. She lay awake all night, eyes clinched, shaking.

. . .

Two days later, Allison's luck ran out in a way she never expected. It almost cost Allison her life.

She was alone at home when she received a call on her cell. A gravelly voice said, "Whatever you do, bitch, don't even think about hanging up."

Her finger hovered over the disconnect button.

"I know your husband just left for work, and your beautiful son and daughter just went off to school. I know 'cause I watched them."

The statement gave Allison a chill.

"And don't go running to the window. I ain't out front anymore … Now… bitch… tell me why I shouldn't just come back there right now and pop a cap in your ass. Tell me why I shouldn't do the same to that asshole husband of yours and your kids."

She tried to quell the fear in her voice as she responded, "Look, who is this?"

"Never fucking mind who this is! The only shit matters right now is, I know who you are."

"What have I done to you?"

"You know damned well what you done. You killed one of the best dealers I ever had. You can't imagine the money that cost me."

"Sir, you have the wrong…"

"Don't give me that shit! Jeremy checked in with me every night. He told me about your little rendezvous. Last night the cops found him, right where you left him."

Trembling, Allison willed herself not to reply.

"This morning I drove down to Peachtree City thinking, I'm gone kill this bitch. It wasn't until I stopped outside your lovely home and gazed around at your little white bread neighborhood that I asked myself, *how could I make something good out of this?* Then it came to me.

You see, Allison, in my line of work, I got competition. From time to time, I need to take one of 'em out. Problem is, some of these folks live down there in your part of the world, and anybody I send after 'em gone be suspect number one, know what I'm saying? What I need is somebody nobody's gone suspect, somebody I can count on, somebody who's just cold enough to pop a poor little kid like Jeremy, dump his ass in a parking lot, and go right on about her business."

He took a deep breath before continuing. "You know why I can count on you, Allison? 'Cause I know you can't go to the police without admitting you shot Jeremy. Besides, they ain't gone believe some wild story about a scary black man threatening to kill you. Hell, I don't believe it myself. And when it's all done, I'll just come back down there and take care of you and your family like I promised I would."

He waited a moment to let this home movie play out in Allison's mind.

"Now I know, after a while you're gone want out of this deal. You'll come up with some scheme to get away from me. Maybe you'll leave your husband and kids and run off somewhere. I'm sure that thought's crossed your mind already. But you know I can't allow that, Allison. Right now, I need your services. So, here's what I'm gone do.

Your first hit is payback for Jeremy. We'll call it a 'training' exercise. After a while, I'll up the contract a little. One of these days you'll have enough money to go somewhere nobody'll ever find you. Maybe take the kids with you. You'd like that, wouldn't you Allison?"

Allison clinched her fists, praying for this nightmare to stop. When she said nothing, he went on.

"You know, Jeremy told me all about that cheating husband of yours and that bitch... What's her name? Ah, yeah. Wendy Miller... Now, Jeremy was one stupid little dude, eighteen-year-old punk let his dick do his thinking for him. I'm sure it never occurred to you all that pillow talk going in his ears would eventually come out his mouth. I don't forget stuff like that, Allison. In my business, information is money. Maybe someday you can take care of Rob and Wendy too... someday... not now."

The man instructed Allison to buy a prepaid, throwaway phone, take the battery out, and hide it somewhere no one would find it. Each morning, she would go to a busy location, like a mall. There she'd be just another anonymous face in the crowd. She would insert the battery, check for a numeric text, and call him at that number. The calls were always brief. Every few days she'd buy a new burner for cash, ditch the old one and text him her new number.

"One more thing, Allison. I gotta stop calling you by your real name, just in case somebody's listening. You need an alias. What you want it to be?"

For a moment, she was lost for words. *This seems so surreal.* Then it came to her. She'd recently re-read James Joyce's *Ulysses*. "M. Bloom," she gasped.

"Fine. M. Bloom it is. Another thing. Once you work off this little debt you owe me, how you wanna get paid? I ain't writing no checks, for obvious reasons. And if you get caught carrying around some serious cash, you gonna have some explaining to do. Know what I'm saying? And then your problems become my problems."

Allison was out of her depth and sinking fast. "What... what do you suggest?"

"Lemme give you a lawyer I know. If he asks who sent you, you don't remember. Just tell him you got some money you need to stash offshore. That's all he needs to know. He ain't the kind to ask a lot of questions." He gave Allison the office number for Ryan Flynn.

When he hung up, Allison stumbled backward and slid down the wall into a fetal position. She began to cry in huge, wracking sobs. What had come over her? *How could I fuck up like this?*

Slowly, the crying subsided and reality set in. Allison had no alternatives. Somewhere in the back of her mind she heard a door click shut.

. . .

A week later, with a little coaching, Allison made her first hit. Her biggest surprise, when it was over, was that she felt nothing. It wasn't as though she had a choice. It was more like a business transaction, no different from Denise making an insurance sale. Besides, the victim was just another drug dealer, and the world was better off without him.

Before long, Allison began to anticipate each job, stalking her prey, seeing the surprise on his face, dispatching him, and making her escape. The thought of a secret life, one no one would ever suspect, took her breath away. It was so much simpler than she'd expected. Each successive hit became that much easier.

Most of them occurred in smaller suburbs, like Griffin and Douglasville, where Allison, a young white female, could easily blend in. She'd pose as a housewife on a shopping trip or as a fitness-conscious young woman out for a run, roles in which she was naturally comfortable.

When, in late August, the calls stopped, her thoughts turned from anguish to doubt. Had the man with the gravelly voice been arrested... or worse? In time, her worries abated, and she heaved a sigh of relief, thinking her troubles were over.

CHAPTER 2
FELIX LOPEZ

Midtown Atlanta
Friday, October 12

Felix Lopez stepped onto the patio of his Midtown bungalow and closed the French doors behind him. It was good to be home after so long. For the past two weeks, he'd been in the Dominican Republic following a month in Puerto Rico. He visited his cousins, many of them still digging out from the carnage of Hurricane Maria. He smiled to think how it must gall them to accept help and money from the little maricon they'd tormented so much when he was younger.

He settled into his chaise lounge and took a deep breath of cool night air redolent with the aroma of wood smoke from a neighbor's chimney. Felix's tenant, an elderly man living in the house behind him, had brought in his mail and newspapers. Felix would get to them later. All he wanted now was to relax.

Beneath the steady thrum of traffic on Ponce de Leon Avenue he heard the low murmur of his next-door neighbor's television. From somewhere down the alley, screened from view by overhanging dogwoods, came the sounds of a party on someone's rear deck. A woman laughed. There was Reggae music and the rustle of indistinct voices.

Despite the proximity of adjoining homes, Felix enjoyed relative privacy, thanks to the high privet hedge surrounding his back yard. He and his lover had moved in a year ago. Two months later, following a brutal fight, the partner moved out. Felix relished the tranquility of living alone.

The sun had already set, and the last vestiges of twilight were fading away. Felix had turned off all his interior and exterior lights and now sat in complete darkness. The sky was so clear he could make out some of the brighter stars, though they were mere pinpricks of light. He pulled a joint from his pocket, lit it, closed his eyes, and inhaled the acrid smoke.

Felix was glad to be home and anxious to get to work. He had a major trial starting in two weeks. In his mind he recited his opening statement. He pictured the scene in detail, down to his crisp, cream-colored shirt, the three-piece suit, and the two-tone wingtips that would complete his ensemble.

This was why he became a defense attorney. Born and raised in the worst part of Queens, he'd witnessed first-hand the uselessness and inequity of drug laws. He'd seen what they did to so many young men, especially those, like himself, whose principal crime was being born the wrong color. Other lawyers had warned him not to get involved with drug dealers. They'll only drag you down, they said. Felix would prove them wrong.

His current client, with three priors, had what some might consider an unwinnable case. The prosecutor had an impressive array of evidence, including photos of more than fifty industrial trash bags filled with pot. But Felix had a few surprises for the narc who'd be testifying for the state, a crooked cop with a long history of planting evidence. This trial would make Felix famous... or perhaps infamous. He didn't care which.

The fact that this client was also Felix's personal supplier played no part in his decision to represent the man. He pictured the smug look vanishing from the police officer's face, closed his eyes, and let the warm glow of the cannabis suffuse his body.

At thirty-two, he was still single. He was young, handsome, and virile. He'd soon find someone else to keep him company.

He took another drag. With the music and the noise from next door, Felix never heard the muffled footfalls on his patio. He never saw the gloved left hand or the silenced .22 caliber revolver. He felt but a moment's pain as the first bullet entered the center of his sternum, flattened out, ripped apart his aorta, and lodged between two thoracic vertebrae.

The sounds of the neighbor's television continued uninterrupted. The woman at the end of the alley laughed again, this time louder. The music played on.

The gloved hand placed two more bullets into Felix's head, one in the center of each eye. Before leaving, the left hand reached out with a pair of scissors and removed a lock of Felix's hair.

Quiet footsteps retreated into the night as a thick, dark pool spread across the concrete pavers Felix had laid with such loving care. Neighbors would later report seeing a large man in a hoodie running down the street in the middle of the night.

. . .

The phone rang on Beth Long's bedside table. Seven AM. For a heart-stopping moment she thought she'd overslept. Then she remembered it was Saturday, her day off. She lived alone in a cramped downtown loft she'd chosen for its proximity to work. She had almost no life besides her job and cared nothing for the teeming bars and restaurants nearby.

Her next thought was that the caller might be Brandon Markham, her former psychologist. Their six-month affair had been little more than an outlet for her pent-up energy and frustrations, an opportunity to get some exercise and satisfaction through strenuous sex.

She had to admit the man was good, especially for his age. She told herself that was all he wanted from their relationship. He was, after all, married with four daughters. And he had his professional standing to think about. Beth had visited his office only once, on the advice of a friend from work, and one thing led to another. He left her apartment only six hours earlier. *What in the hell could he want now?*

The phone grew more insistent. She picked it up and read the display, "Don Walsh." This could not be good. She let out a deep sigh and answered the call.

"Hey"

"I need you over on Vedado Way." He gave her the address.

"What happened?"

"Another shooting. Another lawyer."

"Oh shit!" Long rubbed the back of her neck. She could already feel a headache coming on. "Same MO?"

"Same MO."

"Ah shit!"

"I talked to Paxton. You can skip roll call. Just get over here."

"I'll be there in fifteen... make that twenty."

She rang off, hauled out of bed, stumbled to the closet, retrieved her police sergeant's uniform, and hung it on the doorknob. On her way to the shower, she again exclaimed, "Ah shit!" She was wide awake now, heart pounding. She reminded herself this was why she'd become a cop.

CHAPTER 3
TOM WILLIAMS

Midtown
Saturday, October 13

Traffic's light, the air crisp and cool as I set out for my morning run. The sun, peeping over the treetops, momentarily blinds me as I make the turn at the old Kodak building. I'm headed downhill toward Ponce City Market. My four-year-old pointer, Bogie, trots at my side on a retractable leash. A block away an ambulance pulls out of Charles Allen Drive, lights flashing, no siren. Behind it trails a cop car, presumably on its way to Grady Hospital.

Atlanta's Ponce de Leon Avenue starts at Spring Street, across from the Varsity Restaurant. From there, it runs some five miles eastward to the city of Decatur where it becomes West Ponce de Leon. Along the way, it passes several of Atlanta's older and more colorful neighborhoods. It gets its name from Ponce de Leon Springs, a health spa that once occupied the current site of the Market. Occasionally, people will give it some butchered semi-Spanish version of the old conquistador's name. Those who know better pronounce it "Ponce."

My wife and I moved to Midtown forty years ago. We renovated a classic two-story Victorian where we raised our daughters, Kathleen and Marie. Colleen's gone now, a victim of lung cancer. The girls are both grown and married with children of their own, leaving Bogie and me to shift for ourselves.

As we turn at the Kroger parking lot and make our way home, I'm already planning how we'll spend the rest of our day, me sprucing up the lawn and cleaning house, Bogie chasing squirrels across the back yard.

Lately I've developed a love-hate relationship with this place. It has so many memories and ghosts. I just can't picture myself doing yard work and repairs for my remaining days. Again, and again, my mind turns to fantasies of moving on.

All I've ever wanted to do was write. Now I dream of becoming a literary journalist. Maybe I'll author an occasional novel or short story. I could sell my house, rent an RV, and take to the road with Bogie, like some aging Hunter Thompson or Jack Kerouac. I figure I'll drive out west, meet a lot of people, visit interesting places, and write about them. I'm still in good health, for my age, and maybe, if we're lucky, my warranty and Bogie's will run out at the same time.

I'm wondering how to break the news to Kathy and Marie. I'm sure they concluded long ago that I've gone nuts in my old age. Kathy's a pediatric oncologist at Emory Orthopedic, her husband, Sean O'Meara, a medical researcher at Emory. Marie followed in her mother's footsteps, becoming a defense attorney in D.C. There she married a State Department official named Bill Wakefield. What the man does for a living I'm probably better off not knowing.

There's an old Hebrew proverb. "Man plans. God laughs." I unlock the front door in time to hear my phone ringing in the study. It's Mitch Danner, a long-time friend and writer for the *Atlanta Journal-Constitution*.

"Hey," he asks, "You hear about that shooting last night over on Vedado?"

"No."

Vedado Way is a couple blocks east of me. I awake to local news on WSB radio every morning. I must have missed this one.

"Another lawyer," says Danner. "That makes three, all within a mile of you. Same MO. Shot through the eyes at close range with a small caliber weapon. No witnesses. I'm telling you; this is starting to look like a serial spree."

A month ago, someone murdered a Midtown attorney in his own living room. Two weeks later, someone gunned down another when he came to his front door in the middle of the night. Both victims lived alone. The speculation is it's a single perp.

"Wow!" I exclaim. "Three murders so close together! And in Atlanta, no less! Even if they aren't serial killings, think what a story that'll make!"

"Alright, smartass! You'll wish you were on top of this before it's over. It's like 1980 all over again. I've talked to some cops I know, and, so far, they don't have a clue who the shooter is."

"So, where are you getting this stuff about him being a serial killer?"

"A guy I met. Writes for a small startup called *Biz Atlanta*. Lives near you, in Buckhead."

Only someone like Mitch, who lives out in the burbs, would think Buckhead is anywhere near Midtown.

"His name's Ambrose Mangham."

"Ambrose Mangham... Never heard of him. Where's he getting this information?"

"Says he knows some cops. Claims they told him, off the record, that the perp collects trophies, goes through some creepy ritual... stuff like that. He says the police are trying to keep a lid on it while they put together a profile. I'm not sure the guy knows what he's talking about, but it may be worth looking into."

"If he's a reporter, why doesn't he cover it himself?" I ask.

"*Biz Atlanta* doesn't carry murder stories. It's a small business tabloid. Most of their stuff is puff pieces about their advertisers and entrepreneurial advice from SBA bureaucrats. Mangham reached out to the *AJC*, but, so far, they're not buying his story. The real reporters don't trust him. He has no crime creds, and he's a bit of a whiner. Seems he took up reporting a couple of years ago as part of some mid-life crisis. Now he thinks he's Bob Woodward."

"Why aren't you working this yourself?"

"The boss has me covering the story about the housewife up in Cartersville."

"The one attacked and murdered in her home, supposedly by her Mexican gardener?"

"That one. Anyway, I thought you might be interested. It's right there in your backyard. You won't even have to back that heap of yours out the driveway."

"Yeah." I turn the idea over in my mind for a moment. "You know, this might be interesting. I'll ask around… see if anybody's heard anything."

"You do that. And if you get anything, give me a call. I'll put in a word for you at the paper."

"Thanks, Mitch. I owe you."

"That you do, my friend."

"By the way. Do you have a number for this Ambrose Mangham? Maybe I'll call him."

"Sure." Mitch looks up the number while I retrieve a small notebook and pen from my desk. It's nice to know someone besides my daughters worries about me having too much time on my hands.

I owe Mitch more favors than I can count. Over the years we've shared leads and even co-written stories. Two years ago, he helped me track down the real identity of Dawn Sawyer, alias Dina Savage, a young woman on trial for murdering the man she claimed raped her.

As I open the back door to let Bogie out, my thoughts drift again to the idea of selling the house and renting an RV. Maybe I'll postpone that trip.

Through the kitchen window I watch Bogie investigating something in a far corner of the yard. My phone rings again. This time it's Marie. She's taken to calling me several times a week, worried I might run off and do something stupid.

"Hey, Mo." Kathy and I are the only people still alive who can get away with calling her that.

"Hey. What're you up to?"

"Nothing. Just standing here watching Bogie leaving a little gift in the back yard. He was supposed to do that earlier when I took him for our morning run."

"You need to carry a plastic bag, Dad."

"Yeah. I know… What's up with you?"

There's a long pause, which my mind soon fills with all manner of horrible possibilities.

"Dad, I'm leaving Bill. I've put the house on the market. I've spoken to the folks at Mom's firm. They'd like to take me on as a partner, handling criminal cases, like she did. I'm bringing the boys with me… I was wondering if we could maybe stay at your place, just long enough for me to find something out in Cobb County, closer to the office."

"Sure. There's plenty of room. It'll be great having you guys. I'll fix up the guest rooms. When are you getting here?"

"I'm still packing. I'm putting most of our stuff in storage for now. I'll be there day after tomorrow."

Trying to work some sincerity into my voice, I add, "Sorry to hear about you and Bill." The truth is I can't stand the guy, always trying to impress people with his importance and his pedigree. Now maybe I can stop pretending.

Marie fills me in on more details of her pending breakup than I want to know. When she finally rings off, I open the door to let Bogie in.

"Well, Bogue. Looks like we're going to have company." With Marie and the boys moving in, the RV and the open road are now little more than a fading image.

My thoughts return to what Mitch said. "You'll wish you were on top of this before it's over. It's like 1980 all over again."

From 1979 to 1980 someone killed thirty of Atlanta's children and young adults, all from poor African American homes. This came on the heels of Atlanta being named murder capital of the country. Homicide detective Paxton Davis worked several of those cases and was one of the first to mention the possibility of a serial killer. Until then, the murders received scant attention in the media.

When police finally caught Wayne Williams dumping a body into the Chattahoochee River, prosecutors were quick to link him to *all* the victims, despite their differing profiles and the circumstances of their deaths. In a moment of frustration, Paxton mentioned to a reporter that he didn't think Williams was the sole perpetrator, that he was just a convenient fall guy. This comment nearly ended Paxton's career and went a long way toward explaining why he never made it past lieutenant despite having the best clearance rate on the force.

It was during that time that Paxton and I first met. Over the years I've turned to him many times as a confidential source. He's usually happy to cooperate when he thinks it might shake loose information that'll help solve a crime, especially when the story embarrasses people higher up in his chain of command.

I have Paxton's home number and his cell, but one reason we have such a good working relationship is that I don't abuse it. I'll call him Monday.

. . .

Later, seated in the enclosed sleeping porch I've converted to a home office, I boot up my laptop and begin searching information on serial killers, including Wayne Williams. Williams was, at one time, an *AJC* employee. I met him once, coming out of a dark room.

The definition of a serial killer is someone who murders three or more people for some form of gratification. Sometimes there's sexual contact, as with Williams. Often there's not. The perps tend to be unemployed, single, white males in their thirties with a history of isolation or abuse.

Serial murder has been around for centuries. Over time it's become fodder for media sensation, owing to its randomness and its ability to create mass hysteria. The last thing cops want to do, if they can avoid it, is classify a string of homicides as serial.

Typically, there's something about the victims, their gender, age, ethnic background, or profession that attracts the killer's interest. The most common denominator is they're less able to defend themselves. Many of them, like prostitutes or the homeless, are less likely to draw attention from law enforcement when they turn up missing. Nowhere do I found mention of lawyers as victims.

As I'm pondering this, the doorbell rings. Standing on my front porch is a man I peg immediately as plainclothes officer. He wears a tan corduroy sports coat over a black polo shirt and gray slacks, complemented by expensive Oakley sunglasses and a well-worn pair of tasseled loafers. He looks to be about forty, still in good shape, with peroxide blonde curls going gray at the temples.

"Mr. Williams?" he asks.

"Yes."

"I'm Detective Walsh with Atlanta Police. I apologize if I'm disturbing your weekend."

"No worries." It's not like I'm going anywhere.

"There was a shooting on Vedado Way last night. We're just checking with neighbors to see if anyone might've seen or heard anything unusual."

"Detective, I've lived in this house for forty years. I've learned to sleep through sirens, fights in the street, all-night partying, you name it. The most unusual thing I could imagine around here would be peace and quiet. I first heard about this murder an hour ago from a friend. I wish I could help."

"This friend of yours, does he live in the neighborhood?"

"He lives in Roswell and writes for the *AJC*. What little he knows probably came from police sources."

Walsh hands me a card with his name and phone number. "If you hear anything, would you give me a call?"

"Sure."

He's about to turn away when I have a sudden thought, a long shot. "Um, Detective, I know you're busy right now, and you're probably anxious to get home, but I was wondering if maybe you could tell me a little more about this shooting. It might help jog my memory."

All this brings is a smirk. "Afraid not. Like you said, I'm busy."

• • •

It's still light outside, so I stroll over to Vedado to see what I can find out. It's a short walk, and I'm there in five minutes. The address Mitch gave me turns out to be a modest craftsman bungalow set atop a hill. Three people have congregated at the end of the driveway.

One of them, an older man in a Panama hat, Hawaiian shirt and khaki shorts, is describing the grisly scene he discovered early this morning while walking his dog. No doubt he's told this story many times over the course of the day. His latest audience, a young woman in a grey running bra and tight shorts and a young man in a wife-beater and cutoffs, listen in rapt attention.

As I ease up and join the little gathering, I resist the temptation to pull out my notebook for fear it might frighten them into silence. The narrator stops in mid-sentence and introduces himself as Oscar Arrington, a retired social worker. The woman in the running bra is Diane Hampton and the younger man is Jay Wallace. Though I live only a few blocks away, I've never met any of them.

"Hi. I'm Tom Williams."

Arrington's eyes narrow. "You must be Colleen Williams' husband."

Figures. Colleen knew everybody in the neighborhood.

I nod. "Yep."

"I was so sorry to hear about her passing. She was a wonderful woman. We're all going to miss her."

"Thanks." I work up a wry smile. "I'm missing her already."

According to Arrington, the homeowner, one Felix Lopez, lived alone following the departure of his partner a couple of months ago. Arrington, who lives on Greenwood, was walking his dog, a pug named Waldo, this morning. When they got to Lopez's house the dog suddenly broke free and ran up the driveway. Arrington chased after him, as best he could, and caught the dog in the back yard.

There he found Lopez, sitting in a chaise lounge on his back patio, with a bullet hole in his chest and one in each eye. The remains of a reefer lay on the concrete beside him. Waldo was licking at a pool of congealed blood.

A distraught look comes over Arrington. "You can imagine how horrified I was. My God, for all I knew the poor man was HIV positive, and here I was pulling Waldo from a puddle of his bodily fluids. I even got some on my shoe."

Arrington says he called the police on his cell and waited until they arrived. He's been here most of the day, filling in passersby on what he found and enjoying his role as amateur reporter. One of the neighbors told him earlier there was a party on the rear deck of a home on Monroe Drove. No one reported hearing a gunshot, an argument, or anything unusual.

"Was one of the policemen you met a detective named Walsh?" I ask.

"Yes. He asked if I knew anything. I told him no."

"Did he ask anything that might have implied a connection between this homicide and the two previous murders of attorneys?"

"No. He just wanted to know what I knew about Felix. I said I knew him in passing and had seen him down at the park on the occasional evening."

"So," I ask, "how many possible suspects do we have?" I begin ticking them off on my fingers. "There's the ex-lover, a disappointed client, somebody who hates lawyers... anybody I'm leaving out?"

"Somebody who hates gays," adds Arrington.

"Of course."

Diane Hampton speaks up, and suddenly I realize I've passed her several times on my morning runs. To be more accurate, she's passed me. She gives me a wide-eyed, innocent stare. "This is really creepy, having something like this happen so close to home."

We all nod in agreement.

Wallace comments that every household in Midtown should arm itself with rifles. The others ignore him.

"Oscar," I ask, "did you get a good look at the corpse?"

He shudders. "I'm afraid so."

"I don't mean to be morbid, but how did the bullet holes look? Were they large or small?"

For the first time, he's hesitant. "I don't know. They were small I guess."

"You don't know if they made exit wounds, do you?"

He closes his eyes and shakes his head.

Seeing that I'm creeping him out, I change directions. "Oscar, I'm a freelance writer, and I may end up covering this for the local papers. As I come across more information, would you mind if I dropped by just to see what you think? I wouldn't have to quote you or anything."

He considers this, warming to the idea. "No. I don't suppose I'd mind."

I pull out my notebook and pen. He gives me his phone number, and I promise to call.

"While I've got you," I ask, "what do you know about the two previous victims?"

Arrington says he never knew the second victim, a tax attorney named Jacob Epstein. "I knew the first one, though. He was Lyle Mallory, a tireless activist for the LGBT community. He had such a bright future ahead of him. People were urging him to run for mayor… until a few years ago, when he got caught up in some scandal."

"Do you recall what that scandal involved?"

"Something to do with the IRS. That's all I remember. I can find out if you like."

"That'd be nice. Right now, I'd like to get a look at the crime scene. Wanna join me?"

"No. I think I've had enough for today."

The other two show no interest, so I climb the hill alone. By the time I get there the only remaining evidence is the dried blood on the pavement. The chaise lounge still sits where Arrington found it this morning.

In my mind's eye I picture a man reclining in the chair smoking a joint. The fact that he's made no apparent attempt to get out of the chair tells me he either knew his assailant or didn't hear him walk up.

There's a wooden fence at the back of the property with a gate. I examine the gate. It's shut but not locked. The shooter could have entered from the adjoining property. The house is locked, which tells me nothing. The police probably went in to investigate and locked up behind themselves when they left. Not having my Nikon with me I pull out my phone for a couple of quick photos.

On my way home, I make a note to speak with Father John O'Malley, a retired priest at the Shrine of the Immaculate Conception, where Colleen and the girls attended church. The padre and I have become close friends since Colleen's death, and we meet weekly at a nearby Starbucks just to chat. It's supposed to be some sort of therapy. It helps to talk with someone who isn't judging me and doesn't think I'm crazy because I'm not ready to spend the rest of my life in a rocking chair on the porch.

A former homicide cop from Chicago, O'Malley retired and became a priest following the death of his own wife. He moved to Atlanta to be with his sister, who came here years earlier with her late husband.

Already I'm feeling it. I'm getting hooked into this story. Gone, for the moment at least, are any thoughts of travelling. I can do that later, after Marie and the boys settle into their own place. In the meantime, I have something to keep me occupied. I'll cruise back by Lopez's place later. This time I'll bring my camera and get some more pictures.

I'm almost at my door when it hits me. All three victims were lawyers. My daughter's a lawyer. Granted, she's just moving here, and no one knows her, but I'm not taking any chances.

I go up to the attic and find my dad's old .45. If this person, whoever he is, brings a weapon to my house, I'll just have to have a bigger weapon. I'll take it out on the patio to clean it, so the gun oil doesn't stink up the house.

Bogie meets me at the door. He wags his tail and jumps on me as though I've been gone all day. I let him out in the back to take care of his business and then call him back inside.

Not long after Colleen died, I set up a bedroom for myself in my downstairs office. It's convenient, and, if I'm honest, the thought of sleeping in the bed we shared for so many years is just too much. Tomorrow I'll prepare the upstairs rooms for Marie and the boys.

For now, I'll do some more online research. First, I google the name of Felix Lopez. I find a website for his law practice. It seems he specialized in criminal law and civil litigation. It mentions a couple of honors he received from the Atlanta Bar and the Georgia Trial Lawyers Association but little else.

There's even less on Jacob Epstein. He moved to Atlanta a couple of years ago and joined one of the larger firms as an associate. I look to see where he went to school, on the off chance he might have known the other victims. Epstein, it turns out, graduated from my alma mater, the University of Florida, while Lopez was a Virginia grad.

I switch to Lyle Mallory and hit pay dirt. There are articles about his many accomplishments and his years of community service. He's a former president of the Midtown Neighborhood Association. Colleen would've known him, I'm sure. There's no mention of the scandal that ended his political prospects.

My thoughts return to Ambrose Mangham. An exhaustive Google search turns up nothing. It seems the man was born about eight months ago. His LinkedIn account lists him as a "correspondent" for *Biz Atlanta*, but nothing else. Mitch mentioned he'd taken up writing as part of a mid-life crisis. Whatever he did before that's a mystery.

None of the Internet information contains street addresses of the victims. So, I pull out my aging phone directory.

By the time I glance up from my laptop, it's well past supper time. I haven't been to the store, and there's nothing in the refrigerator. Now that I'm by myself I've begun cooking less and eating out more. I decide to go to Manuel's Tavern for a bite.

CHAPTER 4
DON WALSH

Atlanta, Georgia
Saturday, October 13

It was nine PM, and every table and barstool at Manuel's was full. In the last booth, across from the bar, Detective Don Walsh nursed a beer. He faced the rear entrance, out of sight of other customers.

He'd spent all day walking the streets of Midtown, with little to show but tired, sore feet and had no time for small talk. He was here to meet one of the confidential informants he'd developed while working in Narcotics.

Among Manuel's patrons were blue-collar workers, artists, yuppies, newspaper writers, politicians, television reporters, and other off-duty cops. Back in the days when he could end his shift and leave the work behind, Walsh had been a regular. One of the bartenders waved, and Walsh gave him a nod.

DeKalb County CEO, Manuel Maloof bought the bar in 1956. Manuel died in 2004, but the place still bears his name. Pictures of celebrities and politicians, most of them Democrats, fill the walls. A large portrait of Franklin D. Roosevelt hangs above the bar.

Walsh hadn't seen the interior since it reopened following a complete electrical upgrade, but it was exactly as he remembered. The owners took pains to photograph and catalog the pictures, booths, and wainscoting and put them back precisely as they'd been.

Walsh had considered another, less crowded venue for tonight's meeting, but this was his turf. Besides, no one here was likely to recognize the man who, hopefully, would walk through the door at any moment.

As he waited, Walsh went back over what little he had on the Midtown murders. Lyle Mallory, immensely popular, moved among the power circles of Atlanta. His assailant was almost certainly someone Mallory knew. The shooting occurred in his living room at close range. Lights were on throughout the house. There was no sign of a struggle or forced entry.

Jacob Epstein went down in his foyer with the front door open, as though he'd just answered a knock. Felix Lopez, the little scumbag defense lawyer, died in a chaise lounge on his back patio while smoking a joint. Walsh, had run up against Lopez more than once as a narc and found this both fitting and ironic.

Investigators had ruled out robbery as a motive. None of the homes had been ransacked.

As Walsh pondered all this, Rollo Witherspoon appeared, looking out of place in his stained t-shirt and faded jeans. He gazed around timidly for a moment, spotted Walsh in the corner, and joined him.

Rollo had lived nearby until a couple of years earlier, when two of his associates wound up on the wrong end of a gun fight behind an abandoned warehouse. The murderer, a Russian hacker, went down in a hail of bullets a week later, but Rollo wasn't taking any chances. He moved in with his sister in a Southwest Atlanta apartment complex.

"Hey. What's up?" asked Rollo. "You say you got something to talk about."

"Just wanted to check in with you, Rollo, see how you're doing. You been staying out of trouble?"

"Best I can… long as I don't have to come around meeting no police."

"Hey, it's cool, Rollo. Nothing to worry about. I was just hoping you could provide some information."

"Man, I start giving you information, I end up wearing a toe tag."

"You know I've always taken care of you, Rollo."

Rollo studied the cop for a moment but said nothing.

"I'm sure you heard about me moving over to Homicide."

"Congratulations." They'd known each other for years, ever since the day Walsh decided Rollo would be more valuable as an informant than as a small-time drug arrest.

"Thanks, Rollo," he smiled. "My lieutenant has me working the murder of that attorney last night. You probably heard about it."

"Yeah. I seen it on the news. Felix Lopez."

"You knew him?"

"I knew him. I bet you knew him too. All his clients were dealers."

Walsh pursed his lips. "Maybe."

Rollo looked away and shook his head as though Lopez were a close friend. "They saying on the news it was a serial killer."

"Yeah. Well that's the thing, Rollo. This one looks just like the other two murdered lawyers. Maybe it's the same guy. Maybe not. But that doesn't make it a serial killing, if you know what I mean."

"Yeah. Well them three lawyers are just as dead... if you know what I mean."

Walsh traced his finger in the condensation on the side of his mug. "I'm not asking you to become a junior detective, Rollo. I just want you to do what you do best, keep your eyes and ears open and let me know what you find out. You think you can do that for me?"

Rollo took a deep breath and exhaled. "Maybe."

"That's good, Rollo. I wouldn't want anything to happen to our mutually beneficial relationship."

"What am I supposed to be looking for?"

"Each of the victims was shot at close range with a small caliber pistol, first in the body, and then in each eye socket."

Rollo winced.

"The crime scene guys say it was a .22. The thing is, he never uses the same one twice. The ballistics don't match. That means he's tossing the gun somewhere and buying another one every time, no doubt from illicit dealers.

For reasons I won't go into, our profilers peg him as a male, somewhere between thirty and forty-five, most likely a white guy, well-educated, professional. A guy like that making regular gun purchases on the street is probably gonna stand out. He's not your regular customer, right? I figure, with your connections, you could ask around and perhaps come up with a name. You might also check to see if the Lopez hit has anything to do with our... mutual interests. Do that, and I promise I'll make it worth your while... maybe next time I'm visiting my friends down in the property room."

"Yeah. And what's behind Door Number Two?"

Walsh leaned across the table and gazed into the man's eyes for what seemed to Rollo an eternity. "You don't want to go there, Rollo. Word gets out you're helping the police..." He smiled and shrugged.

The smile reminded Rollo of a snake sizing up a small rodent. "Yeah, sure. Whatever you say, officer."

"I knew you'd see it my way. Listen, I know you're a busy man, Rollo, so I won't keep you. Just let me know what you find out. Okay?"

"Sure."

Rollo seemed more than happy to get away from Walsh. He'd provided the narc many tips over the years resulting in arrests. Newspaper and TV stories lauded Walsh's superb police work and courage under fire. What they didn't mention were rumors he and his partner had ambushed their suspects, without warning, and absconded with hundreds of thousands of dollars.

Walsh studied Rollo as he exited the bar, passing an older man coming in. He recognized the newcomer as Tom Williams from their conversation a few hours earlier. Williams, he knew, had been a reporter for the *AJC*. Like Walsh, he seemed to know everyone in the place.

Williams glanced at Rollo as he passed in a way that made Walsh think he'd seen him before. A veteran reporter like Williams, Walsh figured, would have a mental catalog of names and faces dating back years.

Before Walsh could find a menu to hide his face, Williams caught sight of him and waved. "Detective Walsh, mind if I join you."

"No," he said reluctantly. "Have a seat."

A waiter appeared, and Williams ordered a Dos Equis Amber. "You must be pretty tired," he said to Walsh. "I bet you've had a long day."

"Yeah. You do what you have to," Walsh said and forced a smile.

"I spoke to a couple of neighbors about Lopez. They brought up the other lawyers murdered recently. What do you think about the rumors of this being a serial killing spree?"

"That's bullshit!" Walsh said.

Walsh regained his composure. "We don't have any evidence of that. The similarity of the murders alone doesn't mean there's a serial killer."

"What else do you think might have connected these homicides?"

This prompted the standard police response. "Come on! You know better than that. We can't say anything at this time. This is an ongoing investigation. We're not ruling anything out."

Williams laughed. "Yeah. I bet you guys have that printed on the back of your Miranda cards." He glanced at a waitress as she passed. "Rumor has it no one witnessed any of the killings, and nobody heard a thing. Do you think the killer might have used a silencer?"

"We don't even know it's the same guy. I'm afraid I can't help you."

Walsh stared at Williams. "You know, I asked around. I understand you're a freelance reporter now. If you don't mind my asking, who are you working for?"

"Nobody... at the moment... I'm retired."

"Yeah. Right," Walsh smiled. "You guys never retire."

"Tell me," Tom asked, "did you notice the gate in the fence across Mr. Lopez's back yard?"

Walsh gave him a look typically reserved for obdurate children. "Mr. Williams, tell me you weren't trespassing on Mr. Lopez's property."

Tom's only reply was an innocent smile.

"Yes," Walsh replied. "We checked with the back-door neighbor, who, it turns out, was Mr. Lopez's tenant, an elderly gentleman who was at home the whole night. He says he saw no one come through his yard. The crime scene techs found no recent fingerprints on any part of the gate."

Williams changed the subject. "How long have you been with the force?"

"Six years"

"With Homicide?"

"Nope. Until a few weeks ago I was in Narcotics."

"How do you like the change?"

"It's different, more challenging. It's harder to set up a sting to catch a killer," he grinned.

"Yeah. I imagine that'd be difficult. Do you see anything in the fact all three victims were gay?"

Walsh could tell Williams was fishing. "Nope."

Walsh clammed up. If Williams wanted more information, he would have to get it somewhere else. They made some more small talk as Williams finished his beer.

"Well," said Williams. "I hope you catch whoever it is before he does it again."

"Yep. Me too."

"Meanwhile, I've got your card. You asked me to call you if I heard anything." Tom pulled it out as if confirming the fact. "I'll do that."

"I'd appreciate it," said Walsh.

Walsh went back to his beer. Tom excused himself and walked over to the bar, where he ordered a BLT and another Dos Equis. Before long he'd taken up a conversation with an Atlanta city council woman seated nearby.

Tired as he was, Walsh had other pressing business. The recurring talk of a serial killer was preying on his mind.

• • •

Two months earlier, Walsh made a major drug bust. It went sideways. In the ensuing shootout, he suffered a minor leg wound. Everyone else, including his partner, died.

The target of the arrest was Maurice "Kingfish" Hamby. Among evidence taken from Hamby's apartment was a laptop and a couple of burner phones. Walsh neglected to turn them over to Property. If caught, he could claim he'd been distracted by the leg wound and forgotten about the equipment. At worst, he'd get a reprimand.

Later, after transferring to Homicide, Walsh removed the laptop and burners from beneath the seat of his truck and hid them in his Smyrna apartment. With the help of a lab technician, he opened the phones and noted the contacts and their numbers. One of them bore the name "M. Bloom."

Checking the outbound texts on each phone, he found they contained a ten-digit phone number. In each case "M. Bloom" had called Hamby immediately afterward. Within days of each text, one of Hamby's competitors south of Atlanta turned up dead. Hamby always had an alibi. Walsh wondered now if there might be a connection to Felix Lopez.

He filed that thought away as he left Manuel's. His mind turned to his ex-wife and the young son he'd never see again.

CHAPTER 5
REVEREND JOHN O'MALLEY

Midtown
Monday, October 15

Father John and I chose the Starbucks on Monroe more for my convenience than his. It's a short walk from my house. He offered to meet me here the day he gave Colleen her last rites. It's been our spot every Monday morning since.

I settle into a booth with a copy of the *AJC* and a tall black coffee. While I'm waiting, I call Paxton Davis. It goes straight to voicemail. I leave him a message to call me when he has a moment.

Minutes later, the padre appears at the door, decked out in a tan windbreaker, clerical collar, and jeans. Sunshine reflects off his thinning white hair, giving it the look of a tonsure. He waves, goes to the counter, orders some sort of Frappuccino, and joins me at the table.

"Thomas, how are you doing this morning?" He's the only person who calls me Thomas, perhaps something to do with my lack of faith.

"I'm okay."

His sympathetic nod tells me he knows better. I take a deep breath and gaze out the window. All these months and I'm still amazed at how this guy can get people to open up so easily.

"I guess I'll never get used to life without Colleen," I add. "I still find myself thinking of things I want to tell her."

"So, tell her."

"Oh, I do. But it's not the same. I'm not used to getting the last word."

He laughs. "So, what are you doing with yourself in the meantime?"

"Well, I was thinking of putting the house on the market and doing some travelling, but something's come up."

"What's that?"

"I got a call from Marie on Saturday. She and the boys are coming to visit."

The priest's face brightens. "That's wonderful! I'm sure you're excited. It seems only yesterday she and Kathleen were having their first communions. And what about her husband," he glances heavenward as he retrieves the name, "William?"

"Bill isn't coming. He and Marie are going through a… separation."

He looks at me like I just told him I have a terminal disease. "Oh, I hate to hear that. I certainly hope they can work things out." He pivots the conversation, his brogue noticeably thicker. "When does Marie get here?"

"Late this afternoon."

"Well, maybe Marie's visit will provide a welcome diversion."

"Yeah. I suspect part of the reason she's coming is to keep me from doing anything crazy."

"You mean like running off to Texas chasing down some story about conspiracy buffs?'

"Yeah." I smile. "Like that."

"When my Martha left us, and I told my kids I was becoming a priest, they thought I'd lost my mind." He takes another sip of coffee. "You know, it's been almost two years, Thomas. Are you seeing someone… or are you perhaps considering the priesthood?"

I nearly choke. "No. There's no one else, at least not yet. Nobody's beating down my door."

He laughs. "Wait until the widows in the neighborhood discover you. They'll be at your door, alright, steaming casseroles in hand."

"Actually, I did get a call a few days after the funeral. I haven't thought about it since. A girl I dated in high school…" I catch myself. "She's hardly a girl anymore. Anyway, she's divorced now. We talked for a while. I told her I'd call sometime, maybe meet her for lunch… but I never did."

"You should. It may be an opportunity to rekindle your relationship."

"Even though she's divorced? Doesn't the church frown on that sort of thing?"

"Perhaps we can arrange an indulgence," he says with a smile. "They're half-off this week."

I glance out the window. "You know... I love my family and I'm glad to see them. It's just... living alone has given me the opportunity to take stock of my life and where I should go from here. I've had this dream, for years now, of writing a book."

"And you see this visit from your family as interrupting your plans. You resent it and you feel guilty about the resentment."

"Yeah. I probably do."

"Thomas, things don't happen on our timetable. They happen on God's. Maybe this is just a brief delay... So, besides taking care of your family, what else are you up to?" I love how he makes his point then changes the subject.

"I'm working on a story for the paper. You've probably heard about the recent shootings around here. The press is calling them the 'Midtown Murders'."

"Yes. I heard."

"The last victim was only a couple of blocks away, on Vedado."

"Oh. That's a bit close for comfort. I hope they catch this poor soul before he kills anyone else."

"We don't even know the murderer's a 'he'."

"I guess you're right, but they usually are. We'll say 'he' for now and correct ourselves later if needed."

I fill him in on what little I've learned from Oscar Arrington and from Mitch. "There's a rumor going around these are serial killings. The victims are similar in age and are all lawyers. The MO is the same. The perp shoots them in both eyes from up close."

Father John scratches his chin. He's shifting from priest mode now to ex-cop. "None of that necessarily indicates a serial killer. Shooting out the eyes sounds like a crime of passion, like the shooter knew his victims and was acting out of rage or guilt. But the silencer would indicate a professional. Either way, there might be some connection."

"At least two of the victims were gay, but that might not mean anything."

"I'm sure the police are looking into it. Maybe it's a hate crime."

"Or a jilted lover." I add.

"Nope." The priest shakes his head. "That I did hear about. It seems the police automatically suspected Mallory's partner and hauled him in for questioning. That's usually where you start. But the partner had a solid alibi. The LGBT community raised a stink about it, and the chief had to issue a public apology. I don't think they'll make that mistake again.

You know, back in Chicago I worked the Richard Speck case and helped Cook County with John Wayne Gacy. There's something different about this one. I don't think these were random victims."

I give this some thought. "I need to find out more about Epstein and Lopez. I ran into a Detective Walsh last night at Manuel's. He's the lead investigator. He wasn't much help. All he did was stonewall me."

"That's his job, Thomas. You'll have to find a less involved source, someone more likely to run his mouth, as long as he doesn't get his name in the paper."

"When I brought up the serial killer angle, Walsh acted like I'd insulted his mother."

"Cops don't like rumors, Thomas, especially ones that make them look like they don't know what they're doing. You'll have to get your information elsewhere."

"Maybe I can get a name from my friend Mitch Danner. He knows more cops than I do."

"Do you think this has anything to do with the victims being lawyers?"

"I don't think so. Lopez was a criminal defense lawyer. Mallory was some sort of rising political star, and Epstein was a tax attorney… I hope that's not the reason they were killed, given I have a lawyer near and dear to me."

"I can imagine," he chuckles. His voice takes on a more serious tone as he returns to his reason for meeting me here. "Thomas, I want you to know God has a purpose for all of us. We can't always divine what it is. Saint Paul tells us to pray without ceasing. I hope you'll do that for me, Thomas. You're here, alone though you may be, because the Lord still has work for you. Maybe it's to write the story of these murders. Maybe it's to care for your family. Or just maybe it's to write that book of yours. He'll help you figure out what it is. Meanwhile, I'm glad to hear you're coming out of your shell and getting to know your neighbors."

Uncomfortable with this topic, I glance at my watch and drain my coffee. "I'm afraid I'll need to cut this session short. I have work to do before Marie and the boys arrive."

He stands. "Same place next week?"

"Same place," I smile.

We shake hands and leave, he in his aging Pontiac and me on foot.

• • •

Walking home, I pull out my cell and dial Marie. After a couple of rings, her older son, William, answers.

"Hey, Pops." Only my grandchildren call me "Pops."

"Just thought I'd check and see where you guys are."

"We just passed Raleigh," Marie says in the background.

"Good. You should be here by suppertime. "Drive safely."

I'm back at the house when the phone rings. It's Mitch.

"Hey," I answer. "I was about to call you. I followed up on what you told me Saturday. First, a homicide cop named Walsh came by, canvassing the neighborhood about Lopez. I told him I didn't know anything. Then I tried to get some information from him. He suddenly remembered a pressing engagement."

"Walsh... I think know him. Curly blonde hair, snappy dresser?"

"That's him. I ran into him later at Manuel's. He said he used to be in Narcotics."

"Yeah. He had a reputation as a cowboy, a rule breaker. But his arrest rates were phenomenal."

"I tried again but couldn't get anything out of him. I was wondering if you knew somebody else who might talk, off the record."

"There's this one narcotics officer named Gwynn, Lyman Gwynn. I believe he worked with Walsh. He isn't on this case, naturally, but he works your area, and he hears stuff. He gives me tips occasionally, as long as I keep his name out of it."

"I understand."

I pull out my notebook and take down the cop's name and number.

"You up for a round of golf this afternoon?" Mitch asks.

"Can't. I meant to tell you. Marie and the boys are gonna be staying with me a while, until she finds her own place. She's finally leaving that prick she married. I have to get ready."

"Hey, that's great! Just don't let the word out she's a lawyer."

"Yeah. Really."

Mitch hangs up, and I call Gwynn.

"Yeah?" he answers.

"Detective Gwynn, this is Tom Williams. I'm a friend of Mitch Danner's. He thought you might be willing to help me with something."

His voice goes from gruff to wary. "And what might that be?"

"I'm working on a story. A neighbor of mine was murdered Friday night, over on Vedado. I'm sure you know about it. I was wondering if you could provide some background. It'll be strictly confidential."

There's silence on the other end, and for a moment I think we've lost our connection.

"I could meet you somewhere for lunch," I offer. I cast about for a place where we aren't likely to run into other cops or reporters. "How about The Albert?"

He considers for a moment then agrees.

I glance at my watch. It's five minutes to eleven. "We could meet at eleven thirty. That way we'll miss the lunch crowd. I'll go early and get us a booth."

"Alright, I reckon. Long as you're a friend of Mitch."

. . .

Thirty minutes later, I'm sitting at a back table, facing the front door and enjoying a veggie burger and iced tea. A tall, burly African American cop walks in. He's in uniform. His bald scalp reflects the overhead lighting, matching the spit shine on his shoes. He glances about, like he's worried somebody might recognize us.

I wave him over.

A young waiter with mutton chops and shaved head takes Gwynn's lunch order, a burger and Dr. Pepper.

As the waiter leaves, I pull out my pen and notebook.

"The first victim, Lyle Mallory, was shot at closer range than the other two," says Gwynn. "Looked like they struggled. Epstein and Lopez went more peacefully."

"Did the techs find any transfer evidence?"

"There were recent blood stains, very small, on the carpet near the body. We don't know if they're the perp's, but they ain't the vic's."

"Well, that should help."

"Not really. We ran it against the FBI database and came up blank. Whoever they are, they ain't been busted for a violent crime... at least not yet."

"So, the evidence isn't much help?"

"Not unless we're lucky and get a DNA hit. Finding a killer takes real police work. It ain't like the TV shows. Most times it just helps us get a conviction later."

"Okay. If Mallory let the shooter inside, does that mean he knew him?"

"Probably."

"What was the shot pattern?"

"One to the gut, two to the eyes. Blood pattern makes us think it was the gut first, easier target. He would have bled out eventually, but it'd take a while. I'm guessing the perp shot him without aiming, then popped him again in each eye to finish him off."

"Okay. So, maybe shooting the eyes was a fortuitous thing with Mallory. Assuming the same guy did Epstein and Lopez, why shoot them in the eyes?"

"I don't know, man. Maybe he was so proud of himself he decided to make that his signature."

"Kind of calls attention to the fact he killed all three."

"Don't it, though." Gwynn leans back and stares up as though visualizing the murder scenes. He shakes his head. "That still don't make him no serial killer."

"Did any of Mallory's neighbors hear or see anything?"

"Not that we know of. That don't mean much neither. Mallory lived in a big house back up off the street. We found his body in the living room, with all the doors and windows closed."

I nod and take another bite of my sandwich, which gives me time to think. "If Mallory, Epstein, and Lopez all knew each other, why wouldn't the other two get scared and call the police or leave town after Mallory got shot?"

"Not sure about Epstein. Maybe it just didn't occur to him. Lopez is easy. He was out of the country and got back right before he got hit. We found all his mail and newspapers stacked in his house like he hadn't looked at 'em."

"So, let me see if I can put this together. The shooter knows Mallory and goes to see him for some reason. They get in an argument. A struggle ensues. The shooter has a gun in his pocket. He pulls it out and shoots the easiest target he can find, Mallory's midsection. Mallory staggers back, still alive. Maybe he starts to scream. The shooter reaches out and pops him in the eye to shut him up, then shoots out the other eye for good measure. Later, he kills Epstein and Lopez, for reasons unknown. Only this time, he plays it safe and uses a silencer."

Gwynn smiles for the first time since we met. "You know, you oughta sign up for police academy."

"I don't think they'll take me at my age."

"You never know," he laughs.

I shake my head. "So, what connects Mallory, Epstein and Lopez?"

"Beats me. So far we ain't found nothing."

I finish my sandwich and drink. "Listen, I appreciate your meeting with me. If I think of anything else, or if you do, maybe we can get together again.

He shrugs. "We'll see. You take care of yourself, Mr. Williams. Don't go getting yourself shot."

"I'll do my best."

We shake hands, and I leave him to his lunch.

• • •

As I'm climbing into my car, my phone rings. This time it's Paxton Davis.

"Tom Williams, what's this shit about you sticking your nose where it don't belong? I've got enough to worry about with these damned murders. My officers ain't got time to waste talking to reporters."

"Hey, Paxton. How are Clarice and the kids?"

"Driving me crazy, as always, and don't try to change the subject."

"Hey, I'm just a curious guy. You know how it is. I'd never turn in anything without running it by you first."

"Yeah, right! Don Walsh tells me you been snooping around the neighborhood asking folks what they know about the murders. That kind of curious can get you killed."

"I suppose."

"He says you tracked him down at Manuel's and tried to pump him for information."

"I didn't track him down. I ran into him. I asked him some simple questions. He wasn't exactly forthcoming."

"The city don't pay him to be 'forthcoming,' especially with reporters. You know that."

"Well, you'd be proud of him, then. He didn't tell me squat."

"Good."

"The thing is, Paxton, if I decide to write something… I'm not sure I will, mind you… But I'll have to go with whatever I have. It'd be good if it came from you."

His tone softens. "Look. I promise I'll call you when we have something. Right now, we don't know what we have."

"Word on the street is you have a serial killer."

"That's bullshit. We know more about this case than those rumor mongers out there, and for several reasons we don't think he's a serial killer."

Hearing this from anyone else, I might be skeptical, but given Paxton's experience, I'll take his word. "Okay. I won't turn in anything until I run it by you." The truth is, I don't want to be embarrassed, as newspaper writers often are, by rushing to print something, and then finding out it isn't true.

"Yeah. I appreciate that," says Paxton. "And, by the way, next time you run into Lyman Gwynn, you tell him I'm gonna kick his ass if I catch him talking to any more reporters. Dumbass gonna screw up my investigation."

"Tell the family 'hello' for me, Paxton."

"Sure, man. How your girls doing?"

"They're fine. You're not gonna believe this. Marie called. She and the boys are moving in for a while."

"Sounds like the Wakefield's having some marital troubles."

"Sounds to me like she's finally come to her senses."

"Okay. Well, you take care of yourself. Don't get in any trouble. I mean it."

"Thanks, Paxton. I'll try."

CHAPTER 6
THE CLIENT

Peachtree City
Monday, October 15

Ragged clouds sailed eastward on a mild breeze. Damp with morning dew, the college track showed footprints as Allison and Denise slowed to a walk and caught their breath. They stopped at a bench long enough to stretch and cool down. From there they took Denise's car to the gym to complete their workout. Denise lowered the top, turned on the seat warmers and flashed Allison a wicked smile.

As they sang along to Little Big Town's "I've Got a Girl Crush," Allison realized how lucky she was to have a friend like Denise. In the four months they'd known each other, Denise had become her confidant, the one person with whom she could share her deepest secrets, including the fact her husband was cheating on her. Had Allison thought a bit longer, she might've realized just how little she knew about the woman.

By the time they finished, it was early afternoon. On her drive home, Allison wondered again what had become of the man with the gravelly voice, not that she missed him. She'd be just as happy to never hear from him again.

Stopping at the end of her driveway, she stared at the house she and Rob had moved into nearly twenty years earlier, the home where she'd raised two children. *Where did I go wrong?* she thought. She couldn't believe she'd murdered total strangers with so little thought. *What else could I have done?*

Then she thought about all that money sitting in the Commerce Bank of Antigua. How would she ever retrieve it?

Another question, still unanswered, was what to do about Rob and Wendy. Allison now realized her chances of killing them and getting away with it were nil. Murdering your husband and his girlfriend brought nasty complications, like an obvious motive, something Allison never worried about when taking out people she didn't know.

She considered telling Lon Miller the whole sordid story and letting nature take its course. Middle-aged and insecure, Lon had a history of violence. Wendy had shown up in public more than once with a black eye. Lon, she thought, could take care of Rob and Wendy. But she wasn't sure how to tell him without anyone else knowing.

She punched the garage door opener.

While undressing in the laundry room, Allison stopped and stared at the clothes hamper. She opened it and retrieved a small, plain pasteboard box from beneath the fragrant pile. She was the only family member who ever washed clothes, and this had been an obvious place to hide it.

The box contained a burner she'd purchased just before the calls stopped. Each day, she'd put the battery in and check the texts. When no more texts arrived, she opened it less frequently. By now, she'd almost forgotten it.

Allison stared at the object as though it were an oracle about to speak. What harm would it do now, she thought, to see if he'd left a message? She inserted the battery, pressed the button and waited for it to power up.

When a number appeared, she nearly fainted. She started to dial it, standing there naked in her laundry room but instead shut it off, removed the battery and put it back in the box. She would make that call, as she'd always done, from a crowded location.

She showered, changed into loose, frumpy clothes, and drove her golf cart to the nearest mall. Along the way her thoughts returned, as they often did, to Jeremy. Poor, pitiful, beautiful Jeremy, so thin, so hard-bodied. Dumb and dangerous as he was, there were nights when Allison missed him so badly, she ached. *If he were still alive, I wouldn't be in this mess... I'd just be in a different mess.*

Breathless, she entered through a side entrance and found the nearest restroom. There, seated in a stall, she powered up the phone. *Why would "the voice" call again after so many weeks?*

As always, there was no message, only a number, one she'd never seen. Did he have a new burner? Was it the same man? This could be a trap, a police sting, or a setup by some rival drug dealer, which could only mean something had happened to him.

Another woman entered the restroom. All Allison saw was a pair of Michael Kors slip-ons. She waited until the intruder left, closed her eyes, and dialed. It rang once.

"Hello." A man perhaps. Allison couldn't tell. It sounded like he was using electronic distortion. Of one thing she was sure. It was *not* the man who had blackmailed her into killing people.

"You wanted me to call?" she asked.

There was a pause. Was he surprised she was a woman? *He must not know who I am.*

"I got your number from Maurice Hamby."

Allison now had a name for "the voice." She made a note to find out more about the man who'd threatened her life and her family.

"Yes?"

"I hear you paint houses."

It took her a moment to get his meaning. She hit the mute button, bowed her head, and began to sob. *He got my number from this Hamby person. He knows I've killed people. I'm trapped. There's nothing else I can do.*

Steeling herself, she unmuted. "What can I do for you?" she asked in a flat tone.

"There's these two people..."

Even through the distortion, he sounded nervous. *That's a good sign*, Allison thought. Her heartbeat slowed. She was gaining control. If she was going to kill for him, this person would pay her a lot more money than Hamby had.

He started to explain why the two people should die, but Allison cut him off. "I don't wanna know," she snapped. "All I need is who they are, where they live, and the places they frequent."

Before disconnecting, she gave him the same instructions she'd given Hamby, right down to the anonymous bank account in Antigua. He gave explicit directions as to how the murder should appear. They were gruesome, but for two hundred grand she could accommodate him.

As she left the restroom, Allison glanced about, wondering if anyone were watching. She caught herself and shrugged it off as paranoia. She would shop for a pair of .22 caliber pistols in the morning. Time permitting, she could stop at an indoor range for some practice.

She also considered going by the library to Google Maurice Hamby, then remembered Kyle and Leslie would soon be home from school. If she weren't there when they arrived, they might wonder. She could do her research and preparation later.

CHAPTER 7
PAXTON DAVIS

Atlanta, Georgia
Monday, October 15

Still seething from his conversation with Tom Williams, Paxton set his phone on his desk, let out a deep sigh and rubbed his eyes. His head ached from lack of sleep.

He'd known Williams for more than forty years. They met when Paxton was a young detective trying to run down the Atlanta child killer. Williams, a newspaper writer, was new in town and looking to make a name for himself. How the hell they became friends, Paxton could no longer remember, nor did it matter.

The last thing he needed was a nosy reporter, especially Tom Williams, stirring things up in the middle of a murder investigation. Already, rumors were flying. Atlanta had another serial killer, or some homophobic hate group.

Williams was as good as reporters got. When he latched onto a lead, he was like a dog with a chew toy. Often, the information he provided helped police clear an investigation. The sonofabitch should've been a cop.

Just as he was wondering what else could go wrong, Paxton's phone rang. The number was one he didn't recognize, a "404" area code.

"Davis," he replied.

"Lieutenant Davis, this is Lieutenant Mavis Wilson with Internal Affairs."

"Yes, Lieutenant Wilson, what can I do for you?" he sighed.

"I need to talk to you about an inquiry. Nothing to worry about. When might you be available?"

"Lieutenant Wilson, I'm in the middle of a murder investigation, and I'm a bit shorthanded. Can you tell me what this is about?"

"I certainly can... in person. How does your schedule look this afternoon?"

"Pretty much like every afternoon, full."

"I understand. Would it be okay if I popped by in a half hour?"

"You might as well come now. I'll be waiting for you."

"It'll take me a few minutes to get my things together. Let's say fifteen."

"Fifteen."

Paxton knew Wilson by reputation only. She was thirty-five years old and a rising star in the darkest corner of the police department. This was due, he thought, to her gender, but he dare not say so. The last thing he needed was a harassment complaint.

To the beat cops and detectives, she was "Hardass Wilson." Even among a species known for eating its young, she stood out in ways that made other IA officers seem lenient. This would not end well for someone, Paxton knew, hopefully not him.

Fifteen minutes later, Lieutenant Wilson and a young corporal walked through Paxton's door, closing it behind them.

"Lieutenant Davis," she began, "let me start by saying you have nothing to worry about. This investigation has nothing to do with you."

"Well, that's a relief."

If she caught his sarcasm, she didn't show it. "This involves a person under your supervision, a recent transfer. I'm here to notify you, in strictest confidence, as a matter of professional courtesy." She annunciated the last two words with feigned sincerity.

"I appreciate that. I suppose you're going to tell me who you're investigating."

"Detective Don Walsh." She pulled a thick manila file from her briefcase, set it on Paxton's desk, and laid her hand on it as if it were nothing more than a prop. She never once offered to open it.

"We have sworn statements from several individuals that Detective Walsh, while assigned to Narcotics, engaged, on multiple occasions, in bribery and extortion. He may also have been an accessory to murder."

Paxton took a deep breath and let it out slowly. "Let me guess. Every one of these sources is an upstanding citizen, pillars of the community, doctors, schoolteachers, maybe a preacher or two, not the kind of folks who'd lie to a police officer."

Wilson gave him an annoyed look. "We also have complaints Detective Walsh used unnecessary force."

Paxton glanced at Mavis' companion. "Well now, that's something new."

She leaned closer and bore into the homicide cop with a cold stare. "Lieutenant Davis, you may have heard that Detective Walsh went through a nasty divorce a while back. At one point, his wife alleged he'd molested their son, charges she later dropped."

Paxton raised his voice just enough to benefit anyone outside his office who might be eavesdropping.

"Lieutenant Wilson, do you think you could get to the point of this visit? Because if you're looking for me to help you crucify one of my officers, you can think again. Even if I didn't have a multiple murder investigation, I wouldn't have time to help you with your witch hunt."

"Lieutenant let me assure you this is not a 'witch hunt,' and there's nothing I need from you at this point. Don Walsh is going down, Lieutenant, and when he does, you'll want the record to show you did everything you could to assist us. Like I said, this is just a courtesy call. But I can also assure you, if you don't cooperate, you may find yourself retiring sooner than expected."

With that, she picked up the envelope and stormed out, the young corporal in tow.

Paxton sat back and stared out the window. He hated dealing with IA. He hated it even worse when their investigations turned up something legit.

He'd known Walsh only a short time. He knew precious little of the man's tenure in Narcotics and nothing about his personal life. Perhaps he could speak with Walsh... later. In the meantime, Paxton would find out more about him. He could contact the head of Narcotics but preferred to remain discreet.

Instead, he picked up a phone and called Lyman Gwynn. Paxton and Lyman grew up together, and Gwynn was the only narc Paxton knew or trusted.

"Lyman!" he said when the man answered.

"Paxton Davis! Been a long time. What can I do for you?"

"You got time for a cup of coffee?"

Gwynn knew this was more than a sudden need for caffeine and company.

"Sure. What you got in mind."

"Mickey D's down the street."

• • •

It was late afternoon. The supper crowd hadn't arrived yet, and business was slow. The MacDonald's Paxton chose was just far enough from the precinct that few officers ever came here. It was perfect.

He ordered a tall coffee and took a window booth with a view of the parking lot. Lyman showed up moments later and slid in across from him with a large Coke and couple of fried apple pies.

"What's up, Paxton?"

"I need your help on something. You know I got that homicide investigation, the one with the three lawyers."

"You want my help with that?"

"No, Lyman. The only thing I need you to do is stop talking to reporters, especially Tom Williams."

Gwynn looked abashed.

"Meanwhile, I got another problem. I got a visit this afternoon from Mavis Wilson."

Gwynn's eyes bulged. "Hardass Wilson?"

"Uh huh."

"What's she investigating you for?"

Paxton shook his head in derision. "She ain't investigating me, man. She's investigating one of my detectives."

"Do I know him?"

"Yeah, and I need you to keep this under your hat. Can you do that?"

"You know me. I won't say nothing to nobody."

Paxton considered a reply to that, but let it drop.

"Lyman, I ain't helping Mavis with nothing. You understand, right? I just need to know if there's truth in what she's saying. I need to know if I'm gonna lose one of my lead investigators."

"I got you."

"You think you can help?"

"I'll try. Who is it?"

"Don Walsh."

Gwynn shook his head. "Now, that is one mean ass redneck. He's a good cop though. There was this one time he took a straight razor off a dealer and held it to his neck until backup arrived. Then he kicked the sonofabitch's ass."

Paxton grinned. "Now Lyman, you and I may not see anything wrong with that, but Mavis would have a different view. Know what I'm saying?"

"Yeah. I bet. At least Walsh didn't cut the dude with his own straight razor."

"Have you heard anything about Walsh taking bribes or ambushing a dealer?"

Gwynn scratched his chin and thought. "Nah, he had that shootout a few months ago, but that was righteous, Paxton. The board cleared him. He's one of the best cops I ever worked with."

"Well, you are in Narcotics," Paxton smiled. "Listen. Keep an eye out for me, if you don't mind. But don't go asking questions. I don't want folks thinking you're working for Mavis."

"I hear that."

"The same guys who won't tell her shit will tell everybody else as soon as she's gone. You know how it is."

"I know how it is."

"What's Mavis' problem anyway?" asked Paxton.

"Word is, years ago, when she was little, her older brother got killed by a cop."

"No shit! A white cop?"

"Nope. But the brother's just as dead. He was a small-time dealer, and rumor was the cop was shaking him down. He snitched on the cop and got his ass popped."

"I can see how that might color Mavis's attitude toward the men and women of our profession… Now don't start asking questions. Just give me a call when you hear something. We can meet back here." Paxton glanced down at Gwynn's empty tray. "Maybe I'll buy you a Big Mac and fries to go with that shit."

Lyman grinned. "Sounds good."

"Later."

"Later."

· · ·

Allison pulled a jar of spaghetti sauce and a bottle of olive oil from the cupboard then pretended she was looking for noodles. There was an unopened box in the back corner. With a sleight of hand, she hid it behind the canned vegetables.

Leslie listened to music from her phone while pretending she was doing her homework. Allison pulled out an ear bud, much to her daughter's annoyance.

"I have to run to the store to get some pasta for supper," she said. "Need anything?"

"Nope," said Leslie, cramming the bud back in her ear.

Allison made a mad dash to Publix then stopped at the library to research Maurice Hamby. She was about to step from her golf cart when she spotted Wendy Miller strolling down the sidewalk, followed by her daughter, Madison. Madison was a schoolmate of Leslie. From her expression, she'd rather be anywhere but here.

Madison didn't strike Allison as the studious type. Long before Allison tumbled to Wendy's affair with Rob, the woman suggested they get their daughters together. Allison broached the idea to Leslie.

"Uh, no, Mom," she said, "Madison Miller is the school slut."

Allison smiled and watched the pair disappear into the library. The apple, as they say, never falls far from the tree. Madison had been a chubby little girl but had grown into, Allison had to admit, a beautiful young woman. Beneath her exterior, no doubt, she still carried the scars of an unhappy childhood.

Not wanting them to see her, Allison decided to come back later. "Later", she realized, would mean tomorrow. Already, her evening forays were attracting unwanted attention from her family. She'd wait until they were at work and school.

CHAPTER 8
THE ARRIVAL

Midtown
Monday, October 15

It's late afternoon. I'm sitting on my porch swing enjoying the cool dry air when a dark gray van pulls into the driveway and disgorges three weary passengers. I greet my daughter and grandsons with open arms. The boys head straight to the door before their mom yells at them.

"William, Henry, get back out here and grab your bags! I'm not carrying them for you."

With heavy sighs, they return to the van and haul out their luggage.

"Let me give you a hand," I offer. "You guys are in the large room upstairs. Your mom gets her old bedroom."

"Where are you going to sleep?" Marie asks.

"I set up a bed in my office a few months back. I don't sleep much these days."

She nods and looks away.

"I talked to Kathy yesterday," I add. "She and Sean and the girls are coming over for supper."

"Wonderful."

"What are we having?" Henry asks.

"*Food*, Henry," sighs his mother, "and you'll eat every mouthful."

"I'm grilling chicken," I say, "with squash and asparagus."

"Great!" says William.

Too late, I remember Henry doesn't like asparagus. Tired as he is, though, he's nice enough not to remind me.

From the backyard, Bogie barks. Henry runs through the house, joined by his older brother. They grab a chewed-up Frisbee I keep on the patio.

I gaze at my younger daughter. She gives me a sheepish grin.

"Here," I say, "Come sit on the swing. You look exhausted."

She takes a seat, and I lean against the railing.

"So, tell me. What's going on?"

"I've had it, Dad. Bill's gone all the time. When he gets home, he's too tired to do anything with his family. I feel like I've taken in a boarder who expects to sleep with me."

I feel compelled to defend the man, as much as I dislike him. "He has to make a living somehow."

"Not like this he doesn't." Her eyes flash in anger. I know I've hit a sore spot. "It's not like he's the sole breadwinner. I have a career too, but I manage to get home, cook supper, and supervise homework every night. Do you know he was offered a professorship at George Washington, and turned it down? It's all about his ego. He's a bigwig now, and he gets to hobnob with all those world leaders. He's so excited, because he's going to *Davos* this year."

I had no idea he'd risen so far. Maybe there's more to him than I suspected.

"I'm finally doing what I should've done long ago," says Marie. "I'm taking that offer with Mom's firm. If Bill decides his family's more important than his career, he can come down here and join us." She catches my momentary panic and adds, "as soon as we get our own place."

"Well, I hope he comes to his senses." It takes me a second to realize I mean it. Whatever I think of Bill, I want what's best for Marie and the boys. "You just sit here and relax," I add. "Can I get you something, water, lemonade, Diet Coke? I could add a little something to it, if you like."

She smiles. "I'll take my Diet Coke straight up."

I return with a cold can and glass of ice. "Just relax here while I get the grill going."

For decades, I managed with an old Weber and charcoal. Then, two years ago, Colleen insisted I install a Char Broil with an in-ground gas supply. This is the first time I've used it since she died. I pour myself a glass of wine and set to work.

Watching William and Henry throwing the Frisbee for Bogie, I realize how much I've missed them. Before long, they'll be in school and Marie at work. That'll leave me time to write during the day. Maybe when they move into a permanent home, Bogie and I can take that road trip.

From the front come the sounds of car doors slamming and the squeals of two young girls running through the house. As they streak past, I yell, "Hey you two!"

They stop in their tracks. Eight-year-old Mary Frances jumps into my arms with her full weight and nearly knocks me down. Her older sister, Lauren, wraps herself around me in a tight hug.

Marie appears on the back steps with her sister and brother-in law. They settle in on the patio, while I step into the kitchen to fetch more glasses of wine. When I return, the girls have joined their cousins in a circle, trying to keep the Frisbee away from Bogie, who's beside himself with excitement.

Later, as I pull the chicken and vegetables from the grill and turn off the heat, Kathy and Marie set the table. Kathy recites the Catholic blessing Colleen taught them then gazes at her sister. "Well, it appears we've slaughtered the prodigal chicken in honor of the fatted..."

"I'd choose that next word carefully if I were you," snaps Marie.

Kathy turns to William and Henry. "Are you guys involved in sports?"

"We were," Henry mutters as he picks at his food.

"I run track," says William. "He plays basketball."

Lauren pipes up, "Me too. And I'm going out for cross-country this spring." She's a few months younger than William and almost as tall.

"Mary Frances is at Paideia. Lauren goes to Marist," says Kathy. "Both schools are excellent. You should check them out."

"I need to figure out where we're going to live first," says Marie. "I have a meeting with the partners tomorrow morning. Then I'm going house-hunting."

"Where?" I ask, trying not to sound too excited.

"I thought about Vinings, but I'm not sure I can afford it. Smyrna's closer, but I understand the East Cobb schools are better."

"If you're looking in East Cobb, there's a great parochial school in Roswell," says Kathy.

Marie's getting tired of this subject. Grasping for something else, she turns to the girls and asks what they want to be when they grow up.

"I'm going to be a ballet dancer," says Mary Frances.

"I want to teach high school English," says Lauren.

"You don't want to be doctor like your mom?" Marie asks.

"I don't think so."

Kathy smiles at her daughter. "What about you guys?"

Henry shrugs without looking up.

"I want to be a newspaper reporter, like Pops," says William.

I glance at Marie. She rolls her eyes.

"That's great!" I say, as much to annoy Marie as anything else.

"Yeah. I've been writing for my high school paper... and some other stuff."

"I'd like to see it sometime."

Marie changes the subject again. "I keep wondering what Dad's going to do when he grows up."

"Well, I *was* planning on travelling, maybe writing a book." No sooner are the words out of my mouth than I realize the implication that Marie's arrival has interrupted my plans.

If she catches this, she doesn't let on. "Tell me you're not still running," she says.

"All the time," Kathy chimes in.

"Whenever I can. I used to run with Lauren, but now she runs off and leaves me."

"I'd like to run with you," says William.

"I get up pretty early."

"That's okay. I don't mind getting up early."

"I'll wake you up at 5:30 then. How about you, Henry?"

He shakes his head.

Kathy's expression changes. "What's this I hear about another shooting over on Vedado?" She catches Marie's startled look but presses on. "Another attorney... the papers are calling them the Midtown Murders."

Marie does a slow pan in my direction. "Uh, Dad, when were you planning to mention this?"

"I haven't had a chance to tell you."

The girls were young at time of the Atlanta Child Murders, but they're old enough to remember.

"I spoke to some of the officers investigating the case. You remember Paxton Davis. He has several leads. They should catch the killer soon." This is total bullshit, and my daughters know it. All I want right now is to reassure them.

"So, Sean, what have you been up to?" I ask.

It's as though everyone suddenly remembers he's here. He looks up from his meal and brightens. "I'm working with an engineer from Tech. We're developing a microchip. You implant in the brain of a patient. It monitors his vital signs and relays them back to his doctor on the Internet. In most cases, it won't even require an office visit."

Marie is stunned. "Wow! You sound like Dr. McCoy on 'Star Trek.'"

"Exactly," Kathy butts in. "And that's just the first step. Before long, the chip will be able to release nanoparticles that'll repair or remove damaged cells."

"Nano what?" asks Marie.

"Tiny particles," Sean explains. "They're molecular computers built from carbon compounds. Everything we need is right there in the body. The microchip serves as a little manufacturing plant. The doctor can monitor and direct it remotely."

This stuff amazes me. "So, what you're saying is you can treat just about any disease or injury without surgery or drugs."

"Eventually," he says. "We're not there yet. Naturally, we'll start with things like cancer, Alzheimer's... stuff like that."

"And then you can work your way around to obesity, acne... flatulence," I add.

This brings guffaws from the kids and a disapproving look from Kathy.

"Someday," she adds, "we'll be able to treat psychological conditions, like bipolar disorder, hyperactivity..."

Marie's skeptical. "Who defines psychological disorders?" For once, she's beaten me to the punch.

"Naturally, we'll need oversight," responds Sean.

"Naturally," I join in. "We wouldn't want someone defining homosexuality and political incorrectness as psychological disorders. These nanoparticles could tell us what to think and how to act."

"Participation will be voluntary," adds Kathy.

"That's how it starts," says Marie.

"There'll be regulations too," Sean blurts out.

"And that," I conclude, "is where the *involuntary* part begins."

"Dad, you read too much Orwell and Huxley," says Kathy. She gazes at the food in front of her as a single tear forms in the corner of her eye. "The work Sean's doing will someday ensure that no one has to die the way Mom did."

As I'm taking this all in, I gaze around the table at my grandchildren to gauge their responses. They're the ones who'll live in Sean's brave new world. William and Lauren seem fascinated. Mary Frances looks bemused, and Henry's gone back to picking at his food.

"Why can't we go home?" he mutters under his breath.

Before Marie can say anything William pipes in. "Why don't you stop being such a wuss?"

Without warning, Henry turns and punches his brother on the shoulder.

"Stop it!" Marie yells. "I'm tired of this. If I hear anymore, I'm sending you both up to your room for the night."

• • •

As I'm putting away the leftovers, Marie's phone rings. She checks the readout, gives a deep sigh, and steps out on the patio. Through the open window I overhear her.

"Bill, I've explained all this. I've made up my mind. I'm not taking any more of your shit."

I glance at Kathy. She's heard it as well. I point to the dining room and she nods.

Moments later Marie returns, wiping tears and working to regain her composure.

"Hey. Mo," says Kathy, "Why don't you let us clean up? You guys need to rest. I'm sure you have a big day tomorrow."

Later, as I'm on the porch saying goodbye to Kathy and her family, a man in a dark hoodie and sweats runs past. He's wearing no reflective gear. He must think he's invincible. I go back inside, and the image leaves my mind as quickly as it appeared.

By now the grill has cooled. I put the protective cover back on and smell the barbeque from next door. The guys are partying with their friends in the hot tub and singing along to show tunes.

The leaves overhead have begun to turn. In a week or so I'll get out my yard broom. This year, at least I'll have help from my grandsons. Maybe I'll clean out the playhouse and convert it to a gym for them. I can bring down my old weights from the attic.

I finally have something I've been missing since Colleen died, something to look forward to. Despite all our losses, life's good.

For the moment I forget that within the past two months, three of my neighbors have been gunned down in their own homes.

CHAPTER 9
ROUGH JUSTICE

Midtown
Monday, October 15

Stately, plump Lou Allen sat at the antique roll top desk in his upstairs bedroom. It was a gift from a wealthy, unmarried uncle in Montgomery, a criminal defense attorney of some renown. Lou chose divorce law, instead.

This came in handy for him. Before coming out of the closet, he'd been married fifteen years to a woman who'd borne him a son. The ex-wife and son still lived in suburban Lithonia. Nowadays she only spoke to Lou through lawyers, the son not at all. Lou missed the Boy Scout campouts and church outings. But if he had to do it over again, he'd gladly trade all that for his new life... or so he told himself.

He was quite good at what he did, thanks to a repressed memory specialist who worked with young children, all of them alleged victims of sexual abuse. If pressed on the subject, Lou would admit Eleanor Heinz was even better at what she did than he was.

Eleanor rarely accepted new patients, except by referral from divorce attorneys. After hooking up with Lou, she moved into the lucrative role of an expert witness. Now more than ninety percent of the children Lou referred to her could describe, in lurid detail, the perverted things one or the other of their parents had done to them. Naturally, they all gave videotaped testimony, to spare them the additional trauma of appearing in a crowded courtroom.

Tonight, Lou was putting together an invitation list for his annual Halloween costume party. Booked as a traditional masque, the autumn soiree had become the talk of the Midtown social circuit.

Each year he pulled from the desk a stack of index cards containing data on everyone he knew. In what had become a meticulous ritual, he leafed through the cards, putting those he planned to invite in one pile. Anyone who'd incurred his wrath in the past year went in the other. Perhaps by next year they would redeem themselves.

From time to time he'd stop, take a puff from his elegant cigarette holder and study the smoke patterns as they drifted toward the twelve-foot ceiling. Seated in his dragon print dressing gown, he gazed at his reflection in the window and watched the passing headlights on Monroe Drive. His classic home stood high enough to provide an excellent view.

A light came on in the bedroom window next door. It was the room of that handsome young man, the one with the learning disability. For a moment Lou imagined the boy was looking at him, silhouetted in the faint illumination. He smiled to himself and wondered what it would be like to spend some time with the lad.

. . .

An only child, Ben Hogarth had the mental maturity of a ten-year-old trapped in a young adult body with all its hormonal urges. Diagnosed at age six with Asperger's syndrome, he spent most days in his room, expressing himself in charcoal, pastels and paper.

When Ben was younger, when his mother was still alive, she and his father would take him to church, in the fervent hope that something of salvation might sink in. As an emergency room nurse, Marsha Hogarth worked nights. Her husband, Max, worked days. They took turns caring for Ben and making feeble attempts to home school him.

Following Marsha's death, Max retired early. Nowadays, neither he nor Ben left the house, except for the occasional doctor's visit. A relative stopped by to see them once a week and ran to the grocery store for whatever they needed.

Tonight, the object of Ben's effort was a pastel drawing of a dragon, seated atop a pile of brocaded cushions, puffing on a hookah, and wearing a silk dressing gown. The dragon had a broad smile, but it was not a friendly one. This dragon, Ben knew, was evil beyond imagination. The drawing would someday become the cover of a graphic novel like the ones the relative purchased for him each week out of her own funds.

Ben glanced up and saw the man next door staring back at him. In an instant, he turned off his desk lamp and continued staring from his darkened room. After a time, he grew weary of watching the man flip the small, white cards, and instead counted the cars passing on the street. Coming down the sidewalk he saw a figure wrapped in a long coat.

• • •

The night had grown late, too late for Claire Dowdy to be walking home alone. There were no other pedestrians, and the cars passing on Monroe did little to reassure her. The half-moon overhead brightened her path, illuminating the hexagonal sidewalk tiles, many of them broken and shoved out of place by the roots of surrounding trees.

She no longer carried a purse when walking home at night for fear of having it snatched. Her wallet, shoved into her right pocket, bulged under the threadbare overcoat her grandmother gave her when she was in high school.

Simeon Weems, a coworker at Popeye's Fried Chicken, had offered to walk her home, but she turned him down. The dweeb was five years younger than her. Now she felt like an idiot walking by herself in the dark.

This wasn't the first time she'd done this, but tonight felt different. She nearly stumbled on a loose stone and looked down for a moment to regain her balance. When she looked up again her breath caught as a thin young man stepped down off the porch steps in front of her. There was something about him that frightened her, the slow, casual way he moved, staring at her.

A large vehicle passed a few feet away. Claire had nowhere to turn. The man, walking toward her, seemed to sense this. His leering face shone in the light of a streetlamp. She was about to say something when, from behind her, a thick forearm clamped around her throat.

She noticed something else, as well, though she couldn't register what it was, a small, dark object weaving its way slowly uphill from a block away, unnoticed by either of her assailants. What, or who, it was Claire had no idea.

As they dragged her under the low-hanging branches of a Magnolia, she twisted in a frantic effort to free herself. It was no use. She lifted her left foot, as her brother had taught her years ago, and brought it down with all her might on what felt like an instep. She heard a satisfying crunch, followed by a muffled scream.

"You little cunt," the fetid breath gasped in her right ear.

Again, she saw the figure working its way uphill, now closer. It seemed to be another person, perhaps a large man, but by now it was too late.

The assailant tightened his grip on her neck. Images around her began to fade as dots swam before her eyes. Another pair of hands grabbed her flailing legs and pulled them apart. They were taking her behind the house, away from the street and the passing cars.

Suddenly the grip on her legs loosened, as did the forearm at her throat. "Get him," the man behind her called out.

Claire collapsed to the ground and rolled under the cover of an Althea bush. Through the branches she watched as one of her assailants went down and then the other. They made sickening sounds as the man in the dark hoodie kicked them repeatedly.

One struggled to his feet and started to run. He tripped over a tree root and came down hard on his face. For what must have been several minutes, the man in the hoodie kicked each of them in the ribs, the head and the kidneys. The only sound either of them made was a persistent whimpering when the man in the hoodie finally stopped, placed his hands on his knees, and caught his breath.

"You alright?" he asked Claire. He stared directly at her in the shadows of the bush, but she couldn't see his face. Covered from head to toe, he looked to be the same height as the two men at his feet, but twice as wide in the shoulders. He wore thin gloves that matched the rest of his outfit. From his voice, Claire guessed he was black. She wasn't sure.

She gasped and felt the cold night air rush back into her lungs. "I'll be okay," she croaked. She almost laughed as she realized how ridiculous she sounded, then added, "Thanks."

She was about to say something else when the man straightened up, nodded, and without another word, turned and jogged uphill toward Ponce.

She struggled out from under the bush, started to follow, then turned as if she'd forgotten something.

Carefully she stepped over one of the young men lying on the ground. With a deep moan, he began to come around. When he started to roll over, she kicked him with all her one hundred fifteen pounds. The toe of her shoe landed in his left eye socket, unleashing a gush of blood and clear liquid. As she did so, a large truck trundled past. In the noise and distraction, Claire never heard the crack of bone on bone. Nor did she notice the unnatural angle of the man's neck.

As she turned to go, she looked up at a bedroom window, just in time to glimpse Ben Hogarth's face in the passing headlights. Ben closed his curtains and turned on his desk lamp. He put away the pastel of the dragon, pulled out his charcoal, and went to work on his next composition. This would be a work of painstaking care.

An hour later he leaned back and studied the results, a series of panels, the first a small rendering of a beautiful woman walking down a broken sidewalk beneath a single streetlight, the next a circular close-up of her frightened face as two young thugs grabbed her, one of them pulling at her clothes.

In the ensuing scenes, a large figure, his face buried in a hoodie, suddenly appeared. He went through a series of martial arts moves, taking down both assailants. The man in the hoodie wore leather gloves, dark trousers and boots. There was nothing visible of his face. In the final panel, his work completed, he jogged away, as the woman kicked one of her assailants in the eye with the pointed toe of her shoe.

Ben permitted himself one of his rare smiles. His cast of characters had a new hero. He dubbed him "The Dark Avenger."

Exhausted, Ben brushed his teeth, changed into his Spider Man pajamas, and went to bed. Next door, Lou Allen did likewise. Neither of them was awake, an hour later, when revolving blue lights shone through their windows and washed across their ceilings.

CHAPTER 10
WILLIAM AND HENRY WAKEFIELD

Midtown
Tuesday, October 16
Today, I'm up before sunrise. I pull my warmups over a tee shirt and running shorts and pad upstairs where I awaken William, careful not to disturb his brother.

While William splashes water on his face and dresses, I put on an extra-large pot of coffee and let Bogie out into the back yard. I wait for him to scamper around sniffing every corner as though it were a new discovery. He finally returns and barks at the back door for me to let him in.

William joins me for my morning run. Today we make our way over to Monroe and down to the Beltline, a popular route for runners. We turn south and pass Ponce City Market. We're almost to North Highland before we turn back.

On our return we pass Diane Hampton, who smiles and waves.

"Hey, Tom."

I wave back and glance at my grandson as a grin spreads across his face.

"Whoa! Is she a *friend* of yours, Pops?"

"She's a *neighbor*, William. I met her this past Saturday."

"I think I'm gonna like this neighborhood."

"Yeah. You'd better start liking your homework."

When we get back to Monroe, several cop cars have gathered in front of a large craftsman home. William wants to go check it out, but he needs to get ready for school. I'll go back later, when Marie and the boys have left for the day.

William and I return to find the house in an uproar. Marie's standing in the hallway, dressed and yelling upstairs to Henry to hurry up and get out of the shower. William goes to his mother's bedroom, where he shucks out of his clothes and uses the master bath.

I trundle off to the kitchen to prepare breakfast. Bogie, unaccustomed to this confusion, runs circles barking for attention. I hand him a snack and turn to find Henry, standing in the doorway ready for school.

Marie has gone back upstairs and is now yelling through the bathroom door at William. "Hurry up! It's time to leave! You need to be there early."

"Good morning," I say to Henry.

"Good morning."

I'm struggling for words. "I understand you like to play basketball."

He gives me another of his signature shrugs.

"If I could get tickets for some Hawks and Georgia Tech games, you think you might want to go?"

He brightens. "Sure."

Another moment of awkward silence, and finally I blurt out, "Look, I know it's tough being separated from your dad. I wasn't much younger than you when both my parents died. My grandparents did the best they could, and now I miss them too… but they weren't my parents. Know what I mean?"

He nods.

"I just want you to know I'm gonna do everything in my power to take care of you, your mom, and your brother. Okay?"

He nods again and turns away. After a moment, there comes a muffled "Thanks." He picks up his book bag and walks out to the van.

I turn to see Marie standing in the hall, tears pooling in her eyes. She quietly walks over and wraps me in a tight hug.

· · ·

When everyone's left, I shower and change into jeans, a long-sleeved shirt, and my old running shoes. It's a ten-minute walk back to Monroe.

The cops are still there. Don Walsh, standing just outside the yellow tape, is talking to two uniformed officers. He glances at me. His look tells me he's not happy to see me.

"Mr. Williams, this is an active crime scene. You'll need to move on and let these men do their work."

He looks like he spent the night under a bridge.

"What happened here?"

"You can leave now, Mr. Williams, or I'll have one of my officers run you in."

I cross the street and turn back to watch as crime scene techs crawl about like ants, bagging leaves and debris. A police photographer captures images of numbered markers placed in key spots. My first thought is there's been another shooting.

Next door, a portly man in purple silk bathrobe and bedroom slippers walks out onto his porch carrying a coffee cup and saucer. Walsh glances at him then turns abruptly and walks up the street to his car.

Now that he's gone, I can move in for a closer look. The crime techs, intent on their work, and the uniformed cops, intent on watching them, ignore me.

One of the police officers, a female, questions the man on the porch. From his gestures and facial expressions, he has no information for her.

The techs complete their work and carry the evidence bags back to their vehicles. The other officers depart, leaving the female cop alone at the scene.

To the right, another neighbor comes out to watch. He looks to be in his mid-sixties. I walk up and introduce myself. His name's Max Hogarth.

"Any idea what happened here?" I ask.

"Nope."

"How long have you lived here?"

"About thirty years… My wife and I moved in before our son was born. She passed fifteen years ago."

I nod. "I lost mine almost two years ago. We raised both our daughters in this neighborhood."

We're discussing how much the area has changed when the female officer comes over and asks if we saw or heard anything last night around ten PM. Maybe she assumes Max and I live together. She introduces herself as Sergeant Beth Long. She's medium height, athletic build, with brown hair pulled back in a ponytail. I'm guessing she's about thirty.

Max and I assure her we heard nothing last night.

She takes our names and asks if there's anyone else in the house.

"Just my son," says Max. "He has... um... Asperger's."

"Oh. Well... Do you think he'd be able to tell me if he heard or saw anything?"

"I doubt it. He usually turns in early and doesn't have much to say. Do you mind if I ask what happened here?"

"There was some altercation. We think it involved drugs. One man was killed, and another's still at Grady. Do you mind if I speak with your son?"

Max considers then agrees, as long as she keeps it brief.

He goes inside. Long follows, and I fall in behind them, looking like I belong here but maintaining a respectful distance. If this bothers Max, he doesn't mention it.

"Ben?" he calls out. From upstairs comes the sound of footsteps on a wood floor.

A young man appears at the top of the stairs. He's dressed in cutoffs and a black tee shirt with a grimacing image of the Hulk. He's a tad overweight and looks to be in his mid-twenties. He wears heavy horn-rimmed glasses and stares at his feet.

"Ben," says Max, "this nice officer is trying to find some bad guys who were outside our window last night. She has a couple of questions for you."

The young man shows no reaction. He stares at his feet and begins to rock back and forth.

On the wall are several pictures, one of a much younger Max with a woman, presumably his wife, and their son. In the picture Ben must be about three.

There are also several charcoal and pastel drawings. They resemble the panels in a comic book, the kind many young adults read. The technique is excellent, though many of the scenes are dark and violent. The characters have exaggerated features. Most of the women are large-breasted, the men tall and muscular. The only thing missing is dialog.

"Did you do these, Ben?" I ask.

Long shoots me a suspicious look. Before she can ask if I live here, I notice one of the drawings. Newer than the others, it shows a large, hooded man roundhouse kicking another man in the face.

Cowering against a tree trunk is a beautiful young woman in a torn dress. The tree is identical to the magnolia between this house and the one next door. Beside it is an althea bush, where another man lies, apparently unconscious.

"Ben likes to draw comic book pictures," Max explains.

"Graphic novels," Ben mumbles. His voice startles us.

I turn back to the drawing. "Max, how long ago did Ben draw this?"

"This is the first I've seen it. It must've been here when I came down this morning."

"Do you think Ben may have drawn it last night?"

Sergeant Long edges over for a closer look. She sees what I've seen.

"I think we may have a witness," she says softly.

Max stares at us and then back at his son, who continues to rock back and forth, arms folded, staring at his feet. "Ben," he asks, "can you tell us about this?"

There's no reaction. The rocking becomes more pronounced.

Long turns to Max. "Mr. Hogarth, we have an officer, another woman, who specializes in interviewing young people... like Ben. She's very kind and patient. If you don't mind, I'd like to have her talk to him."

"I'll agree under one condition. She interviews him *right* here. If Ben starts to get upset, she'll have to leave right away."

"Agreed. Meanwhile, would you mind if I borrowed this picture?"

"Come back later," Max says under his breath, "when he's gone back upstairs."

Long smiles and nods.

As they work out the details, I wave to Max and pantomime that I'll see him later.

· · ·

Walking home, I pull out my cell and call an old friend, Bonnie Baron. Bonnie and her life partner run a gallery and art agency in Decatur. I tell her about Ben and his drawings. I detail his circumstances and the quality of his work.

Bonnie seems interested, but hesitant. She starts to say she's never represented an autistic artist, then stops. I wait. The only word she utters is, "Liam."

A couple of years ago, Bonnie introduced Colleen and me to a promising young painter, Liam Sanstrom, and his date, Dina Savage, at an outdoor concert. Later that night, according to Savage, he tied her up and raped her. When a Cobb County jury failed to convict him, Savage gunned him down on the steps of the courthouse.

"Let me see what I can do," Bonnie finally says.

"Thanks, Bonnie." I fumble for something else to say. All I can think of is, "Give me a call."

"Sure."

I return home, settle into my office chair and transcribe notes onto my laptop. When I finish, I pull out the number Mitch gave me for Ambrose Mangham.

The man answers after six rings. He sounds sleepy. It occurs to me not all news writers get up at five AM for a morning run.

"Mr. Mangham, this is Tom Williams. I got your number from Mitch Danner with the *AJC*."

"Yes." He sounds perturbed.

I glance at my laptop, which doubles as my clock these days. It's ten AM. The man's obviously a night owl.

"Mitch tells me you have some inside information on the police investigation into the Midtown murders."

There's a noticeable shift in his tone. "Well, I've spoken to police I know, and yeah, they told me things they haven't made public."

I start to wonder how much of this is bullshit.

"Mr. Mangham..."

"Call me 'Ambrose.'"

"Sure... Call me Tom. Mitch and I have known each other for years. I'm retired now, but I still write occasionally for the *AJC* and the *Georgia Globe*."

"I've heard of you. In fact, I read your interview with that woman over in Mississippi, the one they sent away for murdering her boyfriend."

"She paid somebody to murder a man who raped her when she was thirteen years-old," I correct him.

"That's right. Now I remember."

"Anyway, I live in Midtown, so I have a keen interest in these murders. The last was a couple of blocks from my house. I was wondering if you might be free to meet, maybe for lunch."

"Let me check." He pauses, and I imagine him pretending to consult his calendar to make it appear he's busy, an old trick I learned from Colleen. "Sure. I'm attending a luncheon for business leaders today. You want to get together tomorrow, say eleven thirty? That way we'll beat the crowd."

"Sounds good. How about someplace near you. I understand you're in Buckhead."

"Yep."

"Are you familiar with the White House."

"Yep."

"I'll meet you there tomorrow at eleven-thirty."

. . .

Bogie and I set out for his morning walk. On Eighth Street we come upon a crew of workmen breaking up an old concrete driveway. An idea comes to me. I ask for the foreman, and one of the men points to a guy sitting in his pickup with his window down speaking on a phone.

I walk over as he finishes his call.

He eyes me with suspicion. "Can I help you?"

"Yeah. I was wondering if you might be willing to take on a small job pouring a backyard basketball court."

He considers for a moment. "Where?"

"A couple of blocks over." I give him directions.

"We're pouring here tomorrow." He smiles. "If there's any left over, I'll come by and take care of that basketball court for you. You have the forms ready?"

"I will by tomorrow."

"I'll call you when we finish up here. I'll need to see the size of the area before I can give you a quote."

I give him my cell number. He hands me a card. Though neither of us brought it up, we both know there'll be extra concrete, already paid for, concrete that would've gone to waste otherwise. He'll quote me a cash price and divide it with his crew. No one at his office will be any the wiser.

• • •

My journey takes me past the home of Jacob Epstein, whose address I remember from my research. A moving van has somehow wedged into the narrow drive, and two men are loading furniture under the supervision of an attractive woman about thirty. She's tall and thin, with long black hair.

I walk up to her. "Hi."

She gives me a look of sadness mixed with annoyance. "Can I help you?"

"I'm a neighbor. I take it you're a friend of Jacob's. I just wanted to say how sorry I am for your loss."

Her expression softens. "Thanks."

"It came as such a shock to all of us. He was such a nice guy." I shift downwind, so she won't catch the scent of bullshit.

"I appreciate that... What did you say your name was?"

"Tom Williams. I just can't imagine why anyone would do something like this."

"That makes two of us." She extends a hand. "I'm Marina Kovacs," she says. "Sorry if I was abrupt. It's just been... a rough few weeks for me." She starts to choke. "And I don't see it getting better anytime soon."

"I was wondering if you're planning a wake of some sort."

"Not really. I suppose I should. The problem is Jacob wasn't exactly religious. Neither am I. I wouldn't even know where to start. I suppose his family's done something already. I only met them once, and... well, we didn't exactly hit it off."

"I understand you two were planning a wedding."

"Not much of a wedding. I'm Catholic and he was Jewish. You can see how that might be a problem for his parents..." She permits herself a brief smile. "Me being a shiksa and all. As for my folks, they still blame the Jews for killing Jesus."

"I see you're moving his stuff out."

"Yeah. We drew up wills before he was… killed. We left everything to each other. The house and the furniture were about all he had. I'll put the furniture in storage while I decide what to do with it. Now I'm moving it out because the house is under contract."

"I'm so sorry," I reply. Then a thought strikes me. "You say you're Catholic."

"Yeah, a bit of a lapsed Catholic, I'm afraid."

"I'd like to introduce you to my priest. I'm not sure what he can do under these circumstances, but it wouldn't hurt to talk to him."

I can tell she's debating this. I have no idea what her history with priests is or why she "lapsed."

"Look, why don't we just get together for lunch or breakfast somewhere, the three of us. I swear you'll love this guy. No commitment or anything. It could be nothing more than just a cup of coffee."

With a bit more wheedling I'm able to get her phone number and a promise to meet Father John. I continue home doing my best not to feel like a complete whore.

CHAPTER 11
THE ASSAILANTS

Atlanta, Georgia
Tuesday, October 16

Paxton sipped his coffee and nearly choked. Someone had filled the percolator with hot water, instead of cold. It tasted like shoe polish. He picked up a report on his desk from the night before, a homicide on Monroe Drive.

Twenty-five-year-old Derrick Lane had staggered into the street bleeding from his nose and mouth. A motorist swerved to avoid hitting him. First responders found another man, Mac Strong, lying on the ground under a bush in the narrow space between two houses. He was dead on arrival at Grady.

Lane was still under observation for head wounds, a fractured forearm, and a concussion. Police were canvassing the neighborhood. Don Walsh had signed the report. Uniformed officers had contacted him, thinking there might be a connection to the Midtown Murders.

Paxton was about to call Walsh when the detective walked in and collapsed into a chair. Judging by the exhaustion on his face, he'd been up all night.

"Walsh, you look like shit!"

"Thanks. I feel like it too."

"I was reading your report. Did Lane identify his attackers?"

"Nope. Swears he'd never seen them before. It was either two gang bangers or three. He can't seem to make up his mind. Says they were on him so fast he wasn't sure."

"Uh huh. Whatcha wanna bet he knows exactly who they are?"

"That'd be a pretty good bet," said Walsh. "Lane, his buddy, and I go way back. They have rap sheets as long as both your arms, from dealing to grand theft. Lane even picked up a couple of assaults. I don't believe a damned thing he says."

"Your report says the two lived on John Wesley Dobbs near Randolph. What were they doing in Midtown?"

"Lane says they were walking home from Hob Nob, up on Piedmont."

"That's a long walk… Your report says Strong was hit in the eye. This seems to be the season for poking folks' eyes out."

"Looks like a coincidence to me."

Paxton was unimpressed. "Yeah."

"Anyway, the crime scene guys were still there when I left, turning over every leaf, twig, and magnolia cone to see what they could find. I need to shower, change, and get back over there."

Paxton wrinkled his nose in mock disgust. "Good idea. I sent Long over to help out."

"Good. Thanks. I'll go by later and see what she's dug up."

Paxton shrugged. "Fine. Go get some rest."

As Walsh turned to leave, a slim white male in a three-piece suit and patent leather shoes stood in the doorway. Walsh glanced at Paxton, who looked like he'd succumbed to a sudden migraine.

The newcomer was in his mid-forties. His light brown hair, parted down the middle and slicked back, fell to his shoulders. There were tiny rhinestones in each earlobe.

"Detective Walsh," said Paxton, "I'd like you to meet the honorable Marcelle Lacroix, Esquire. Mr. Lacroix, to what do I owe the pleasure of your *unexpected* visit?"

Lacroix gave Paxton an oily smile. "I came by and saw your door was open."

Walsh leaned against the doorframe and smiled at the lawyer like a hungry Doberman eying a Chihuahua.

Normally cool in his dealings with civilians, especially lawyers, Paxton was becoming annoyed. "I was meeting with Detective Walsh, Mr. Lacroix."

Lacroix glanced at Walsh and shifted away from him. "Oh. Well. I just wanted to find out how you were coming with your investigation into the Midtown murders."

"You could have saved yourself the trip, counselor. We're still investigating, as we have been since this began. We'll make an announcement when we have a break. Until then, Mr. Lacroix..."

"I'm here representing the LGBT community, Lieutenant, and so far we're not impressed with your investigation. It seems this matter has not received the attention it..."

Walsh interrupted. "Something tells me you got beat up a lot when you were a kid."

Paxton shot Walsh a warning look. "The next time you come in here representing anybody, Mr. Lacroix, I suggest you make an appointment. Right now, I'm going to ask you to leave. If you'd like, I can have Detective Walsh escort you to the street."

Lacroix gave Walsh a sideways glance. "That won't be necessary, Lieutenant. I'll see myself out." He stepped out of the doorway, into the hall, and turned back. "But you haven't heard the last of this. Rest assured, I'll be speaking with your chief ... and the media."

As the lawyer left, Paxton shook his head. "Just what I need, some self-appointed crusader demanding regular briefings. Now I'll probably have the chief up my ass."

"Better than having Mr. Lacroix up your ass," Walsh smiled.

"Don't you even start that shit! I'll sign you up for sensitivity training."

Walsh gave an exaggerated cringe.

As he left, Paxton pondered which was worse, the odor of the unbathed policeman or the lingering scent of Lacroix's cologne.

• • •

Two hours later, bathed and refreshed, Walsh returned to Monroe Drive to find Beth Long still canvassing, alone. He pulled over to the curb and rolled down his passenger window. "What you got?"

Long stared into the dark sunglasses of the man known on the street as "Dapper Don." She felt a sick feeling come over her. Even through the shades she could see he was sizing her up, again.

On two occasions he'd asked her to join him for drinks after work. The first time she gave him an emphatic "no," hoping he'd take the hint. The second time she told him the answer would always be "no." And if he asked her again, she'd report him. For now, she avoided him, as much possible given their work situation, and limited their conversation to police matters.

It was because of cops like Walsh that Long pulled her hair back tight and wore no makeup. She didn't want anyone else hitting on her and thought the butch look might ward them off. She explained about Ben Hogarth and showed Walsh his drawings of the attack.

"Who's this?" Walsh asked, pointing to the image of the hooded figure.

"There's a note on the back."

He flipped it over. At the bottom, in block figures so small he could barely read them, were two words, "Dark Avenger."

Walsh started toward the Hogarth home, but Long stopped him. "Ben has communications issues, Don…"

"I don't care."

"Yes. You do. Right now, if he gives you anything at all, it'll be worthless. If you get him upset, we'll lose him completely. We need to approach him cautiously. We need to let Edith Campos talk to him. I promised his dad."

"Fine. I want her over here right away. I'll wait outside while she talks to him."

Long returned an hour later with Campos. A transplanted Californian, she was a twelve-year police veteran with a master's degree in child psychology from UCLA. She specialized in victim interviews and worked extensively with children who'd witnessed violent crimes.

Max Hogarth met them at the door. From the look on his face, he still had doubts about the interview.

Campos explained she'd worked with hundreds of special witnesses over the years. Max finally relented and went to get his son.

Ben descended the stairs slowly, avoiding eye contact with the women seated in the parlor. Instead, he froze in the doorway and began rocking back and forth.

"Ben," said Max, "you remember Miss Long. She came by this morning. She liked your drawings so much she brought a friend to see them."

Long, meanwhile, had placed the charcoal drawings of the Dark Avenger, the young woman, and her attackers on the coffee table. Ben glanced at them, and a look of concern came over his face.

"Hi, Ben," said Long. "I'd like you to call me 'Beth.' Would you do that for me?"

When he didn't reply, she continued. "Ben, this is my friend, Edith. I showed her the pictures you did last night. She thinks they're great."

"Hey, Ben," said Campos in a voice so modulated it sounded like an elevator recording. She began with general questions. "Do you spend a lot of time drawing?"

This elicited a quick nod, but he still wouldn't look her in the eye.

She asked him more questions to determine the time of the drawings. He never replied.

A half hour later, the women rose to go. Campos handed Max her card. "Ben, we'd like to come by sometime and see more of your drawings. Would that be okay?"

Ben nodded. Long and Campos thanked him. Max escorted them to the porch.

"Sorry. I was afraid of that," he said.

"No worries," said Campos. "These things usually take time. We appreciate your letting us speak to Ben. He's a wonderful young man... And, who knows, maybe he'll come up with something. If we have any other questions, would you mind our coming by again?"

Max shrugged. "I guess not. Ben seems to like both of you. If you'd brought in a male officer, I doubt I could've gotten Ben in the room." Tears came to his eyes. "Ben's a smart kid, and very talented. He just can't seem to bring it out. You know what I mean?"

The women nodded.

Out on the street, Walsh was still waiting. He stared at Long, who held back and allowed Campos to brief him on their conversation with Ben.

Long pulled her phone from her pocket and turned toward St. Charles Avenue, where she'd parked. She dialed Brandon Markham. The three days since she'd last seen him had been rough, and she needed company.

Listening to his phone ring, she wondered if she were becoming too dependent on him.

When he finally answered, he sounded out of breath, as though he'd gone somewhere to take the call in a more private setting.

"Hey," he said. I can't speak long. I'm at home getting dressed for my daughter's recital."

"Oh! I was hoping we could see each other tonight. Sounds like you're tied up."

"Uh… yeah. The next few nights aren't good either. Maybe we can get together on the weekend. Lisa's taking the kids to see her parents, and I can tell her I have an important client appointment."

"So," she quipped, "I'm an important client now?" She immediately regretted this. She sounded so needy.

"I'll give you a call on Friday. Right now, I gotta go." He hung up without saying goodbye.

. . .

Seated at a computer in the Peachtree City Library, Allison searched Google for background on Maurice Hamby, a name more common than she'd imagined, even after filtering on "Atlanta."

Rob and the kids were out of the house, and Allison and called Denise and begged off their morning workout, saying she had errands to run. Denise assured her she understood, but something in her voice said otherwise. *Was it hurt, disappointment… perhaps jealousy?* Allison had no time to think about it. She had to find out who this man was who'd threatened her and her family.

With patience and effort, she located, in a back issue of the *Atlanta Journal Constitution*, the story of a shootout in the Summer Hill neighborhood. Among the dead was one Maurice "Kingfish" Hamby.

The narcotics officer leading the raid, Detective Don Walsh, was the sole survivor. According to the article, he was on administrative leave pending investigation.

Allison opened her burner and made careful note of the names mentioned in the article.

• • •

Madison Miller collected her books from her locker. Behind her in the crowded hall someone called her name. She ignored them. Something strange was going on with her parents. Her dad was away more than usual, and her mother was acting weird, jumpy. Last night she'd bitched Madison out for no good reason. Wendy was only thirty-eight. Wasn't she young to be going through her "changes?" Madison wasn't sure.

As she closed her combination lock and spun the dial, she turned to see Kyle Embry drifting down the hall discussing something with a teammate, football no doubt. Madison was in no mood to ride the bus. Maybe she could wait until after football practice and catch a lift with the senior quarterback. That would get the attention of the freshman jocks in her classes. She moved quickly and positioned herself ahead of him, waiting casually outside the door where he couldn't help seeing her as he exited.

Madison smiled to herself. *This'll piss off his little stuck-up bitch sister.*

• • •

Allison had just returned from the library and was catching her breath before preparing dinner. She jumped when the door to the garage flew open. Leslie stormed in and threw her books on the kitchen table. *What now?* Allison thought.

"You are not going to believe what Kyle just did!" Leslie yelled.

Allison stared bewildered, as her son slinked through the door trying not to look guilty.

"He gave that tramp, Madison Miller, a ride home in the Jeep and crammed me in the back so she could ride up front."

"What?" Allison felt like someone had punched her in the gut.

"I was positively mortified. All my friends saw us. Tomorrow they'll be asking me if Kyle's dating Maddie now. I just want to puke."

"She just asked me for a lift home," Kyle interjected. "I've had my license long enough to give people rides."

Allison was apoplectic. Before she could stop herself, she screamed, "What in the hell were you thinking? I don't want you having anything to do with that…"

She stopped short at the wide-eyed looks on her children's faces. "I mean…" Allison tried to calm down. "I mean, your dad and I gave you that Jeep, Kyle, on the condition you would give your sister rides wherever she needs to go. It wasn't so you could chauffeur girls like Madison Miller."

Leslie turned to her brother with a triumphant look. Allison saw the red creeping into his normally placid face. "Look, I'm sorry Kyle," she said. "It's just… I've had a rough day. I didn't mean to yell at you. Just… Just be more considerate of your sister next time."

As she turned her attention back to supper, she saw in the reflection of the window her children exchanging curious glances.

CHAPTER 12
AMBROSE MANGHAM

Midtown
Wednesday, October 17

Next morning, when Marie and the boys leave, I get my tools out of the shed and set to work digging out an area beside the house for the basketball court. My plan is to finish the job before everyone gets home so I can surprise them.

I've just finished installing the metal post and nailing together the concrete forms when the alarm on my cell reminds me of my lunch with Ambrose Mangham. I run inside, shower, and change into a black sports coat, gray shirt and jeans.

On my way to Buckhead I call Mitch. He gives me a brief description of Mangham, so I can recognize him. I arrive at the White House a few minutes early and find a table. At eleven-thirty sharp, a man fitting Mangham's description walks in. He's small, middle-aged, and has sandy, thinning hair. I wave him over, and he takes a seat across from me.

He has a broad, flat face with loose jowls and bulging eyes. His tongue flicks the corners of his thick lips, like it's ready to lash out at some passing insect.

I introduce myself as I pull out my notebook. I begin with a few questions. "Mitch tells me you write for the *Atlanta Business Chronicle*." I deliberately get this wrong, so I can gauge Mangham's reaction.

He shoots me an offended look then smirks. "Hardly. They're only interested in big business. I prefer to write about the small entrepreneurs, the people who are truly building the new Atlanta."

"Okay. So, how did you get involved with this murder investigation?" I ask. "Isn't that a little outside your line of work?"

"I heard about the murders on the news. They came up in a later conversation with the CEO of a local company. He was worried this might tarnish the reputation of our city, like those child murders in the eighties. He said a cop told him, confidentially, that this looks like the work of a serial killer. I was interested and started making inquiries."

He glances around at the other patrons as though afraid someone might overhear him. "I thought about pursuing this story myself, but, like you said, it isn't my line of work. I've run into Mitch a few times. He covers the police beat, so I reached out to him."

"Mitch tells me you've only been writing for a year now. Mid-life career crisis?"

There's a momentary flash of anger in his eyes. It passes. "I was in business for myself," he says. "I invested everything I had, along with some family money." He lets out a long sigh. "Long story short, I got screwed out of my business and lost my ass. It was a hard lesson."

"How did you get into newspaper work?".

"I was looking to make a new start for myself. I'd made a number of contacts over the years, including journalists. I showed some of my work to *Biz Atlanta* and they liked it."

My thoughts return, for the moment, to my grandson, Henry, who wants to be a basketball player but will probably wind up short and stout like his mother. Over the years, I've seen countless would-be athletes, unable to realize their dreams, turn to the next best thing, sports writing. I guess Mangham's living out the business version of this story.

"Did this CEO happen to mention why the cops think they're serial killings?"

Mangham gives me a smug look. He holds up his left hand and begins to tick off items on his fingers. "First, you have identical rituals, like shooting out both eyes. Second, all three victims were male and approximately the same age. They were all attorneys. And finally, the shooter takes souvenirs."

"Souvenirs?" This is the first I've heard of this.

"The police are holding that back, hoping to trip up the perp when they catch him. My friend only found out about it because the cop let it slip."

I'm still not convinced, and Mangham can see it in my face.

"I've read up on serial killers," he says. "This has all the hallmarks. The cops don't want to spook people, because they'll panic." He leans across the table and looks me in the eye. "Somebody out there's popping victims who have nothing in common except that they fit a profile. The next victim could be anyone, most likely another lawyer."

For the moment I try not to think about Marie or the fact that these murders are in my own backyard. Something tells me this has nothing to do with the victims being lawyers.

"You know, Ambrose, it's the profile thing that bothers me most. I've done some research myself. The thing about serial killers is they're cowards. They prey on people weaker than they are. It's all about exercising power over those who can't protect themselves, children, homeless people, women, the elderly. Adult male attorneys don't exactly fit that description, if you know what I mean."

"Perhaps. Maybe this guy's more of a risk taker."

"I don't suppose this cop gave your CEO friend a profile of our guy."

"Nope. Probably the usual, white male in his thirties, single, poor employment history, no friends. Lives in his parents' basement..."

I shake my head. "Maybe I'm just not getting it. Even if it's the same perp, he could have some other motive. What do you suppose these victims have in common that would give someone an understandable reason to kill them?"

He gives me an impatient look. "I'm telling you. I've been through their backgrounds, and there's nothing that ties them together, besides their profession."

Another thought comes to me. "Lawyers make enemies. Did you ever think this might be a hired killer?"

He mulls the idea. "Nah! A hit man wouldn't go to this much trouble. He'd double tap the victim and move on."

I can see this conversation's getting nowhere, so I make an excuse about having to meet someone at my house, as I dig into my sandwich and Diet Coke.

. . .

I'm on my way home when my phone rings. It's Bonnie Baron.

"Hey"

"I've been thinking about this autistic kid," she says, "Ben Hogarth."

"Yeah."

"I can't get him out of my mind. This sounds like a fascinating story. I spoke to a friend who publishes art books, and he put me in touch with someone who produces graphic novels. He'd like to come by and meet Ben. Do you think you could arrange it?"

"I'll try. Let me speak to Ben's dad, and I'll get back to you."

I ring off as I pull into my drive.

Moments later, a concrete truck backs up to the curb as close as it can get, and the crew sets to work carting loaded wheelbarrows around to the back. In a short time, they've finished the job and smoothed it out. As expected, they want payment in cash.

As the truck pulls away, William strolls up with a heavy book bag over his shoulder. He's made the short walk uphill from Grady High School.

"Whatcha doing, Pops?"

"Come take a look."

When he sees the basketball court with the pole installed in the concrete, he smiles. "Cool. We can play a little one-on-one." He mimes bouncing a basketball and taking a shot.

"We'll have to let it set first. Then we can take out the forms and put up the hoop and net."

Suddenly I remember promising Marie I'd pick up Henry at Inman Middle School.

"I've gotta go get your brother from school. Why don't you go inside and get something to eat? I'm sure you have plenty of homework."

I find Henry standing by the curb. He climbs into the car without saying anything.

"Hello, Henry"

"Hey." He stares through the windshield, his thoughts a million miles away.

"How was school?"

Deadpan. "It sucks."

"Well, I guess it hasn't changed since I was your age."

There's the momentary flicker of a smile, and his face goes blank again.

"Henry, there's something I want you to help me with when we get home."

He ponders, no doubt weighing this mystery chore against his homework. "Okay."

I pull the car into the driveway and lead him around back. William, I see, has found my ladder and toolbox. He turns and smiles as he tightens the last screws on the hoop and hangs the net.

Henry picks up his pace as he walks over to inspect. "Wow!"

"Looks like William finished it up. You'd better let it set before you play on it."

"Is it okay if we take a nail and carve our initials in it?" asks William.

"I don't see why not. It's yours."

I set to work preparing supper while the boys go upstairs to study.

• • •

By the time we've eaten, the sun is getting low. It's time for Bogie's evening walk. William says he's finished his homework and asks if he can join us.

We walk as far as Monroe, talking about school and writing. I avoid the subject of the murders, trying not to stir up William's active imagination.

"Guess what," William says.

"What?"

"I've signed up to write for the school paper."

"Great! What do you plan to write about?"

"Well, I thought about sports, but that's already covered. I'm thinking of interviewing people like Uncle Sean, who do all sorts of cool research and things."

"That's a great idea. But what are you going to do when your mom moves you out to Cobb County?"

"I can work on a student paper there. If I have the article already written, I can take it to them and see what they think."

As we pass Max Hogarth's house, he's sweeping leaves off his front porch. I tell him about Bonnie, that she has a graphic novel publisher who wants to meet Ben and look at his work. Max agrees, provided it's okay with Ben. I give him Bonnie's number.

On the way home, I explain to William about Ben and how he uses his drawings as a form of expression.

"Maybe you two could team up on an illustrated novel," he quips.

"Maybe."

CHAPTER 13
DARK AVENGER

Midtown
Thursday, October 18

Football practice over, Kyle Embry showered at the gym instead of going home. Decked out in fresh clothes and letter jacket, he texted his mom not to expect him for dinner. Leslie got a ride home with the mother of another cheerleader.

Kyle said he was meeting his teammates at the Avenue for pizza. His homework was done, and he wouldn't be out late. *It's only half a lie*, he told himself. He was, after all, going to the Avenue.

Madison Miller had slipped him a note with her phone number as they passed in the hall between classes. Now she was waiting outside the pizzeria, talking with another girl.

She stood, backlit by the window, and gazed at him. She was so hot. Her jeans and translucent top clung to her tight, little body like an Earl Scheib paint job. The cool night air only enhanced the effect. She was, for all the world, a clone of her mother. It bothered Kyle not the least that she was three years younger than he, Leslie's age, in fact.

Madison said goodbye to her friend and hopped into the Jeep. She leaned across, gave Kyle a long kiss on the lips, and ran her right hand over his crotch. "You're late," she said in a slow, easy drawl.

From there Kyle drove to a secluded spot, where they spent the next hour.

• • •

Miles away, the Dark Avenger ran his usual route. The night sky had grown overcast, with the promise of rain. Following his earlier altercation with the two punks, he'd changed his outfit. To avoid recognition, he pulled a watch cap over his bald head and wore a light sweatshirt instead of the hoodie.

His therapist at the VA recommended regular sessions to deal with his anger issues. This was all the therapy he needed.

As he crossed Ponce, he saw two men enter an all-night market. It was the only place still open this late. Though they were a block away, there was something about them, the way they carried themselves. Something was wrong.

He turned and ran in their direction, arriving just they emerged from the store with large brown grocery bags. From the way they carried them, he could see they were full.

A store clerk emerged. The Avenger recognized him as the owner, a Korean named Kim Soo Young. Kim raised a gun and shot at the fleeing men. One of them returned fire but missed.

By now, the Avenger was within ten yards of the men, running straight toward them. Out of his pocket came a pistol.

The first gunman fired another round at Kim and again missed. The Avenger dropped him with a single shot through the forehead, just above his left eye. Before the other could fire back, Kim put a slug in the back of his head.

The Avenger crossed Ponce, causing oncoming cars to jam their brakes. He disappeared into the labyrinth of alleys that laced the neighborhood, leaving a bewildered Kim to explain the situation to the police. He wondered if Kim had recognized him. Too late to worry about that now.

As the Avenger melted into the darkness, an unseen figure turned and slowly followed him. He'd never catch up with him, but it didn't matter. By now, Ben knew exactly where the Avenger lived and had recognized him despite his disguise.

Max Hogarth was a heavy sleeper, especially after a tall scotch on ice. Had he known his son wandered the streets at night, hiding in the shadows and watching people, Max would have had a stroke.

Ben and Kim weren't the only witnesses. A store security camera beside the market captured a grainy and distorted image, just a few, jerky frames, enough to give Midtown Murder investigators something else to think about.

The shootings occurred too late to make the eleven o'clock news, but featured prominently on the morning talk shows, all of which tried to link them to the three murdered lawyers. Somehow, a shootout involving four men at a convenience store had to be the work of a serial killer, or gangbangers, depending on who told the story. Reporters tried in vain to contact Kim after his questioning by the police.

CHAPTER 14
SHELBY LEWIS

Midtown
Friday, October 19

William and I are out for another run. The air is cool and dry, and we're moving at a good pace, for me at least. Suddenly, William starts asking about the shootings on Ponce last night. We heard about them on the kitchen radio before we left.

I explain that these things happen sometimes. He needs to be aware of his surroundings wherever he goes, especially at night.

"What's the deal with the three lawyers?" he asks.

"That's different. Those guys were all shot, apparently by the same person, while in their own homes. Maybe they knew the killer. Maybe they didn't. But there's something connecting them. We don't know what it was yet, but don't worry. The police will find the shooter and put him away. Don't forget, your grandmother and I raised your mom and Aunt Kathy in this neighborhood back when things were much worse."

He changes gears. "I heard Mom say you shot some people back when you were younger."

"That was a long time ago."

"She said they killed your parents."

"It was a long time ago."

"Would you do it again? I mean under the same circumstances."

I take a deep breath. "*William, it was a long time ago.*" Now I see why he wants to be a reporter.

"What was it like interviewing that woman over in Mississippi, the one who murdered the artist on the courthouse steps?"

I consider this for a moment. "She was a complicated person. I guess that's what made her interesting. She'd been through bad times. She grew up poor and abused. She managed to escape it all, or so she thought. She had cosmetic surgery and built a successful career. It didn't change who she was inside. She was still that skinny, homely little girl everybody picked on. I guess that's why she wanted to be a celebrity. She wanted people to love her."

"What happened to make her murder the artist?"

"She claimed he raped her. When the DA couldn't get a conviction, she took matters into her own hands. She'd been raped before. I guess it was like déjà vu, only this time she was going to make sure the guy got what he deserved. Anyway, the jury in her murder trial acquitted her. Instead, she went away for paying someone to kill the first man who raped her."

"Is it true you and Grandma were standing right beside the artist when she shot him?"

"Close enough"

"What was he like?"

"Talented, narcissistic, probably autistic. His mother coddled him all his life. He had no regard for other people. He used them without thinking of the consequences."

"Wow!"

We run for a few blocks in silence. Then William asks, "Pops, are you trying to help catch this killer?"

"Nope. That's the police department's job. I'm just looking for a story people want to read. If I find anything that helps the cops, I'll pass it on."

"What makes a good story?"

"Interesting characters"

"How do you find interesting characters?"

"This is Midtown, William. There's no shortage of interesting characters. We meet new people every day. We don't always notice them. We get caught up in our own stuff... Tell me about school. Have you met anybody?"

He shrugs. "There's this one guy. He calls himself 'Bill.' Actually, he's Chinese. I think his real name is something like Hung Lo."

"You'd think a guy would be proud of a name like that."

William laughs. "Bill's dad's a prof at Georgia Tech. They live in Virginia Highland. He's promised to teach me martial arts."

"Good. That'll come in handy at Grady. You haven't run into any trouble yet, have you?"

"Nope."

"Met any girls?"

He blushes. "I've seen some. Haven't met them yet."

"You will."

"How do you get to know people?"

"Say hello to them. Find out something they like and learn as much about it as you can. Don't let on what you're doing. Just ask questions, and, most of all, listen. That's especially important when you're trying to meet a girl. Most guys only want to talk about themselves."

He nods as if this makes sense. We return home, and William heads off to school, armed with the wisdom of the ages.

. . .

I get down the leash and take Bogie for a walk, carrying a Publix bag I retrieved from recycling.

I discovered long ago if you want to meet new people, walk your dog. If you meet the right folks, they'll like your dog. If you meet the wrong ones, maybe he'll bite them.

We're on the next block, when Bogie stops and unloads next to the sidewalk. I'm scooping it into the bag when I look up to see an elderly woman standing on her porch. She smiles in approval. She wears a broad-brimmed hat, dirt-stained gloves, and a pair of tan coveralls over a red checked shirt.

I wave.

She waves back.

"Hi," I say.

"Beautiful dog," she says in a thick Brooklyn accent.

"Thanks." I introduce myself as she stoops over to let Bogie lick her hand.

"You're a reporter or something, right?"

"Yes ma'am."

Her name's Helen Weiss. With a few questions I learn she's a widow with no children. Her only living relative is a married niece in Alpharetta who checks on her occasionally.

Her face bears the fine lines of a porcelain vase that's retained its beauty over the years. She keeps herself fit, she says, by working in her yard. Today she's turning over her flower bed, planting pansies and impatiens.

"Have you heard about all these murders?" she asks, her eyes widening behind thick lenses.

"Yeah. Scary, isn't it? What've you heard?"

"Just what they're saying on the news. I hope they catch whoever's doing it."

"Have you noticed anything unusual lately?"

"What? Are you kidding? Everything around here's unusual," she says with a dismissive wave. "You should meet the woman next door. She's weird, I tell you. Sits on her front porch reading Tarot cards. The other day she did a palm reading for a homeless guy. Poor man! Only thing he wanted in his palm was money for a drink. I tell you he was out of here as fast as he could go."

I smile and nod. "Have you noticed anything else out of the ordinary?"

She purses her lips. "Well, there's this big black man lives upstairs from her. He's a scary one."

"What do you mean?"

"Every night I see him from my bedroom window, practicing his karate, whatever you call it. Then he puts on a hood and goes for a run... in the middle of the night for Pete's sake. He's not very friendly either. I think the police ought to question him... see where he's going."

"I'm sure they're questioning a lot of people."

"Well, I just hope they catch him soon."

"Yep."

She goes back inside. I'm about to leave, when the lady next door comes out. Her name, or so she says, is Alicia Moonbeam. She's somewhere my side of fifty, with peroxide hair down to her waist. Her shapeless, full-length smock sways gently in the breeze.

I talk to her a while, thinking of what I told William about meeting people. Again, I wonder how I've lived here so long without meeting my neighbors. Bogie sniffs at her bare feet and licks her toes, which she seems to enjoy.

Ms. Moonbeam gives a very different description of the man living above her. His name's Shelby Lewis and he does something with computers.

"I don't know what I'd do without him," she says. "One night I came in late from my coven, and a man came out of the bushes and jumped me. I didn't know what to do. Next thing I knew, Shelby was right there. He beat the man up and chased him away."

"This Shelby sounds like a hero."

"You bet he is. Boy, was I scared! After that I went right out and bought me a gun." She hikes up one side of her dress to reveal an ankle holster and a small revolver.

I smile and nod in response. Something about this Shelby guy sounds significant, but I can't think what it is.

"Do you think Mr. Lewis is home?" I ask.

"Nope."

She launches into a rambling discussion of Eastern religions and psychic healing. Not knowing what to say, I keep my mouth shut and nod. Then she gives me a coy smile. "Did you know I do palms? Why don't you come inside and let me give you a reading?"

"I really appreciate your offer, but I have to go. Bogie needs to get home, and I have work to do."

. . .

Later, Bogie and I are out for another walk. I see Shelby Lewis returning from work. He glances at me as he steps from his car.

I wave and give him a friendly smile. He's about to ignore me, when Bogie trots over and sniffs at his ankles. He scratches him behind the ear.

"Hi. I'm Tom Williams."

"Shelby Lewis." He extends his hand without even looking up. He's focused on Bogie. "Nice dog."

"Thanks."

I fumble for something to keep our conversation going. "You been living here long?"

"Little over a year."

"My wife, Colleen, and I moved here forty years ago. Colleen passed away a while back. She was the one active in the neighborhood. I'm afraid I'm just now meeting people."

He gives me an appraising look and nods. "I lost my wife too... couple of years ago."

"What kind of work do you do?" It's the question Atlantans ask when they can't think of anything else.

"I'm a data analyst at Turner Broadcasting. You?"

"I'm retired mostly. I write sometimes for the *AJC* and *Georgia Globe*."

His eyes narrow. "You're the one interviewed that woman over in Mississippi, the one who shot the artist in Marietta."

"Yep."

"Man, she must've been something."

I consider for a moment. "You might say that."

"What do you mean?"

"Once I understood where she came from and what she'd been through, it gave me a different perspective."

"Yeah. I can see that." He pauses, like he's thinking of something to say. "So, what do you think about all these murders?"

"There's talk it's the work of a serial killer. I'm not so sure. Usually, with serial killers there's no connection between the victims. I get the feeling these guys knew each other."

He stares into the distance then suddenly remembers something. "Hey, can I offer you a bottled water?" He gives me an embarrassed look. "That's all I got. I don't drink alcohol or sodas. I can fill up a bowl for your dog." He smiles at Bogie. "You want some water, boy?"

Bogie wags.

"Come on up."

We follow him up the outside stairs. Bogie and I wait on the landing while Lewis goes inside.

His home sits on a deep, tidy lot, surrounded by a wooden privacy fence with a small gate in the corner. Beyond it, an overgrown alley runs through the middle of the block. I'd forgotten it was there. Above the trees, I can just make out the roofline of my house. A fence separates my backyard from the alley.

Lewis returns with two bottled waters and a bowl for Bogie. A quick glimpse inside reveals a nicely furnished interior. A set of weights sits in one corner beneath a punching bag. Beside the door a dark hoodie hangs from an old-fashioned hat rack.

"I was walking by this morning, and I met your downstairs neighbor, Alicia."

He chuckles. "Yeah. She thinks she's a witch, fortune teller, something. She's harmless."

"I also met Ms. Weiss next door."

The smile fades as quickly as it appeared.

"Yeah, that woman's a piece of work, always calling and complaining to the city about one thing or another. She needs to mind her own business."

I notice a tattoo of the Marine Corps emblem and the words "Semper Fi" on his forearm. "How long were you in the Marines?"

"Six years. I did two tours in Iraq and one in Afghanistan."

"My dad was a Marine. South Pacific in World War II. I chose the Coast Guard."

He gives me a charitable look. "Were you ever in combat?"

"Yep. We were on patrol off the Vietnam coast in 1965. I got shot in the thigh, and they sent me home."

He nods in approval and holds up his water bottle in a toast.

"You look like you stay in pretty good shape," I venture.

"Helps me relieve stress after work."

"I can imagine."

We continue swapping stories until I realize it's getting late and I need to go pick up Henry. "Shelby, I'm gonna have to get Bogie home. It was good talking with you. Thanks again for the water."

"No problem."

Walking back, I wonder how two neighbors, living next door to each other, could have such different perceptions of the same man.

CHAPTER 15
THE CONTRACT

Peachtree City
Monday, October 22

Allison glanced about before taking her seat at the library computer. Confident no one was watching, she logged in and checked the balance of her Antiguan account. True to his word, the unidentified client had made the transfer. Now what?

She was so sure the nightmare was over when Hamby stopped calling. Now things were worse. She'd graduated from killing drug dealers to murdering innocent people for money.

Allison hyperventilated. She imagined herself passing out here in the library with all her financial information on display. If caught, she'd lose her home, her family, her friends, and her freedom. She'd have no reason for living. For all she knew, this was a setup, and the client was a cop. How could she have fucked up so badly?

She stared at the screen. How would she even get to all that money without anyone knowing?

For better or worse, she was committed. The sort of person who pays that much to have someone whacked doesn't want to hear that you've changed your mind. *He'll just hire someone else to kill her.*

Allison would plan this job as she had all the others, carefully watching her prey, following their habits, and choosing a spot where they'd be most vulnerable. Her gender and her ability to change appearance made her virtually invisible.

The deadline was Sunday. That gave Allison four days. This new client was more particular than Hamby, but for two hundred thousand she could accommodate him. His instructions were explicit. Once both targets were down, Allison would call him and leave an innocuous three-word message, "Come get me."

. . .

Don Walsh carried a large box of files out to his truck. As he reached for the door, his phone rang. The display read "Ardub," phonetic for "RW," Rollo Witherspoon.

"What you got, Rollo?"

The voice on the other end crackled. Loud hip hop blared in the background.

"I got you a lead, detective."

"Okay."

"It's a white dude, kinda small, mid-forties, maybe fifty, gray hair, been buying small pistols from a dealer in Summer Hill, throw-down crap, sorta shit folks in this part of town be embarrassed to carry."

"Does this 'dude' have a name?"

"Dealer calls him 'YT.' I don't think that's his real name."

"No. I don't suppose it is. You got anything else, like where I might find this Mr. YT?"

"Nope. Dealer started giving me the fast eye, like what was I up to. I decided not to press my luck. Know what I'm saying?"

"Okay. So, what's the dealer's name?"

"Man, you trying to get me killed."

"Nobody's gonna know, Rollo."

Rollo took so long to respond Walsh wondered if he'd hung up.

"Hollywood Holmes"

Walsh smiled. "Figures." Holmes had been a runner for Hamby. Walsh had known him since his rookie days in Narcotics. Following Hamby's death, Holmes had gone freelance, working mostly in the Summer Hill, People's Town and Mechanicsville neighborhoods.

"Good job, Rollo. Call me again if you hear anything else. Okay?"

"Yeah. Sure thing, Detective."

Walsh hung up. He reached across and placed the file box on the passenger seat. It'd been a long day.

Later, as he relaxed with a cold long neck, he pored over the crime scene notes. Vague though Rollo's description may be, he now had the outline of a face to go with the killer's profile.

How did he get so close to all three lawyers? Who would they have known and trusted? Was he a professional or just lucky?

An idea occurred to Walsh. Paxton was at a pizza parlor on Ponce addressing a special meeting of Midtown residents. Walsh could be there in twenty minutes.

• • •

Late afternoon shadows crept across Clifton Way near its intersection with Ponce. A late model Acura swung into the parking lot of a fashionable condominium and pulled into to its reserved spot. Out stepped a woman in her mid-forties returning from a busy day at the office.

Single, she now shared her two-bedroom unit with her eighty-three-year-old mom. Mom moved in three months earlier and commandeered the single-car garage for her aging Lincoln. Having her come to stay seemed like a good idea at the time. Now Eleanor wasn't so sure.

She found herself working longer hours just to avoid the incessant carping. Eleanor enjoyed her work. She'd long ago given up finding a man who was worth the trouble. Her "significant other," these days was her career. The assignments were so lucrative she'd soon be able to retire, return to school for a doctorate, and train a new generation of women to carry on the cause.

As she pulled her briefcase from the back seat, a cool, dry gust brought a shower of dead leaves from neighboring trees. A passing car swept the autumn detritus past a young blonde jogging on the opposite sidewalk. She wore a visor pulled low over her face, her hair back in a ponytail. She looked no different from dozens of other women out for a late afternoon run. *How wonderful it must be*, thought Eleanor, *to keep yourself in such shape*. She'd given that up long ago.

A young couple strolled past hand-in-hand. They stopped and spoke to a mother pushing a baby stroller. A man in an unmarked van studied a map. They were no different from people Eleanor saw every day.

. . .

Rob sat in front of the television, as usual, watching "Monday Night Football." Tonight, the Falcons hosted the New York Giants. He didn't look up when Allison entered. It was just as well. She'd rather not explain where she'd been.

Kyle, upstairs in his bedroom, yelled something inaudible to Leslie, who made no reply. Allison went to the bookshelf and found a Sue Grafton novel. She settled into her recliner, took a deep breath and tuned out this diorama of domestic bliss.

Then, in a voice so distinct it penetrated even Rob's hypnotic state, Leslie yelled, "You know, Kyle, if you keep screwing that girl, your dick's gonna rot off and I won't have any nieces or nephews to spoil."

Allison turned to Rob. "Where do you suppose she learned to talk like that?"

He shrugged. "Probably from that crowd she hangs out with at school."

"Since when do you know who she hangs out with?"

From upstairs Kyle yelled back to Leslie to mind her own business.

Rob grinned. "Who do you suppose they're talking about?"

Allison stared at him. How could he find this so fucking funny? Then it came to her. She leaned closer and said "Madison Miller. That's who she's talking about. Your son is fucking Madison Miller."

The momentary look of panic in Rob's eyes as he turned his attention back to the football game was priceless. It brought a warm glow to Allison, as she folded her feet under her and settled into her novel.

CHAPTER 16
NEIGHBORHOOD WATCH

Midtown
Tuesday, October 23

Kyle again drove Madison home. He pulled to a stop in her driveway. She leaned over the console and gave him a long kiss. He smiled back.

"You need to get inside before your mom sees us."

"I'll text you later." She gave him a wink.

Hidden behind her dining room sheers, Wendy watched this happy scene play out, seething with rage. The look on her daughter's face, as she strolled down the driveway swinging her purse, was unmistakable. Wendy was in the kitchen when the garage door opened.

"Hi, mom!"

That Madison was so cheerful only infuriated her more. She took a deep breath and asked in her calmest tone, "Madison, how did you get home?"

"I... um... got a ride with a friend."

"Whose Jeep was that?"

Madison recognized her mother's tone. Beneath the calm façade, Wendy was about to explode. Prevaricating would only make matters worse.

"It's Kyle Embry, mom. He gave me a ride home. *That's all.*"

Wendy lowered her head and took a deep breath. "Where did you go Thursday night?"

Madison's face lost all color. "I told you. I went to the Avenue with Isabel Fernandez."

Wendy's eyes hardened. She pursed her lips and nodded. "I spoke with Isabel's mother." Her volume grew as she spoke. "When she picked up Isabel at eight, Isabel told her you'd met up with a friend. You didn't get home until almost ten. *Stop lying to me*, Madison!" she screamed.

For a moment, Madison was afraid Wendy would backhand her, as she'd done so many times. Instinctively, she collapsed to the floor, sobbing.

"Kyle Embry is a senior," continued Wendy. "You are a freshman. I know what you two have been up to, and if I can ever prove it, that little shit is going to jail." She waited a moment to let the threat sink in. "You are never to see him again. Do you understand me?"

"But, mom..."

"Don't even start. If I find out you're having sex with him, I'm reporting him to the police." It was an empty threat, but Madison wouldn't know. Moreover, she'd never suspect why. This had to stop, now. Wendy watched her daughter, broken and dispirited, repair to her bedroom.

Madison sat on the floor of her closet with the door closed and called Kyle, hoping Wendy wouldn't overhear. When he answered, he said he'd had a similar conversation with Allison.

Now it was Madison's turn to be angry. That bitch Leslie ratted us out, she thought, and then Allison called Mom!

Madison would get back at Allison if it took her the rest of her life. She hung up, wondering what had prompted her mother's outburst. She'd broken curfew with boys older than Kyle. Why was this any different?

• • •

By seven-thirty the dinner crowd at Sergio's Pizza had thinned. Business was slow, and Sergio agreed to open his back room for a special meeting of Midtown Neighborhood Watch. Tonight's special guest was Lieutenant Paxton Davis. Paxton nodded to Tom as he took his seat at the head table. Don Walsh arrived and stood in the back.

At the appointed hour, the chairman stood and welcomed the crowd. Before introducing Davis, he recognized various dignitaries, including a pair of city council members. He described, in detail, the many recent initiatives undertaken by Neighborhood Watch, including a celebration dubbed "Light up Midtown," designed to bring out citizens in a show of unity against crime. Tom wondered if any of them questioned the sanity of leaving their homes unattended all night while they were partying at the park.

By the time the chairman finally introduced Paxton, many were shifting in their seats. Paxton thanked everyone for coming. He introduced Don Walsh and assured them the APD was doing everything in its power to apprehend the culprit. He opened the floor for questions.

The first was whether these were serial killings. "We're not ruling out anything at this point," said Paxton. "But we can't afford to start chasing rumors. We're processing every shred of evidence, and we'd appreciate any information you might have." Paxton winced to think of all the crackpot calls this would bring.

Another neighbor asked if the convenience store shootings on Ponce or the beatings of two men on Monroe Drive had anything to do with the murders. He referred to the perpetrators as "gang bangers." Paxton assured him those events, though unrelated, would receive full police attention.

Sitting near the back, someone stood and shouted, "If you people are waiting for the police to catch this guy, you're crazy. I'm putting my faith in Smith and Wesson."

Before Paxton could reply, a young woman shouted back. "Yeah. That's all we need, crazies like you, running around waving guns. You'll probably shoot one of us… or better yet, yourself."

In the ensuing argument, he called her an "ignorant bitch," at which point her boyfriend jumped him. Walsh and another officer pulled the men apart, cuffed them, and escorted them to separate squad cars waiting outside.

Marie turned to Tom as they left. "Wow, that was constructive."

• • •

Paxton met Walsh in the parking lot. "You got something say, Detective, or you just here for some free pizza?"

"I spoke with an old friend tonight. He told me an interesting story."

"Okay. Spill it. I ain't got all night. Clarice is already pissed at me for working late."

"Ever heard of a dealer in Summer Hill named Hollywood Holmes?"

"I'm not a narc. You think I know all the dealers in Summer Hill?"

"Seems Hollywood's been dealing more than drugs. He's branched out into guns, small caliber, mostly .22."

"So?"

No sooner was the word out of his mouth than a curious look came over Paxton's face.

"From what I hear," said Walsh, "Hollywood has this one repeat customer, a white guy, middle-aged, known as 'YT.'"

"So whaddya proposing, detective?"

"I thought maybe we could set up a sting, pull in Hollywood, shake him down, get him to give up his customer."

"In Summer Hill? I don't know this Hollywood guy, but unless he's got shit for brains, he's gonna see you coming from downtown."

"I can bring in some guys from narcotics. We'll get on top of him in a hurry before he knows we're there."

Paxton considered for a moment. "Okay. But two things. One, I want you to take Lyman Gwynn. And, two, you ain't going in there, gun's blazing, like you did with Kingfish Hamby... Yeah, I heard about that. Last thing I need right now is to clean up more of your shit."

CHAPTER 17
THE CONFESSIONAL

Midtown
Friday, October 26

Jacob Epstein's fiancé, Marina Kovacs has agreed to meet Father John and me at Starbuck's. When I arrive the padre's waiting at our usual table.

We chat for a while. Then I look up to see Ms. Kovacs. She recognizes me and waves as she takes her place in line. Moments later she joins us, steaming Venti Latte in hand.

"Ms. Kovacs, I'd like to meet an old friend, Father John O'Malley."

"Pleased to meet you, Father. You can call me 'Marina.'"

"I'm glad you could join us." I add.

"It's the least I could do, Mr. Williams, given the way I treated you the other day."

"No worries. You've been through some rough times. And call me 'Tom'."

She stares at her folded hands on the table and sighs.

"Thomas told me about your loss," says Father John. "I'm so sorry."

She just nods.

"Tell me about Jacob," the priest says in his confessional voice. "What was he like? How long had you known each other?"

"Wow! Where do I start?" Tears come as she tells how she and Epstein met in law school at Florida. They graduated, moved to Atlanta, and planned to marry. "We were waiting to get on our feet financially. His parents didn't approve. We discussed whether to get married in a church or a synagogue and settled for a civil service."

"You were both lawyers?" I ask.

She tells her story in matter-of-fact tones, as if describing a car wreck she'd witnessed. "I was going to leave my firm and set up a family law practice. Jacob would continue where he was for the time being."

Father John shakes his head. "We can never imagine losing someone so close until it happens. When I lost my Martha, I spent a year wondering what I should do." He stares into his coffee, then chuckles. "When I decided to become a priest, I think I was more surprised than anyone."

Marina's eyes flash as her lower lip begins to tremble. "Then maybe, as a priest, you can explain why this loving God everybody tells me about would let somebody take away my Jacob."

"I wish I could. The truth is, we'll never know until we meet God in person. The more important question, Marina, is why are we still here? Nothing will ever fill the void left by the loss of someone we love. What gets us through is living our lives in a way that would've made our loved one proud."

I've heard all this before. I let it run for a while, thinking of ways to shift the subject. I'm anxious to find out more about Epstein.

"Setting up your own practice, that's a big step," I butt in. "How did you and Jacob plan to raise the money?"

"First, he offered to borrow it from his parents, but I wouldn't hear of it. I certainly wasn't borrowing from mine. Instead, we put aside some savings. Then Jacob lost it all in a business venture." A sour look comes over her. "It almost ended our business plans *and* our engagement."

It's all I can do to keep from reaching for my notebook. "What kind of business venture was this?" Father John gives me a disapproving look. I ignore him.

"It was one of those rapid refund services. They used to set up on Ponce every tax reason. They popped up like mushrooms in January and, by April were gone. Jacob wasn't active in the business. It was supposedly a 'can't lose' opportunity. Then the general partner swindled him. The man opened offices all over Atlanta and hired a bunch of commissioned reps to drum up business. They signed up people for fraudulent tax credits, some three and four times, using stolen Social Security numbers. When it all came down,

103

the IRS swooped in and confiscated everything. They even came after Jacob. He was able to fend off their charges, but he lost all his money and nearly lost his license."

"That hardly seems fair," said the priest. "It sounds like Jacob was what you'd call a 'passive investor.'"

"He was. Unfortunately, the IRS didn't see it that way. They just wanted their money back. They didn't care where they got it. The general partner went to jail."

"Do you happen to remember the general partner's name or the other investors?" I ask.

"No. Jacob wouldn't talk about it, and I never pressed him. I think it was someone Jacob met through another lawyer."

"This other lawyer, might he have been a member of Jacob's firm or a personal friend?"

She considers a moment. "I don't think so. At the time, it seemed Jacob had just met the guy. Like I said, we never talked about it."

The priest starts to say something, but I keep going, to his apparent annoyance. "What was the name of the tax business?"

"I think it was *Rapid Refund*," she mutters as she sips her coffee.

This seems a strangely generic name. "Do you think this had anything to do with Jacob's..."

"Murder?" she shrugs. "I have no idea."

I wonder if this is a missing connection in the Midtown Murders. It seems like a long shot. If anything, Epstein was the aggrieved party. Why would anyone murder him over a bad business deal? He was a minor player and a major victim.

The conversation turns to more pleasant topics. Father John tells Marina about programs offered at the Shrine, including a small, informal fellowship for young, single parishioners. She gives him a noncommittal response.

• • •

An hour later, I'm at home, enjoying peace and quiet. Curious, I open my laptop and Google "Rapid Refund." I get page after page, mostly sponsored links, none of them connected to the late Jacob Epstein. I try variations of the name followed by "LLC" or "Corp." I find a site listing DBA names, nothing else.

At eleven AM, Bogie trots in and nudges my hand. I take him for a walk. Turning onto Greenwood, we encounter Oscar Arrington returning from the Publix on Monroe with a bag of groceries. He's decked out in a black, broad-brimmed fedora, wraparound sunglasses, and a matching black cape over a white linen suit, like some Toulouse-Lautrec character. He invites me onto his porch while he takes in his groceries.

"I would ask you in, but this place is a dreadful mess. Would you like a glass of Pinot Noir?"

"Sure. Why not?"

From inside I hear Oscar's pug yapping.

"Oh, hush up Waldo!" Oscar shouts.

I settle into a wicker chair and let out Bogie's retractable leash so he can explore the tiny front yard. Waldo continues barking while Bogie blithely ignores him.

Oscar returns with two wine glasses. "You'll have to excuse Waldo," he says as he lights a cigarette. "He gets so jealous when there's another dog around."

"No problem. I've been meaning to drop by. I was wondering what else you might've heard about the murders."

Oscar takes a drag from the cigarette, holds it, and slowly exhales. "Nothing else, I'm afraid."

"My daughter and I went to the neighborhood meeting at Sergio's last night. Police Lieutenant Paxton Davis was there. He doesn't seem to be making any progress."

"That's because they aren't looking. If the victims were straight, the police would leave no stone unturned. I heard about that meeting. I knew it would be a waste of time"

"I've spoken to several people in the area, but none of them have anything to offer. They seem as baffled as the police. I did meet one of our neighbors, an elderly lady named Helen Weiss. She's convinced the black man next door to her is the killer."

Oscar gives a disdainful look. "That figures. Always blame the black guy."

"I met the man later. He seems pretty harmless."

"Is he the big one who lives upstairs above Alicia Moonbeam?"

"Yes. Do you know Alicia?"

Oscar rolls his eyes. "Oh, God yes. Everybody in Midtown knows Alicia. Did you meet her?"

"Yeah. She's a character. She wanted me to come inside for a palm reading."

"I'm sure that's not the only thing she wanted. Did she start talking about Eastern religion and mysticism?"

"As a matter of fact, she did." I laugh.

Oscar leans back, releases a smoke ring, and watches it rise. "That woman knows as much about Eastern religion as I do about quantum physics."

"Did you know she carries a gun?"

"Of course, she does," he says with a dismissive wave. "Just about everyone around here has a gun. I'm packing myself." He parts his jacket to reveal a pearl-handled derringer on his right hip. "You can't be too careful, you know."

Shifting in my seat to get away from his cigarette smoke, I suddenly remember Marina's comment about her fiancé's business. "Oscar, when I met you earlier, you mentioned something about Lyle Mallory getting caught up in a scandal, something involving the IRS."

The smile fades as he stares off into the distance. "Yes. As I recall, Lyle invested in some business or other. His partner was found guilty of tax fraud. The IRS investigated Lyle, as well. They never found anything on him, because there was nothing to find. But Lyle spent a fortune defending himself, on top of all the money he lost in the business."

He takes another drag. "The money wasn't much of a problem, you understand. Lyle had plenty. He was the black sheep of a wealthy Buckhead family. The biggest damage was to his political career and his standing in the community." Oscar lets out a long sigh. Half choking, he adds, "And then he went and got himself killed."

"Do you think the murder might relate to the scandal and the tax business?"

Oscar gathers himself and shrugs. "I don't think so. It'd been over for years. The one who was responsible went to jail. I never really thought about it. By the time of the murder, it was yesterday's news."

"This business, was the name 'Rapid Refund'?"

Oscar's eyes widen as if he just remembered something. "It wasn't 'Rapid Refund.' It was 'Rabbit Refund.' I remember thinking, 'What a stupid name for a business!'"

This must have been what Marina was saying as she sipped her coffee at Starbucks.

"And Lyle never mentioned anything about Jacob Epstein?"

"No. Whatever would Epstein have to do with Lyle's tax business?"

"Oscar, I think we just found the connection."

I bid Oscar a hasty farewell and sprint home, dragging poor Bogie behind. This time, rather than Google, I browse Georgia's corporate listings. There, among the names, I find "Rabbit Refund," a limited partnership, now administratively dissolved. Its registered agent was one Joel A. Mangham.

I doodle on my desk blotter as I contemplate my next step. I consider calling Paxton, but something says I should wait.

On the screen in front of me are the notes I'm compiling for my story. At the bottom I type, "Joel A. Mangham?" *Could this be Ambrose Mangham… a relative?*

My phone rings, startling me from my reverie. It's Marie.

"Dad, I'm in a deposition. I just got a call from Inman Middle. You need to go get Henry right now!"

"What happened?"

"He's been in a fight and they won't let him come back until they meet with me."

I let out a deep sigh. "Is he okay?"

"As far as I know."

. . .

Sitting in a principal's office, for the first time since my days in high school, I listen as the petty bureaucrat recites the charges against my younger grandson. Henry slumps in his chair and sulks, a red whelp blossoming around his left eye.

"Mr. Williams, I'm sure you can appreciate why we have a zero-tolerance policy for violence."

In my best imitation of Dr. Phil, I ask, "So how's that working out for you? Did your zero-tolerance policy prevent this fight?"

"Mr. Williams..."

"Did you ask Henry why this happened?"

"There's no excuse..."

"If you don't know what happened, you're in no position to judge that, are you?"

The principal's face reddens. "Mr. Williams, you are here to pick up your grandson. I will discuss all this with his *legal guardian* when she brings him back to school on Monday. I'll decide then whether to readmit him or suspend him."

I wait until we get to the car before saying anything to Henry. "What happened?"

No response.

"I'm on your side, Henry. Just tell me what happened. If you were in the wrong, just say so, and I won't utter another word. If the other guy started it, I need to know."

He doesn't look at me.

"You know what? I can wait here all day. I don't have anything else to do."

He looks out the window. "There's this guy in my class. I think he's been held back. Likes to pick on people smaller than him. He shoved me from behind as were walking into the classroom. I turned around and punched."

Henry smiles. "You should have seen the look on his face."

"Sounds like you were defending yourself. That's what you should tell your mom when she gets home."

"You think she'll understand."

I shake my head. "I can't promise you that. Either she will or she won't. just tell her the truth."

He gives me a puzzled look.

I crank the car and pull away. When we get to Monroe Drive, I turn right instead of left.

"Where are we going?" Henry asks.

"To Sports Authority."

He tries to process this, then asks, "Why?"

To get a speed bag, a heavy bag, a couple of mats, and some gloves. I'm making the playhouse over into a gym. If you're going to make a habit of this, you'll need some lessons… unless you like that look." I gesture toward his eye.

He grins. "Thanks."

CHAPTER 18
AUTUMN SOIREE

Midtown
Saturday, October 27

Lou Allen, in a snit as usual when hosting a party, fussed over last-minute details. Fewer than half his invitees had bothered to RSVP, but he knew every one of them would show. He did, after all, have an exclusive guest list and the finest gala of the fall season.

Caterers and decorators came and went, bringing flowers, balloons, canapes, hors d'oeuvres, and magnums of fine wine. Lou had already sent back one van filled with tropical flowers, totally out of keeping with his Broadway theme.

He fretted over the special sound system he'd ordered to balance music throughout the house. Tonight's selections included show tunes from the forties, fifties and sixties. The technicians were testing with Lou's favorite from *Oklahoma*, "I'm Just a Girl Who Can't Say No."

The doorbell rang. Lou scurried to answer as fast as his bulk permitted. The poor, white-shirted, black-trousered Mormon missionaries who'd chosen to call at this appalling hour hastily vacated the porch under Lou's withering glare.

"Get out of here this instant," he bellowed.

• • •

It was the Saturday before Halloween, and the children of Peachtree City were trick-or-treating early. Rob was out again, this time on a west coast flight. Kyle and Leslie were at a church lock-in. For Allison the timing was perfect.

She gave her disguise an appraising look. The revealing outlines meant few people, if any, would be looking at her face. And then there was the mask and wig. The question was where to stow all this stuff. She couldn't just walk out of the house wearing it. She'd have to find a private spot where she could change, unseen by potential witnesses.

In the end, she wore the outfit under her street clothes and carried the mask and wig, along with her gun, in an old handbag she found at the bottom of her closet. She spotted a gray hoodie and grabbed it also, thinking it might hide her face.

Twenty-four hours earlier, Allison, seizing an unexpected opportunity, had discharged the first half of her contract. The "package," as she called it, lay safely ensconced in a wooded area north of Atlanta. Abandoned near the West End MARTA station, the victim's car was sure to attract the attention of thieves. To make it more tempting she left the keys in the ignition.

Tonight, she would use the same weapon, contrary to her client's instructions. She'd been unable to pick up a second one from a discreet source and resented this person on the phone telling her how to do her job. She was, after all, a professional.

· · ·

Ambrose Mangham, at that moment, was packing for an impromptu, but well-deserved vacation. Humming to himself, he selected a pair of orange Speedos, a white Panama hat and iridescent sunglasses.

Tonight, the children of the neighborhood would be out in force. Though Halloween wouldn't arrive until Tuesday, parents had chosen Saturday as a more convenient occasion for trick-or-treat. He could just see the disappointment on their little faces when they discovered he wasn't home.

A ring tone interrupted his reverie. It was the opening bars of "Also Sprach Zarathustra," from his favorite movie, "2001: A Space Odyssey." The number on the phone's display was unfamiliar. Annoyed as he was at the interruption, something told Mangham the call was important.

"Yes," he snapped.

"Ambrose," said the warm voice, "this is Tom Williams. I hope I'm not calling at a bad time. I'm putting together a story on the Midtown Murders, like you suggested, and I wanted to run something by you."

Tom paused just long enough for Mangham to become mildly annoyed. "I was wondering what you could tell me about a business venture called 'Rabbit Refund.'"

Mangham nearly fainted. He steadied himself as he eased into a nearby armchair. When he regained control, he forced a reply. "I have no idea what you're talking about." In an instant, he knew that was the wrong response. If Williams had such information, then he knew Mangham was lying. Nevertheless, this was his story, and he stuck to it.

"So, I'm to take it, then," continued Williams, "that you and Joel A. Mangham are not the same person?"

"No," Mangham stammered. "Look, you did catch me at a bad time. Can I reach you later at this number?" He drew a deep, slow breath to calm his heart rate. "I'd be interested to find out what else you've learned."

"Sure. I've just started my first draft, and I'd appreciate your input."

Mangham disconnected without saying goodbye. He stared at the half-filled suitcase for several seconds before suddenly dashing to the bathroom and unloading his lunch. *Just that one fuck-up,* he thought, *and I'll spend the rest of my life paying for it. It wasn't even my fault.*

His planned vacation, he told himself, would require but a brief delay. He went to the kitchen and dug through a bottom drawer until he found the old Bell South white pages he used for looking up street addresses.

• • •

The sun had set by the time Tom and Bogie began their evening walk. Tonight, they strolled up to Ponce City Market. Ponce de Leon Avenue teemed with drivers heading for restaurants and theaters where they would stand in long lines waiting for a table or buying tickets.

On his way home, Tom turned at Monroe and made his way down the long hill. On a side street, several cars had parked along the curb. Adults in various costumes greeted each other. One of them, a man wearing a tuxedo and white mask, stepped onto the front porch next door to Max Hogarth. Other guests arrived dressed as sumo wrestlers, cowboys, and ballet dancers. Like the children out trick-or-treating, the adults had moved Halloween to Saturday so they could party late.

As he passed the next street, a woman stepped out of a car parked in the shadow of a large tree. Tom watched, unnoticed, as she removed a gray hoodie and tossed it onto the front seat. Beneath it she wore a full-length, form-fitting costume all in white, a blonde wig, and a sequined mask. Rather than using the sidewalk, she ducked into a darkened alley.

. . .

One by one, the guests arrived. Lou greeted them at the door. They wore masks, as instructed, but he recognized most of them right away. Lou spoke briefly with each before directing them to the champagne fountain and the hors d'oeuvres.

Many were folks Lou had known during his years as a lawyer in suburban Lithonia. Some led double lives, as Lou had before moving to Midtown. One, a middle school principal dressed as Zorro, was regaling Lou with lurid details of a cruise he and his male companions had recently enjoyed.

A short swarthy man in a black tuxedo and tails arrived. He carried sheet music in his hand, lest anyone fail to identify him as an opera singer. He'd darkened his hair and slicked it back. In his white mask he resembled the Phantom of the Opera. Lou and Zorro recognized him immediately.

"Oh, my!" said Zorro, "but isn't that Flaccido Domingo?"

The best response the wounded man could muster was, "Bitch!"

"Not yours, darling," said Zorro as he turned to join another group of guests.

They all commented on Lou's well-stocked library. It included the complete works of Somerset Maugham and biographies of T. E. Lawrence and Field Marshal Montgomery. Lou, none of them realized, had never read any of the books.

The next arrival was a woman, someone Lou couldn't place however hard he tried. She wore a clever disguise and reminded him of Lady Gaga. She replied to his puzzled look with a coquettish smile and a finger to her lips. Lou couldn't wait for the midnight unmasking to find out who she was. *A party-crasher?*

He turned to speak to another guest, and when he looked back, she was gone. Of one thing, he was sure. She was far too thin to be Eleanor Heinz, who by now was more than fashionably late.

Lou seldom watched the evening news, especially when he had business as important as this. Had he bothered he'd have seen the missing person announcement. Eleanor would not be attending tonight's affair.

CHAPTER 19
THE INTRUDER

Midtown
Saturday, October 27
I'm at my laptop, pondering my next step with Ambrose Mangham. Bogie barks and runs to the front door. Muted voices come from the walkway, footsteps on the porch. *More late-night trick-or-treaters*, I think, *probably teenagers with nothing better to do*. I grab the bag of bite-sized Snickers, determined to get rid of the few remaining.

It's Marie and the boys returning from Plaza Theater, a special showing of the cult classic, "Rocky Horror Picture Show." Henry complains, not surprisingly, saying it was a dumb movie.

William thinks it was hilarious. "What do you mean?" he says. "Didn't you think it was cool when the fat guy rode his motorcycle up on the dinner table?"

"But all those dudes dressed like chicks... Yuck!"

"You'd better get used to it," Marie says. "You're living in Midtown now, at least until I can find us a place in the burbs... And by the way, Henry, they're women, not 'chicks.' You know better."

As she passes, I smile. She rolls her eyes.

The debate continues as they climb the stairs to their respective rooms.

As peace and quiet return, Bogie curls up on the rug. I continue browsing for stories on Rabbit Refund. There's a brief news story about Joel Mangham's fraud conviction but no picture or mention of a middle name. The final paragraph mentions Lyle Mallory as an unindicted investor.

There's nothing about Joel on Facebook or LinkedIn. I find a brief profile on newspaper writer, Ambrose Mangham, but nowhere does he call himself "Joel."

Again, I think about Paxton, but decide to call him in the morning. I doze off to the low murmur of Henry's video game overhead.

. . .

Old houses have their own personalities, their unique sounds and smells... much like old people. I've grown accustomed to this place, its creaks and groans, the low gurgle of the refrigerator, the rattle of windowpanes when a large truck labors uphill. By now I've learned to tune it all out. I'm also a light sleeper, which has saved my life more than once. My bed sits next to a window facing the side porch.

What I've just heard is unmistakable. It's a footfall, not from the rooms overhead, but from out front. *Maybe it's Marie having a late-night smoke on the swing.* She usually sits on the back steps, thinking I don't know what she's up to.

Outside, a cloud parts and the room is suddenly awash in moonlight. I rise from the bed to find Bogie pointing at the door, frozen in place as though he's trapped a quail. He doesn't move or utter a sound.

I'm about to reach for the knob, when I hear the sound again. This time it's behind me, at my window. A shadow passes across the wall. It's too tall for Marie or the boys. In an instant, I'm on the floor. Bogie crouches beside me shivering and whimpering.

From beneath the bed, I grab the .45 I retrieved from the attic, cleaned and loaded a week ago. The figure, apparently unaware this is a makeshift bedroom, is working a pry bar under the sash.

As certain as I am that the lock will hold, I'm not about to find out. I come up into a crouch and squeeze the trigger, intending to hit the center of his torso. The explosion shakes the small room, drowning out the sound of shattering glass.

The shadow wheels, grabbing his left shoulder. The pry bar clatters on the porch floor as he tumbles over the railing and into the flower bed. Overhead a shrill voice shouts, "What was that?"

"Dad!" Marie screams, as she runs into the upstairs hall. "Henry, William, stay in your rooms."

Pounding down the stairway, she's almost at my door, when I call out, "It's okay, baby girl. I'm okay." My heart's about to erupt. I struggle to catch my breath. "It was an intruder. I think he's gone. Go back upstairs while I look."

Fat chance! She grabs me as I open the door and presses herself against me. It takes me a moment to remember I'm still holding a loaded pistol. I carefully extract myself from her embrace, engage the safety, and place the gun on my dresser. Bogie peeps out from under the bed.

"What the fuck are you doing with a loaded gun in this house?" Marie screams. "Dad, you could have shot one of us... or yourself."

"Or," I explain with all the calm I can muster, "we could all be dead now at the hands of a home invader."

"How do you know that?"

"I'm pretty sure he wasn't a Jehovah's witness, prying my window open at this hour." I glance at the clock. It's almost one.

Marie's about to come back with another caustic reply when, from behind her, William asks, "You think he was the serial killer?" Standing beside him, wide-eyed, is Henry.

Marie spins on her heels. For a moment, I'm afraid she'll backhand them both.

"Hey." I reassure them. "It's all over. I think he ran away. I'm calling the cops while there's still a chance they'll catch him."

Again, Marie starts to say something, but I hold up my hand. My phone is against my left ear, and a voice answers, "911. What is your emergency?" For a moment I expect her to add, 'Your call is important to us. Please hold.'

I explain I've just shot an intruder. "He was trying to get in through the window. I must have hit him, but I think he got away. We're inside my house. Everybody's okay."

"Sir, a squad car is on its way."

It's fortunate none of us is hurt. The police take twenty minutes to arrive. Meanwhile, I have another thought. I walk over to the chest of drawers and pull out two pairs of underwear. Placing them over my hands so I don't leave fingerprints, I open the now shattered bedroom window. I don't want anyone questioning whether this guy was breaking in.

When I turn back, Marie is staring at me. There's a knock on the front door. I'm about to answer when a male voice shouts, "Come out with your hands where we can see them."

"There are four of us," I yell back, "two adults and two children. We all have our hands in the air."

Marie and the boys follow me as we step into a blinding spotlight. Two cops are standing on either side of the door. One grabs me, spins me around, and pats me down for a weapon.

"Hey," Marie yells as his partner starts to frisk her. She's wearing nothing but a cotton night shirt and panties.

I'm about to say something unwise when a female voice calls out, "That'll be okay. "I'll take it from here." Out of a shadow steps Beth Long, the investigator I met at Max Hogarth's.

I spend the next thirty minutes telling her what happened, while the uniforms proceed to clear the house and yard, including the old playhouse out back.

"And you have no idea who he was?" Long asks for the third time.

"No."

"Have you had a serious dispute with anyone recently?"

"No."

"Mr. Williams, I know you've been talking to neighbors and asking questions about the Midtown Murders. Maybe you asked the wrong person. Who have you spoken to in the past twenty-four hours?"

I'm about to mention my conversation with Mangham, when her phone rings.

"Long," she answers. There's a perceptible change in her bearing. She walks toward the street and continues her conversation out of earshot.

The officers look at each other as if wondering what to do next. The older one, for want of anything better, has me recite my story again while he scribbles notes. His partner, meanwhile, inspects the blood and broken glass scattered across my porch.

Long concludes her conversation and returns. "Mr. Williams, I'm leaving. You'll need to come down to the station and sign a statement. Officers Meacham and White will keep an eye on your house until the crime scene team arrives, but I need you to come straight to the station... now."

At this point, Marie interjects, "Give us a few minutes to get dressed."

"And you are?"

"My name's Marie Wakefield. I'm Mr. Williams' attorney. I'll be accompanying him."

"And we'll want to talk to Paxton Davis," I add.

Long gives Marie an appraising look, no doubt wondering what sort of lawyer spends the night with her client. "Fine," she says. "You have ten minutes."

• • •

Marie insists on driving to the station. Along the way, she has me repeat my story slowly, everything I heard and saw from the moment I awoke. She presses me, as the cops will do, on why I keep a pistol under my bed. I explain I put it there out of concern over the recent wave of murders in the neighborhood and a desire to protect my family.

She smiles. "That's good. Be as honest as possible without saying anything that might incriminate you. Don't sound evasive, but don't volunteer anything they haven't asked. They'll ask you to repeat your story multiple times. Take a deep breath and answer slowly. They'll try to trip you up. Just make sure you don't contradict yourself." Her expression darkens, and she lets out a sigh. "Dad, what were you thinking? You know I hate guns."

"And I hate the thought of being dead... or losing one of you."

In the back seat, Henry and William sit quietly, taking in our conversation.

I pull out my cell and dial Paxton. I can tell I've awakened him. I explain about the break-in and my suspicions regarding Ambrose Mangham. He tells us he's on his way.

At the station, Marie and I are whisked into a small interrogation room. William and Henry sit in the lobby under the watchful eye of an elderly sergeant. We wait for what seems an eternity.

When he finally arrives, Paxton is not happy. "Tom Williams, what have you gotten yourself into?"

Before I can answer, I feel the light pressure of Marie's foot atop mine under the table. "Paxton, you remember my daughter, Marie."

"Marie!" he smiles. "It's been a long time. What brings you down here? Tell me you didn't come all the way here from D.C. just to keep your old man out of jail."

"It's a long story," she says, returning his smile.

"I see. Now, Tom, tell me what happened."

As Marie instructed, I take a slow breath. "Not long ago, I moved my bed downstairs into my study. I awoke this morning to footsteps on my front porch. I got up to see what was happening. Then I heard someone coming around the side of the house to my window. When I turned, he was trying to jimmy it open. I got down and crawled over to my bed, where I keep a loaded .45."

Paxton nods. "You keep a loaded gun under your bed."

"Yep. With all the murders around here, you never know."

"Yeah. Go on."

"The intruder, whoever he was, was opening my window like he was going to climb inside. I saw what looked like a gun in his left hand. I came up and fired. In my excitement, I guess my shot went high. It may have caught him in the shoulder. He staggered back and fell over the railing. I called the police right away. When they got there, he was gone."

"You're lucky as hell you got that shot off when you did," says Paxton. "Meacham and White tell me they found a lot of blood..." He gives me a knowing look. "... and a lot of glass." He knows my story about the window being open is bullshit. He just isn't calling me on it... yet.

He continues, "Whoever he was, he couldn't have gone far. There's a team on their way there now to check out the backyard. So, tell me about this Mangham guy you mentioned on the phone."

"When we spoke the other day, you asked me to let you know if I found out anything about the murder victims... the lawyers."

He leans back. In the corner of my eye I see Marie start to say something. I press my foot against hers beneath the table and continue my story.

"I was talking to Jacob Epstein's girlfriend, Marina Kovacs, yesterday. She said Epstein lost a bunch of money a few years ago in one of those rapid tax refund schemes."

"Yes."

"At first, I thought she said its name was 'Rapid Tax.' Later, I was speaking with a neighbor who knew Mallory. He said Mallory had been involved with a tax filing partnership called 'Rabbit Tax.'"

Paxton lowers his head and lets out a sigh. "How in the hell could we have missed that?"

"I'm sure nobody thought it was important at the time. Anyway, Marina said the business was a limited partnership. I looked it up on the Secretary of State's web site. Turns out the registered agent was somebody named Joel A. Mangham. One of my sources was an Ambrose Mangham. He writes for a paper called *Biz Atlanta*."

"I never heard of anybody named Ambrose Mangham or any paper named *Biz Atlanta*."

"You wouldn't have. I just met him the other day. He said he had sources in the police department telling him there was a serial killer."

Paxton jumps up and begins to pace. "Tom, why the hell you just now telling this? You got my phone number."

He's right. I take a breath and continue. "I know I should've called you sooner. At first, I thought the guy was just a flake… and then yesterday…"

I glance at Marie. She nods. "Yesterday, I found out about Rabbit Refunds. I was debating whether to dig some more or call you. This afternoon I called Mangham to get his reaction."

"And?"

"He became evasive. He said he didn't know any Joel Mangham, and then he cut me off."

Paxton stops pacing and stares at me. "This biz whatever dude said he had police sources."

"Yeah. He said they gave him information you withheld from the press."

"Like what?"

"That the killer used a .22 caliber pistol up close. He shot his victims, first in the chest, then once in each eye. Before leaving, he took hair clippings as souvenirs."

Paxton's eyes widen, and I realize Mangham's the only person I've heard mention souvenirs. None of the news stories said anything about them.

Paxton pulls out his cell. "Go home, Tom. Don't go anywhere else. I might have some more questions. I'll put a squad car outside your house, in case there's any more trouble. We'll keep looking for this guy."

CHAPTER 20
THE SHOOTOUT

Atlanta, Georgia
Saturday, October 27

The gala was a success beyond Lou's wildest expectations. The Weather Channel forecasted a late evening thunderstorm. So far, it had not arrived.

Exhausted and alone, Lou turned out the downstairs lights and mounted the stairs. He recalled again the woman in the white body stocking. He hadn't seen her since she arrived. She was nowhere in sight for the great unmasking. He'd placed himself near the front door hoping to catch her before she departed. She must have left through the rear.

Stripping out of his clothes, he gazed out his window onto Monroe Drive. The light of a passing car illuminated Ben Hogarth's face peering from his darkened bedroom. Standing naked in full view of the window, Lou smiled and waved as he reached for his robe.

A distant rumble interrupted his reverie, followed by a small, indistinct noise. Lou turned. His smile vanished as he saw her standing in his closet, silenced revolver in hand.

. . .

Hunched against the evening chill, Walsh pulled a cheap fleece hoodie down over his face. He too heard the thunder and hoped like hell the rain held off until he finished his job. In one gloved hand, he held a brown paper bag containing an empty can. The other hand, crammed inside the bottomless jacket pocket, held his Glock. He rocked back and forth, humming a low tune.

He'd bought the fleece from a homeless man on John Wesley Dobbs Avenue under the overpass. It reeked of sweat, piss, and sour wine. When he finished with it, he would toss it into the nearest trash can. The occasional passerby glanced away and gave him a wide berth.

The low wall where he sat was directly across from a Summer Hill apartment building, the residence of Hollywood Holmes. Walsh had called Lyman Gwynn that afternoon, as Paxton instructed, and arranged the stakeout.

Lyman and two plain clothes officers sat in an unmarked car, down the block in the shadows of an abandoned driveway. Its tinted windows precluded anyone seeing inside but gave them a clear view of Walsh.

"Now that is one crazy-ass cracker," remarked the narc in the back seat.

Gwynn shook his head and smiled. "Man, you have no idea."

The front door of the apartment building opened. A dark figure emerged and crossed the street toward the parking lot behind Walsh. It took Walsh seconds to realize it wasn't Hollywood, but a member of his crew, sent out on some errand.

As the man passed, Walsh stood and set the paper bag aside. In one smooth move, he clamped his left hand over the man's mouth and jammed the barrel of the pistol into his right ear. The suspect winced in pain then froze.

"Make one wrong move, motherfucker," whispered Walsh, "and I'll spatter your brains all over the street. Nod your head slowly if you understand."

The man nodded.

"Now," said Walsh in his most soothing voice, "we're going to ease over there and you're going to ring Hollywood's buzzer. Whatever you do, don't get stupid. I'm not here to kill you or Hollywood. I just have a couple of questions for him."

As his hostage reached for the buzzer, Walsh broke the light bulb above the door with the butt of his pistol in case Holmes had an outside security camera. The man flinched so hard Walsh almost lost his grip. Gwynn and the other officers took up positions a few feet on either side of him.

"What?" asked a gruff voice over the speaker.

"Sorry, man! I forgot my wallet," said the runner.

The voice grumbled, "dumb motherfuck!" The door buzzed and clicked open.

In seconds, Walsh, Gwynn, the other officers, and their prisoner were inside the building. An elderly woman opened her apartment door and looked out. Before she could scream, a plainclothesman clamped a hand over her mouth and shoved her back into her room.

Another pushed past Walsh to the unit at the end of the hall. Walsh stood back as he swung a fifteen-pound sledge, sending the door crashing into an adjacent wall and splintering the frame.

Startled, Hollywood Holmes stared up from a coffee table on which he was rolling a joint. Before he could reach for the Makarov at the end of the couch, Gwynn levelled his service revolver at Holmes' forehead. "Don't do it, Holly. You'll lose."

Holmes slowly returned his hand to the coffee table, where he lay it, palm down beside the other. He looked up at Walsh, lowered his eyes, and shook his head.

The plainclothesmen cleared the apartment, retrieving weapons, emptying their magazines and placing them on the floor in the corner. One of them dumped the drugs into plastic evidence bags while the other radioed for backup.

Minutes later, uniformed officers led three of Holmes' men in handcuffs to the squad cars awaiting them on the street. Walsh stayed in the apartment with Holmes who lay, face down on the floor, his hands secured behind him.

"Ok," Walsh whispered in his ear. "This is how it's going down. You're busted. You've got a lot of stuff here, Holly, pot, smack, coke, meth. As I'm sure you know, some of it could disappear between here and downtown. Some of it might even make its way back to you. I just need your help on something." He waited a moment. "Do I have your attention, Holly."

Holmes nodded.

"I need information about a white dude, known as 'YT,' mid-forties. He's been buying little piece-of-shit .22s from you, throwaways."

Holmes became very still.

"C'mon, Holly. You don't have any reason to protect this man. Nothing you tell me will come back on you, and you know it. Besides, he's going down anyway. It's not like you're gonna get any more business from him. We're about to pin three murders on him, maybe more. You don't want any part of this action. Next to this, what's a small-time drug bust? Hell, we could even make this whole thing go away."

Walsh waited.

Holmes shook his head. "Man, I ain't no snitch."

"Shit, Holly! This ain't snitching. What's a little asshole like this YT to somebody like you? All I need's his real name, and I promise you won't see me again."

Holmes tried to bury his face in the avocado shag carpet. "I caught his name from the dude who put him in touch with me. I pretended not to hear it. It's Ambrose something. I mean… I remember thinking, 'What a pussy name! Just like some pansy-ass white boy… no offense, man."

"None taken. You know, Holly, we might make a standup citizen out of you yet."

"Yeah. Well, just don't tell nobody. Okay?"

"Don't worry. This'll be our little secret. Meanwhile, you'll need to come downtown with us, so we can handle some paperwork."

Walsh escorted Holmes to a waiting squad car. He'd just settled into his unmarked unit when his phone rang. It was Paxton.

"Hey, Boss. Whatcha got?"

"Where are you?"

"We're bringing in Hollywood Holmes. He gave me a name."

"You need to get over to Tom Williams' place right now. He shot somebody climbing in his window. The dude got away, but he couldn't have gone far. I've got Meacham and White over there babysitting until the techs arrive. I'm at the station interviewing Williams."

"Any idea who it was?"

"Williams thinks he was somebody named 'Ambrose Mangham.' I don't have any details yet." Paxton said. "Look. I gotta go. Long's calling me."

Walsh slammed the car into gear before Paxton finished speaking. "I'm on my way."

Heart pounding, Walsh hit the light bar in his grill and floored the accelerator. He had to get to Mangham before anyone else. He remembered the location from canvassing the neighborhood following the Lopez shooting. In ten minutes, he was in front of Williams' house.

He found Meacham and White on the front porch alone and bored. The crime scene techs still hadn't arrived, and Williams wasn't back yet from the station.

"Ok," he asked. "Where did it happen?"

White walked him around the corner of the porch. He showed him the shot-out window and broken azaleas where the intruder fell over the railing.

"Ok," said Walsh. Go around there and keep Meacham company while I have a look."

"You sure you don't need backup?"

"I'm sure," he said. "Now just fucking do what I tell you."

It took Walsh minutes to find the pistol in the bushes beside the porch. It was an aging Ruger .22, as Holmes had said, as likely to blow up in your hand as to hit its intended target. Two feet away lay a puddle of blood about twelve inches in diameter. Bloody handprints smeared the bannister. Walsh donned latex gloves and carefully lifted the gun.

Hiding it behind his back he leaned around the corner of the house far enough to see Meacham and White standing on the steps, engrossed in a quiet debate over who was the greatest wrestler of all time.

"You boys stay there and wait for the techs. I'll go see if I can find out where this guy went."

Walsh held the Ruger in his left hand with his flashlight, which he played over the ground where the man had fallen. He pulled out his Glock with his right. A few feet away a large dollop of blood glistened on a fallen leaf. A wooden privacy fence blocked his path. Near its top he saw another bloody handprint.

On the other side, the trail continued across Williams' back yard. Walsh zig zagged to avoid stepping in dog shit. Slowly he worked the light back and forth, locating more splotches of red. On the far side, he found a bit of cloth clinging to a curled section of chicken wire at the bottom of the fence. It looked to be part of a torn trouser leg.

He scrambled across and found an overgrown alley running through the middle of the block. A footprint in the sand indicated the perp had turned right, along a path that led toward Charles Allen Drive. Walsh followed it to the end and looked up and down the street. There was no one in sight.

Doubling back, he noticed a gap in a chain link fence behind a house on the next street. He saw another piece of torn cloth matching the earlier one. He worked his way through the opening.

Five feet away stood a shed made of rough wooden planks. It leaned to one side. Two of the planks were missing, and the door hung open on its hinges.

Walsh stepped closer with his flashlight trained on the ground in front of him. He stopped and reached the light around the door before peering inside. From the shed came a low cough. Peering through a gap he saw the outline of a man lying on the ground. A sudden flash of lightning illuminated his face, the eyes clinched tight in pain. Leading with the Glock, Walsh shifted until he saw him completely.

Mangham's breathing was ragged. His feet dug into the soft dirt floor.

Time to put this sonofabitch out of his misery, Walsh thought. He stepped into the doorway and placed a single shot through Mangham's heart. He timed it so the thunder would help mask the sound. The body lurched, and the head lolled to one side.

Walsh was leaning over to place the Ruger in Mangham's lifeless hand when a noise interrupted him, like someone clearing his throat. He spun to see a dark form looming just seven feet away. He'd been so focused on Mangham he hadn't heard the man come up behind him.

As he raised his pistol to fire, a burst of flame erupted from the man's extended hand. The first bullet caught Walsh in the right shoulder, sending the Glock spinning into the nearby brush. The second caught him in the forehead, ripping away the back of his skull.

Moving quickly, the man retrieved the Ruger. He placed his own gun in Mangham's hand and fired another round into the dirt, leaving gunshot residue on the dead man's body. Investigators might eventually realize Mangham didn't killed Walsh, but by that time he would be long gone.

A half block away, as the crime techs arrived, Meacham and White heard the shots. Working carefully across the back yard with White in tow, Meacham scanned until he found the spot where Mangham and Walsh had climbed the fence. He followed Walsh's steps to the shed where the two bodies lay. He turned and looked at his partner. An already long night had become much longer.

Neither of them saw the pair of eyes watching them closely from behind the stand of bamboo that marked Helen Weiss's property line.

CHAPTER 21
SUMATRA SIMMS

Midtown
Sunday, October 28

So exhausted they could barely move, Tom, Marie, and the kids returned home in the predawn hours to a major crime scene investigation. Police cars and media vehicles lined both sides of the narrow street. Flood lights bathed the yard as investigators combed the flower beds on their hands and knees. A local TV reporter spoke into a microphone as curious neighbors looked on, some waving at the camera.

Working his way past the crowd, Tom caught the reporter's eye. She recognized him and called out. He turned to her, shielding Marie and the boys from the camera long enough for them to escape into the house.

"Hey, Sumatra." He flashed the reporter a weary smile. Though much younger than Tom, Sumatra Simms was already a veteran journalist. They had run into each other many times over the years.

She faced the camera as she spoke. "I have here Tom Williams, who, earlier tonight shot and wounded a man trying to break into his Midtown home. Police now believe the man was Buckhead resident Joel Ambrose Mangham, found dead in a dilapidated shed behind a nearby residence. Mangham died in what appears to have been a shootout with Atlanta Police Detective Don Walsh, also dead at the scene. We tried getting down there, but the police have blocked off both ends of the alley leading to the shed."

Simms turned and placed her free hand on Tom's shoulder. He stood frozen in silence, stunned by the news of Mangham's and Walsh's deaths.

"Mr. Williams," she asked, "Were you aware that the man you shot was Joel Mangham."

Tom recovered long enough to choke out, "No. I wasn't."

"We understand you just returned from the police station, where you gave a statement about the attempted break-in. Do you have any idea why Mr. Mangham tried to burglarize your home?"

Tom took a deep breath and tried to recover. He pictured Marie gazing down from an upstairs window, willing him to keep his mouth shut. "No. As you can imagine, Sumatra, I'm in shock right now. I need to spend some time with my family. We've been through a terrible ordeal."

Sumatra tried to interject another question, but Tom ignored her. He turned on his heels and strode toward the house. Another reporter blocked his way. A police officer intervened just as Tom was about to punch the man in the face.

Safely inside, Tom and Marie made sure the boys were in bed and then met in the kitchen. Tom made a pot of coffee. Neither had any hope of sleeping with news crews and cameramen camped on the lawn.

Tom stared into his daughter's haggard eyes. "Well, counsellor, what's next?"

"What's next is we sit tight and wait for this to blow over. The reporters will eventually get tired of swapping lies and go home. Right now, you have nothing to worry about. Just don't speak to anyone without my being there. Understood?"

"Understood."

She bit her lower lip as if holding something back. "Dad, I'm getting the boys out of here as quickly as I can. I wish you'd consider selling this place and moving somewhere closer to us."

Tom sighed. "I'll think about it."

CHAPTER 22
AFTER PARTY

Midtown
Sunday, October 28

At the end of the alley, Paxton Davis parked his SUV and climbed out. A group of police officers cleared a path through the television crews camped nearby hoping for a glimpse of the bodies.

"Alright," he said. "Show it to me."

Meacham led him to the scene, sweeping his flashlight along the narrow path in front of them. Careful not to get blood on his shoes, Paxton stooped beside the man who, only hours earlier he had sent to investigate a home invasion. The body lay face up with a hole the size of Paxton's index finger in the middle of the forehead. A halo of blood and brain tissue encircled his head.

The eyes stared up with a look frozen in amazement. The irises had already begun to fade. Paxton studied them for a long time. Lightning flickered across the sky, its reflection creating the momentary illusion that Walsh was looking back at him trying to say something.

Paxton stood and walked to the shed for a closer look. Mangham lay in the dirt, eyes closed, arms outstretched in a gesture of supplication. A crime scene tech motioned Paxton to step aside as he got one last shot, a closeup of the .38 in the man's right hand.

"He fired two shots, said Meacham. We found one of the slugs in the ground over there." He motioned to a hole in the dirt. The techs bagged it and are taking it downtown. We believe the other one went through Walsh. They're still scouring the area for it."

Paxton pretended to listen as he studied the positioning of the body. There was something odd about it. He'd seen the aftermaths of many shootouts in his career. This man, he was certain, had not been an active shooter when he died. "I need everything I can get about Mangham. Something about this doesn't look right."

He made a note to put Long on it. By now, though, she had gone home. He considered calling to tell her about Walsh and Mangham but decided it could wait until morning. He spoke with the crime techs, who said it would be hours before they completed their work. Reluctantly, he headed home to get some sleep. As he drove away, the skies erupted.

"Just fucking great," said Meacham. "I knew this circus was missing something."

• • •

The low rumble of distant thunder awakened Beth Long. A pale finger of predawn light filtered between the blinds of Brandon Markham's bedroom. His wife and daughters were still out of town, and Long had agreed to come over for the evening.

Atop a chest of drawers on the other side of the room her phone rang. The clock on the bedside table read six-thirty. Markham stirred beside her.

"Sorry!" she said. "I meant to turn it off."

It rang again before she could get to it. She read the caller ID.

"Paxton?" she answered, her voice still raspy from sleep.

"Hey. Sorry to call so early. I need you over on Monroe right away, Lou Allen's home. We already have uniforms there. I'll be there in twenty minutes."

• • •

Shivering inside their yellow slickers, Meacham and White spent the remainder of the night at opposite ends of the alley holding civilians and media at bay. The rain slowed to a steady drizzle. Having made their deadlines, the news crews decamped, and the neighbors went home. The sky had begun to brighten above the trees by the time the two officers met in front of the Williams home.

They were about to return to the station and file their reports when Meacham's phone chirped. He pulled it from his pocket and listened intently as the caller spoke. He placed a hand over his eyes. "Got it" was his only reply. He ended the call and turned to White. "That was Long. We've got another one."

Three blocks away, they pulled into a side street and walked the short distance to the home of Lou Allen. Long met them at the door. There were no media or nosy neighbors yet, the arrival of police on Monroe Drive being more commonplace than on Eighth Street.

"Whatta ya have?" asked White, in his best imitation of the wait staff at the Varsity Restaurant.

"Lou Allen, divorce attorney, had a big party last night," said Long. "A guest came back for something he'd left. He found the front door open and discovered Allen upstairs, lying naked in a pool of blood. The body's still there. Paxton should be here soon."

"Don't tell me," said Meacham with a sigh, "one in the body and two in the eyes."

"Precisely."

"Shit!"

As they climbed the stairs to Allen's bedroom, the officers explained what had happened at the Williams house, culminating with the deaths of Mangham and Walsh. Long staggered for a moment then recovered.

"I know you guys are tired," she said, "but I need your help."

White turned to his partner and smirked. "What the hell! We're already on overtime."

Long filled them in. "The call came in at six AM. Two uniforms responded. They found a guest, Stan Hadden, sitting on the porch crying. He was still crying when I got here.

He says he left the party about two. Allen was still alive. When he returned Allen was dead. That places the time of death within a four-hour window. We'll know more when the ME gets through with him. The MO is the same as for the other three lawyers. When I spoke to Paxton, he was ready to pin those murders on this Joel Mangham."

Meacham took a moment to process. "Williams reported the break-in at his place a little after one. Mangham never made it away from there. So, Mangham's not our Midtown murderer."

"Or," said Long, "he was, and we have a copycat. This one could be a psychopath or just someone with a grudge." She squatted next to Allen's corpse and studied the entry wound. "What kind of gun did Mangham have?"

"We found a .38 revolver on him," said White.

"This looks like a smaller caliber, maybe a .22, like those used to kill the other lawyers... And you didn't see one anywhere at the Williams place?"

"Nope." said White.

They stood silent for several seconds letting this sink in.

"We don't know what we have yet," said Long. "And we won't know until the investigators finish. When Paxton gets here, we can ask him what he thinks. Meanwhile, when the media gets wind of this there'll be a shit storm. Until you hear otherwise from Paxton or me, you don't know anything. *Am I clear?*"

The officers nodded.

CHAPTER 23
THE ARTIST

Midtown
Sunday, October 28

Ben Hogarth watched the police from his window. He'd lain awake all night after trailing the Dark Avenger to the abandoned alley where he shot the policeman. Afterward, Ben followed him home and watched from outside as the man hastily packed and left. Ben wasn't sure what to make of this or how it fit it into his emerging story. *Why was the Dark Avenger leaving?*

Carefully avoiding lighted areas, Ben walked home and crept in through his back door, leaving the lights off, not wanting to awaken his dad. He stripped out of his clothes and was about to go to bed, when he looked out his window and saw the fat dragon next door enter his bedroom and undress.

Without warning, a strangely clad woman stepped out of the dragon's closet with a small gun in her hand and shot him, once in the chest and again in each eye. She then took a pair of scissors from her pocket and, for some reason, clipped off a lock of his hair.

The woman wore a white body stocking so tight Ben at first thought she was naked. A white sequined mask covered most of her face. Waves of blonde hair fell across her shoulders. To Ben she was the "Ice Queen." He didn't know yet if she were a good character or bad. The man she'd just killed was as evil as anyone Ben could imagine.

Ben spent the next four hours capturing the whole episode in bright pastels, setting off the virginal white of the woman's outfit against the purple of the dragon's robe and the rich crimson blood spatter on the wall. He was just applying the finishing touches when he looked out and saw the lady officer standing on the porch next door. She had a kind face, and Ben liked her very much. She reminded him of an old photo of his mom. That photo was Ben's only memory of her.

An older man arrived, the same one who came by the morning after the Dark Avenger beat up the two bad guys. He spoke to the lady cop, then glanced up at Ben staring down from the window. He pointed, and she turned her head.

. . .

Tom had grown tired of hanging out at the house. When Marie went upstairs to shower, he and Bogie ducked out for a walk. Finding the police at Lou Allen's home, he struck up a conversation with Meacham and White, who, in direct disobedience of Long's instructions, filled him in on everything they knew.

When he saw Ben staring from his window, Tom wondered if the young man had witnessed Allen's murder. Long was about to tell him to leave, when Tom pointed to the window and suggested he might've seen something.

"Maybe," said Long. "but what good will it do if he won't tell us anything?"

"He might've made another drawing. It wouldn't hurt to check."

Long glanced back at Lou Allen's house. She knew Tom was right, but she needed to get him out of there.

"Mr. Williams, this is still an active crime scene. I appreciate your wanting to help, but I'm going to ask you to leave. If we have any more questions, we'll give you a call."

As he crossed the street, Tom glanced back to see Paxton's Escalade pull up to the curb. Meacham was on the sidewalk fending off nosy pedestrians, while White stood at the edge of Monroe trying to keep traffic moving without getting hit by a car.

Paxton eyed Tom. He started to say something. but decided it could wait. He turned to Long. "What you got?"

"This is our theory, so far. When the last of Allen's guests left, he went upstairs to turn in. The killer was waiting for him. Based on blood spatter, we think he was in the closet. The killer stepped out and surprised him. We have GSR on the carpet but no shell casings. It might have been a revolver."

"I'm almost afraid to ask."

"Small caliber. One in the chest and one in each eye..."

"Ah shit! And the time of death?"

"We don't know yet. It had to be somewhere between two AM and six when no one else was here. Meacham and White told me about Walsh and Mangham. I understand Mangham was a suspect in the attorney shootings."

Paxton let out a sigh. "He *was*. Based on the time of the break-in and Mangham's subsequent death, Mangham couldn't have done Allen. By the time all this went down, Mangham and Walsh were well on their way to ambient temperature."

Long glanced across the street at Tom. "Could he have been wrong about the time of the break-in?"

"Nope. The 911 came in at a few minutes after one. And then there's the .38 we found on Mangham. It doesn't fit. That don't mean Mangham didn't do the other lawyers. But he sure as hell didn't do this one."

Long shook her head in frustration and forced a smile. "Yesterday, we had no suspects. Now we have too many." She looked around the room. "And too much evidence."

"Look, Beth, uh... losing Walsh has put me in a bind. I'm gonna need you to take over for him until we can get another detective up to speed." Paxton failed to notice the brief flicker of a smile on her face. "And, while I'm here," he said, "you might as well give me a quick tour."

She led him through the house, careful where she stepped and staying out of the way of the crime techs. Traces of white powder covered a coffee table in the living room. The dining room looked like it'd been used as a frozen margarita machine. Broken glass littered the kitchen floor. Spilled drinks had begun to sour, and the place had the aroma of ripe garbage. Upstairs, they passed a guest bedroom just as a tech with a pair of long tweezers dropped a used condom into an evidence bag.

"This must be what Bourbon Street looks like on Ash Wednesday morning. This is the worst crime scene I ever saw," he said in disgust. "It might as well be a MARTA station. Do we have a list of Allen's guests?"

"I've been looking for one. The man who called this in was in hysterics and couldn't help us."

"Any chance he might have shot Allen?"

"I don't think so… something about the way he acted. I got his number and copied the address from his driver's license."

"Okay. Send Meacham and White home. You too. I'll get some uniforms on the streets and see if the neighbors noticed anything."

Long stopped suddenly. "You know, Tom Williams was just here. I was about to make him leave, when he noticed the neighbor's son peering from an upstairs window."

"Yeah, and what you gonna get from him?"

"We could go over there and see if he has any more pictures."

"Okay. But I mean what I said about you going home and getting some rest. You're as white as a bedsheet. I don't need you passing out here."

She glanced at the house next door and shook her head. "I don't think this can wait."

• • •

Max Hogarth watched the police from his living room window. He wandered out onto his porch as Long and Paxton came over. They asked if he'd seen anything during the night.

"No. Was it Mr. Allen?"

Paxton ignored the question. "Do you think Ben might've seen something?"

Max started to say no again, stopped, and shook his head. Ben, he explained, was still upstairs. Beth asked if she and Paxton could take another look at Ben's pictures.

"Let me see." Max invited them into his living room while he went upstairs. He said something to Ben they couldn't make out. He returned with a stack of papers and handed them to Long, who thumbed through them until one of them caught her eye.

"Whoa!" she said. "These are new."

Max confirmed that this was the first time he'd seen them. One sketch, in charcoal, showed a man in profile, surrounded in semi-darkness. Moonlight illumined his face. It was a remarkable likeness of Don Walsh.

In front of him, also lit by the moon, lay Ambrose Mangham, eyes wide, cowering in terror in the corner of a small shed. Walsh fired his gun and at the unarmed Mangham.

The next page contained a sequence of panels in which Walsh turned, an exaggerated look of shock on his face. Silhouetted in the moonlight a large, hooded figure held a pistol in his extended hand. Walsh pointed his weapon, but the other man shot first. The final drawing showed the hooded man placing his weapon in Mangham's right hand and retrieving from Walsh a small pistol.

Long stared for several minutes, trying to take it all in. "Do you think this explains why Mangham had a .38?"

Paxton made no reply. He handed her a pastel of a slender, well-endowed woman in a white body stocking. In her hand she carried a laser pistol. She was blasting the head off a dragon in a purple robe. The inscription on the back read "Ice Queen." "What in the hell do you make of this?"

It took them a moment to recognize the scene as Allen's bedroom, where they'd stood only fifteen minutes earlier. They were now looking at it from the perspective of someone peering in Allen's window. Their eyes locked.

"Well, boss," said Long. "Looks like Allen's shooter may have been a woman. But I don't know what to make of these scenes with Walsh and Mangham. It looks like this mystery man shot Walsh in self-defense and then tried to make it look like Mangham shot him." She thought for a moment. "I suppose he was afraid no one would believe him."

"Smart man," said Paxton. He pursed his lips. "This shit just gets better and better."

They sat in silence for a long time. "Get me Edith Campos and a sketch artist," Paxton said in a low voice. "See if he can convert these to something we can use." Gone suddenly were any thoughts of Long going home and getting some rest.

"I'll try…" she said.

"Just do it. I'll wait next door."

• • •

Long left Paxton sitting in a swing on Lou Allen's porch as Campos and the sketch artist arrived together in her late model Audi. The artist, whom Long had never met, looked to be twenty years old, at most. Maybe Campos drove because he didn't have a driver's license.

While Max went to get Ben, Sedgewick, Campos and Long waited in the parlor. Sedgewick occupied his time rendering a quick sketch of Long. He was just finishing when Max walked in with Ben trailing behind.

Ben stopped in the doorway. He said nothing but looked at the feet of the guests seated on the couch. He stole furtive glances at Long and Campos before settling, not on Sedgewick, but on the sketch pad in front of him.

Max introduced Ben to Sedgewick, who looked up and started to say something. Campos placed a firm hand on Sedgewick's shoulder to silence him.

"Hey, Ben," she said in the same even voice as before. "You remember me. I was here the other day with Sergeant L… Beth."

Ben smiled without looking at either of them, his attention still focused on the pad in front of Sedgewick.

Sedgewick glanced at Campos. She gave a slight nod, and he put the finishing touches on the sketch of Long. Next to it, on the coffee table, lay Ben's drawing of the "Ice Queen." Sedgewick looked at it as if seeing it for the first time.

Slowly he turned his pad to a new page. Ignoring the skin-tight leotard and oversized breasts, he studied those portions of the woman's face that were visible around the mask. He began with the shape of her head. The blonde hair was an obvious wig, so he gave her a neutral shade and provided some different styles.

As Sedgewick started on the eyes, Ben became agitated. Campos was about to call a stop when Ben grabbed the pad from the startled Sedgewick. He pulled a charcoal from his pocket and started making changes. Then, without looking up, he set to work on the lips. When he was done, he set the finished product in front of Sedgewick.

"Very good," Sedgewick murmured. He picked up the picture of the younger woman Ben saw outside his window a week earlier and made his own rendering of the young woman showing only her face. Ben studied it for a moment and nodded.

Long smiled. Her witness was talking.

• • •

Paxton meanwhile had lost patience. He was about to go next door to find out what was happening, when Long, Campos, and Sedgewick emerged.

"Show me what you got." He studied each of the drawings. He turned to Sedgewick. "Thanks. I'll make copies of these when I get back to the station. Y'all go home. I'll see you in the morning. Enjoy what's left of the weekend."

"Paxton, I can visit Stan Hadden and see if he recognizes this woman in the body stocking."

"No. That can wait 'til tomorrow. Go home."

The crime scene investigators had finished, leaving yellow tape strung across Allen's porch banisters and rear entrance. Paxton called the station and had a uniformed officer come by, ostensibly to keep an eye on the place but more to protect Ben and Max, in case the murderer returned. When the officer arrived, Paxton climbed into his car and drove to the home of Tom Williams.

CHAPTER 24
SUPPER GUEST

Midtown

Sunday, October 28

Returning from the back patio, I set a plate of grilled pork chops on the counter beside a platter of sautéed Brussel sprouts and pour myself a Malbec. Marie dons a pair of mitts and pulls from the oven a dish of macaroni and cheese for Henry. She pours herself some wine and goes to retrieve her sons, who are shooting hoops out back.

We're about to put supper on the table, when the doorbell rings. Through the curtains I see Paxton Davis, carrying a large manila envelope.

"Paxton!" I swing the door open far enough for him to see Marie and the boys in the dining room and catch the aroma of food. "You're just in time for supper. Marie, would you set another place?"

"No!" he says. "I didn't mean to interrupt your dinner. I was just finishing up over on Monroe and thought I'd stop by. I can come back tomorrow."

Now he has my attention. "It's no trouble. You're welcome to stay."

I turn to find Marie standing beside me. "Yes, Paxton," she says. "We have plenty of food. Why don't you join us?" Despite her warm welcome, her tone tells me she's wary of another visit from the police so soon after the shootings.

The aroma works its charms on Paxton. "Well, okay," he says. "I'd better not eat too much. Clarice will have a big dinner ready when she gets home from choir practice."

Marie adds another plate and Paxton takes a pork chop and some mac and cheese.

"Can I offer you some wine?" I ask.

"Now, Tom, you know I'm a Baptist," he smiles.

"So am I." I raise my newly filled glass.

"You a lapsed Baptist is what you are."

"He's not much of a Catholic either," Marie scoffs.

Later, as the boys clean the kitchen, Paxton, Marie and I retire to the front porch.

"So, tell me about Lou Allen," I ask.

It takes Paxton a moment to decide what he can disclose. "From what we know, the probable time of death was somewhere after the Walsh and Mangham shootings, so that rules out Mangham. We have two other persons of interest. One of them we're pretty sure was a witness to the shootout, so he's not likely to have killed Allen. We still wanna talk to him."

I glance at Marie. She seems relieved we aren't discussing my involvement with Mangham.

I've been wondering since Paxton arrived what's in the large manila envelope he's holding. He pulls out some pages torn from an artist's sketchpad. "These are police composites taken from some drawings by Ben Hogarth. I was hoping you might be able to identify these folks. Maybe you've seen them in the neighborhood."

The first shows a woman who looks to be in her mid-twenties. "Our sketch artist did this from Ben's drawing you saw the other day, the young lady we think was attacked outside Allen's house."

"Have you found out who she is?"

"Not yet, but Ben's picture of her walking down the street tells me she lives nearby."

He pulls out another sketch, this time a different woman, very attractive, upper thirties, maybe forty. "How about this one?"

"Nope."

"Seems she was a guest at Allen's party last night. We're trying to figure out what she looks like without her costume."

"Her costume?"

He hands me a third drawing. "We got her from another of Ben's sketches. We think she's the same woman. Here she's in costume. Ben calls her the 'Ice Queen.'"

"I saw her last night... early evening. Bogie and I were out for a walk. She parked on Greenwood under the shade of a tree. She was wearing a hoodie, but she took it off and tossed it in the back seat. At first, I thought she was butt naked. She turned into the alley instead of using the sidewalk on Monroe."

Paxton leans forward, his eyes narrowed. "Was she by herself?"

"Yes."

"You get a good look at her car?"

"Nope. Like I said, I was looking at her."

"Did you notice anything else?"

I stop to think. "Yeah. I doubled back and saw her come out the other end of the alley near Allen's house. None of the other guests acted like they knew her."

Paxton rubs his chin. "Okay. Then she's probably not from the neighborhood."

"No. I don't think so."

"What if her name wasn't even on the guest list, like she was..."

I finish his sentence. "...crashing the party?"

Paxton pulls out a drawing of a black man in his thirties. "This is another of Ben's drawings, a superhero, the 'Dark Avenger.'"

"I think I know this guy," I say. "We met the other day... big guy named Shelby Lewis. He has an upstairs unit on the next street, right beside where Walsh shot Mangham. Do you think he's involved in the Allen shooting?"

Paxton ignores my question. "Next door to Helen Weiss?"

"You know Helen?" I ask.

"Not yet. I need to talk to her, though, find out what she might have heard."

"Mind if I tag along? I could introduce you to her... and Shelby if he's there."

I glance at Marie. She rolls her eyes and shakes her head.

CHAPTER 25
THE FUGITIVE

Midtown
Sunday, October 28

We find Helen Weiss in her yard pulling weeds. "If you're looking for that Shelby what's-his-name," she yells. "He's not there. Moved out in the middle of the night, right after all that shooting."

"Did you hear or see the shooting?" Paxton asks.

"I heard it. Woke me up... that and all the sirens. I certainly wasn't going outside to see what was happening."

"But you saw Shelby Lewis."

"I saw him from my window. I heard a noise next door and looked out to see what it was. He was in such a rush, banging around, throwing stuff in his car."

"How long after the shooting?"

"Maybe fifteen minutes."

Paxton glances at me and turns back to Weiss. "Does his landlord live downstairs?"

"Lord, no! The landlord lives out in Gwinnett County somewhere."

"Do you think the person downstairs might know where he went?"

"I don't think so. That lady's nuts," she snorts. "I wouldn't believe anything she says."

I turn and murmur to Paxton, "I've met the downstairs neighbor. She's a bit strange, but she might know something. Let's ask her."

Alicia Moonbeam, it turns out, isn't even aware Shelby has skipped. Her eyes widen when Paxton shows her his badge and begins asking questions. She asks Paxton what his sign is, and for a moment I'm afraid she's going to invite him in for a reading.

Desperate to keep the conversation on track, I ask, "Alicia, has Shelby ever mentioned relatives or friends?"

She furrows her brow. "No. Not that I recall."

"Do you think it would be okay if we went upstairs for a look?" Paxton asks.

She looks him up and down. "Well, you're a policeman. I guess it's okay."

We climb the stairs and try the door. It's locked. We peep through the window. Everything's gone but his barbells. Paxton calls for a uniform to keep an eye on the place while he gets a search warrant.

As we return to my house, he mentions Ben's drawing of Walsh shooting Mangham in cold blood. Walsh then turned to see Lewis and tried to shoot him, but Lewis shot first, killing Walsh. Lewis then placed his gun on Mangham to implicate him.

I point out that Shelby, if he is this Dark Avenger, is, at worst, a vigilante. He could be guilty of manslaughter but appeared to be acting in self-defense. He can claim he carries the gun for protection. He might even have a permit.

None of this impresses Paxton, though right now he has bigger fish to fry. The idea of a self-appointed, armed guardian of the neighborhood seems to bother him worse than me. I'm hoping he'll focus on catching the killer instead.

Paxton mentions an Internal Affairs investigation of Walsh on allegations he killed several drug dealers without justification. He supposedly stole and marketed narcotics taken from crime scenes.

I'm slowly putting together what I've learned. "So, if Shelby was busy skipping town, he couldn't have whacked Allen. Besides, what motive would he have? As far as we know, they never even met. We can scratch Walsh and Mangham. Who does that leave?"

Paxton shakes his head. "Looks like our top suspect right now is this 'Ice Queen'."

"How are you going to find her?"

He shrugs. "The best we can do now is get names of all the folks at the party and see what they remember."

We walk the rest of the way in silence. We're just stepping onto my porch when, for no apparent reason, I think back to the day, two weeks ago, when I first met Walsh and then ran into him later at Manuel's.

"Paxton, you remember the man you questioned a couple of years ago following the shooting of..." I stop to recall their names, "Ron Dalrymple and David Curry, the Penguin?"

"Skinny little dude... looks like he's afraid of his own shadow?"

"That's him," I say. "I remembered him from the news."

"Name's Rollo Witherspoon. Why?"

"I saw Rollo at Manuel's with Walsh the night after Felix Lopez got shot."

"What would he be doing there?" Paxton muses. "He used to be a small-time dope dealer. His last bust was possession of stolen property several years ago. Last I heard he was hiding out somewhere in West End."

"Do you think he may have been an informant for Walsh?'

Paxton ponders and slowly nods. A smile crosses his face. "Maybe I'll pay Mr. Rollo a visit."

As he leaves, I turn to Marie and ask what she thinks.

"I already told you. You need to put this place on the market and move in with us while we find you a condo in the suburbs."

"Speaking of which, any progress on your house hunt?"

"I'm meeting an agent in Smyrna tomorrow. Why? Are you anxious to get rid of me?"

"Smyrna?"

She catches my dubious tone. "You wouldn't believe what they've done there, Dad. People are renovating old houses. They have a village green now with shops and a music venue. It's a lot safer than Midtown was when you and Mom moved here. The house is near Campbell High School. Campbell has an international baccalaureate program. It would be perfect for the boys."

Your ex-husband will be so proud, I think, but I keep that to myself.

My mind turns to Lou Allen and his masquerade party gone wrong. Then a thought hits me. "What do you suppose will become of Allen's law practice?"

"I imagine he has some buyout arrangement with another divorce attorney who'll come in and take over his clients." Her eyes narrow. "Tell me you aren't going to start snooping into Allen's background, not after what happened Saturday night."

"What happened Saturday night was that I shot and wounded a man in self-defense. He was later killed by a cop, perhaps murdered. Either way, I don't see…"

"Dad, you need to distance yourself from this. You don't want it coming back to haunt you… and we don't need another break-in."

CHAPTER 26
THE PARALEGAL

Atlanta, Georgia
Monday, October 29

Marie's mention of another lawyer taking over Allen's practice gives me another thread to pull. I'm about to turn into the parking lot of Allen's office when I notice Beth Long getting into her car. I pass by and loop around the block hoping she hasn't seen me. When I return, she's gone.

Located on Piedmont Avenue in a beautifully restored home surrounded by high rises, the office features an open plan downstairs with twelve-foot ceilings and enlarged double-hung windows. The floors are polished oak inlaid with rosewood; the walls eggshell white with Corinthian-style cornices.

Its lone occupant is removing files from drawers and stacking them in banker's boxes. He's slender and diminutive, has shoulder-length blonde hair, and appears to be in his mid-twenties. He moves like a patient dosed on Xanax.

I introduce myself. He tells me he's Wayne Perkins. He's been Allen's paralegal for the past five years, ever since Allen divorced his wife. He tells me he's boxing up Allen's files for Amanda Helmholtz, the divorce attorney who'll be taking over the practice.

Helmholtz's office, located at Tower Place in Buckhead, has three associates and four paralegals, all female. Perkins will be unemployed by the end of the week.

He collapses into a swivel chair and places his head in his hands.

"I'm so sorry for your loss," I say, unable to think of anything else.

"Oh, it's absolutely wretched," he moans.

"What was it like, working for Lou?"

"We had our moments. He could be very kind sometimes. At others he was such a beast."

"And now you're losing your job."

His head snaps up, a flash of anger in his eyes. "That, I must say, is the one little ray of sunshine in an otherwise dreadful week. Amanda's a witch. There's simply no way I'd ever work for that woman. Besides, I don't have the right equipment, if you know what I mean."

"What do you plan to do?"

"I don't know." His gaze sweeps the room and the wreckage of file boxes. "This is all I've ever done. I guess I'll have to find another firm in need of a paralegal."

An idea comes to me. "My daughter's a partner with a firm out in Vinings. I don't know if they have an opening, but I could ask."

"Oh, would you? That would be so wonderful."

"No worries... So, tell me about Saturday night. Were you at the party?"

He bites his lower lip as it starts to tremble. Tears stream down his face. "Yes."

"Did you see the woman in the white body stocking?"

"Oh my God! Who didn't? I tell you she was the closest thing I've seen to bona fide conversion therapy."

"Do you know who she was?"

"No. It's like I told the policewoman who just left, no one seemed to know her."

"Were there other women at the party?"

"I'm not even sure, with some of the costumes people were wearing."

"What women would Lou have invited?"

"I don't know. Not many." He stops and gives me a puzzled look. "Now that you mention it, Eleanor Heinz was supposed to be there, but no one saw her. She's a social worker who specializes in repressed memory. She gives expert testimony in most of Lou's cases... At least she did..."

He looks like he's about to begin blubbering. "What sort of repressed memories?" I ask. I think I already know where this is going.

Perkins takes a deep breath and lets it out. "An unusually high number of Lou's cases involved fathers accused of molesting their children. When the children came to us, of course, they couldn't remember anything. Eleanor helped them. She's gentle, but very effective."

"And Lou usually won his cases."

"All of them," he says with a casual wave.

I nod as I think of what to ask next. "You mentioned that Lou divorced his wife five years ago. What's her name?"

"Tamara."

"What was she like?"

"I never met the woman. The only reason I know her name is that Lou had me send her child support every month. I acted as his personal secretary."

I'm wondering what other services this guy provided, but I chase that thought from my mind. "Would you have Tamara's phone number anywhere?"

Perkins gives me a startled look. "Whatever for? Do you think she might have had something to do with Lou's death?"

"No." I smile. Finally, I let it out. "You see, Wayne, I'm a reporter for the *AJC*."

For a moment I'm afraid he'll crawl under his desk and assume a fetal position.

"Don't worry. I'm not recording this conversation. In fact, I don't plan to use your name at all... that is, of course, unless you want me to."

"Actually, I'd prefer you didn't."

"I was hoping to get in touch with Mrs. Allen, see if I could get a comment from her."

Relieved, he reaches for an old Rolodex and gives me her address and phone number.

"Oh, and while you're at it," I add, "why don't you give me your number so I can pass it on to my daughter?"

"Sure."

"Also, do you know if Lou was familiar with Lyle Mallory, Jacob Epstein, or Felix Lopez."

"I couldn't say. I mean, everybody knew Lyle, but I'd never heard of Epstein or Lopez before I saw their names in the paper. And I doubt Lou knew them."

I thank him again and tell him how sorry I am for all he's going through.

• • •

Ignoring Georgia law, I dial Marie while driving.

"Hey," she asks. "What's up?"

"A couple of things. I just spoke to Allen's paralegal. A divorce attorney named Amanda Helmholtz is taking over his practice. He'll soon be out of a job."

"And?"

"And I was hoping you'd at least talk to the poor guy. He's lost a close friend and now his job. He's distraught."

"And why all this sudden compassion? What's in it for you?"

"You cut me to the quick. I can't believe my own daughter would doubt my motives."

"Perhaps because I know you."

"Well, he did give me some interesting information."

"Surprise!"

"Allen divorced his wife, Tamara, about five years ago."

"Tell me you're not planning to interview the poor woman."

"Nope."

"Then what *are* you conniving?"

"I just thought I might contact her lawyer, as a matter of courtesy, and give him a heads up that the media are about to descend on her front yard with cameras and microphones."

"Dad, you're such a saint."

"Cut me some slack, will you? I just want to know who her attorney was."

She lets out an exasperated sigh and says she'll do what she can.

Minutes later, as I'm pulling into my driveway, my phone rings.

"That was quick."

"Yeah, well. I got her lawyer's name and number. He's Alfred LeMay out in Lawrenceville. The divorce, it seems, was settled in a matter of days."

"Wow! So, he just capitulated?"

"Not likely. Sounds like she had something on him he didn't want to come out."

"Such as?"

"Like I would know?"

"Okay. Well thanks."

I ring off and call LeMay's office. A woman answers. I introduce myself and ask to speak to him.

A gruff male voice comes on. He's either in his seventies or a lifelong smoker. "LeMay."

"Mr. LeMay, I'm Tom Williams with the *AJC*..."

"Now, Tom, what makes you think I'm going to talk to you about anything, least of all the death of Lou Allen?"

I'm taken aback.

"Tamara just got a call from Wayne Perkins," he says, "and now she's calling me."

Recovering, I blurt out, "Mr. LeMay I just wanted to warn you. Several reporters are about to show up at Mrs. Allen's home, and you might want to be there with a prepared statement."

"That's why you called me?"

"That's it."

He hangs up.

I call the paper, and, for good measure, Sumatra Simms. There's no sense promising a media invasion and not delivering.

When I'm done, my phone rings again. It's the number I just dialed for LeMay. But this time it's his secretary.

"Mr. Williams," she whispers, "I hope you'll forgive Mr. LeMay. He can be rather abrupt at times." I can barely make out what she's saying over the copy machine in the background.

"That's perfectly fine, Ms. ..."

"I'd rather not give my name."

"I understand."

"I just want you to know that that man got exactly what he deserved."

It takes me a moment to realize she's talking about Lou Allen. "How's that?"

"I typed up the notes for Mr. LeMay when he first met with Mrs. Allen."

"Yes."

"And the things she said he did to their son you wouldn't believe... I'd rather not repeat them."

"That's okay. All I need to know is, did Mr. Allen molest the boy?"

She takes her time answering. "That's what Mrs. Allen claimed."

"And how did she find out?"

"She came home and caught him in the act."

"I see." I try to think of something else to ask but come up empty. "Thanks. I appreciate this."

She's already hung up.

My next call is to Paxton.

"Tom, tell me you haven't shot any more of my suspects," he says.

"Nothing like that. You asked me to let you know if I came across anything else."

"I shudder to think what tidbit you have for me now."

"I was just speaking with Wayne Perkins."

"Tom, interviewing witnesses is the job of my officers. Beth Long just left there."

"I know. Did she mention an Eleanor Heinz?'

There's a long pause. I hear Paxton shuffling papers.

"No. Who's Eleanor Heinz?'

"She's a consultant, repressed memory specialist. She testified for Allen in divorce and child custody cases. Somehow every child she interviewed remembered being molested by the other parent."

"She sounds like a real upstanding citizen."

"Or, just maybe, somebody who could give you the names of Allen's potential killers."

"Okay. I'll have someone get in touch with her."

CHAPTER 27
CONNECTING DOTS

Atlanta, Georgia
Monday, October 29

Long, Meacham and White, were working the day shift. Paxton gave them a list of Allen's guests from the index cards found in his desk drawer. Beside each name was a phone number and a street address. They were looking for anyone who might remember the Ice Queen. They also carried Ben's other drawings showing the unidentified young woman and the Dark Avenger, on the off chance someone could identify them.

Meacham and White worked the Midtown addresses. Long had already spoken with Allen's paralegal. Next on her list was Stan Hadden. As she turned onto the Downtown Connector her phone rang. Paxton related his conversation with Tom Williams. "Why don't you call Eleanor Heinz next?"

Long made a U-turn and headed east toward Decatur. Instinct told her she should knock on Heinz's door, rather than calling.

An older woman answered, her face drawn. Long badged her and was about to speak when the lady blurted out, "Oh my God! Have you found her?"

Long coaxed the woman back into the condo and got her seated on the couch.

"Ma'am, first let me ask who you are."

"I'm Stella Heinz, and my daughter is missing."

"Take a deep breath and tell me what happened."

"Eleanor left the house Friday afternoon. She said she was going to go meet one of her clients. I awoke next morning to find she hadn't returned. I tried reaching her. I even called her office but got no answer. Finally, I called the police. At first, they tried to tell me Eleanor was okay and would probably show up soon, but I know my daughter. She would never go off overnight without telling me first. I had a time convincing them to file that damned report."

"Mrs. Heinz let me first explain that I'm investigating an unrelated matter. This is the first I've heard about your daughter's disappearance. I just wanted to speak with her about a party she attended Saturday night."

Stella gave her an indignant look. "I'm trying to tell you my Eleanor is missing. I can assure you she wasn't at any party on Saturday night."

"Okay. Tell me everything you remember about what Eleanor said. Did she mention her client's name?"

"No. I just got the impression it was a woman. Most of Eleanor's clients are women."

When Long had everything she could get from the woman, she promised she'd follow up on the Missing Persons report. She dialed them from her car. Her next call was to Paxton.

• • •

Paxton was still at his desk when the call came from the medical examiner. Lou Allen's time of death, somewhere around two AM, confirmed Paxton's suspicions that Mangham wasn't the shooter. This "Ice Queen," whoever she was, was looking better and better.

The lab had a preliminary match of Mangham's blood type to a tissue sample found under Lyle Mallory's fingernails, the apparent result of a scuffle. He also matched the blood found on Mallory's carpet. To Paxton, this made Mangham good for Epstein and Lopez as well. Allen's killer had simply copied Mangham's MO.

Paxton reached for his phone, then stopped. Allen's killer took a lock of his hair, just as Mangham had done with the other three victims. How had she known to do that? Paxton had made a point of withholding that detail. Only his investigators and the Midtown murderer should have known. Was there a leak in his department? Had Mangham mentioned souvenirs to someone besides Tom Williams?

His phone rang again. Long filled him in on her conversation with Stella Heinz. While she spoke, a corporal walked in and handed Paxton the missing person report. Paxton stared at the driver's license photo. "You can forget trying to call Eleanor," he said. "I don't think she'll be answering."

• • •

Paxton's next call came from a very pissed-off Mavis Wilson. "Lieutenant why am I just now hearing about Detective Walsh?"

Paxton tried to work some contrition into his reply. "Good morning, Mavis. I was just about to call you. Why don't we sit down and go over what I have so far?"

"I'll be in your office in ten minutes."

"No. I'll come to you." It wouldn't do for Paxton's staff to see him talking to Mavis again, so soon after her prior visit.

Fifteen minutes later, he was downtown at APD headquarters, seated across from Mavis. He filled her in on events at Tom Williams' home on Saturday night and his subsequent call to Walsh. Walsh at the time was questioning Hollywood Holmes. Holmes had sold pistols to Mangham like those used to kill Mallory, Epstein, and Lopez.

"I met Williams at the station after the break-in and took his statement," said Paxton. "He couldn't describe the man he shot, but he spoke to Mangham earlier in the day about the three lawyers. Turns out they were all involved in some tax filing scam, and Mangham wound up taking the fall."

"That's just great!" said Mavis, "a reporter playing detective. What does all this have to do with Walsh?"

"I called Walsh and told him to get over to Tom's place. Meacham and White were still babysitting there when Walsh arrived. Walsh made them stay put while he went searching for Mangham."

Mavis leaned back and closed her eyes. "You mean he just took off on his own with no backup?"

"It gets worse. Walsh found Mangham hiding in a shed off a back alley. There were gun shots. When Meacham and White got there, Mangham and Walsh were both dead."

"A shootout?"

"That's what we thought at first. Then we found a witness, a... special needs kid. He was out wandering around the alley and saw the shooting. Name's Ben Hogarth. Turns out he's a cartoonist. Draws pretty good pictures. He gave us sketches of Walsh shooting Mangham in cold blood."

"Then who shot Walsh?"

Paxton told her about the drawings of Shelby Lewis, whom Ben had dubbed the Dark Avenger. "We're still looking for him. We also want to question him about the death, a few nights ago, of a mugger outside Lou Allen's window and the later shootings of two armed robbers on Ponce."

Mavis gave him a pained look. "It's a small world, Lieutenant."

"Especially in Midtown. Anyway, the drawings show Walsh shooting Mangham. Mangham was unarmed in the picture. He must have dropped his weapon earlier. Walsh turned, saw Lewis and was about to shoot, but Lewis got him first. In the final sketch Ben has Lewis putting his gun in Mangham's hand. It was a .38, not the kind of gun Mangham used on the lawyers. Lewis must've wanted it to look like a shootout."

Mavis shook her head. "If Mangham was unarmed, then why did Walsh shoot him? The man was cold-blooded, but that makes no sense. And what does this have to do with Allen?"

"Beats me."

They thought about this a while then Paxton said, "It's like Walsh never intended to take Mangham alive."

Paxton pulled out the sketches of the Ice Queen. "The Hogarth kid puts this woman in Lou Allen's bedroom. He actually saw her shoot him."

"He was peeping in the victim's window?"

"He lives next door. His bedroom looks straight into Allen's. Looks like the woman forgot to pull the curtains."

"How reliable is this kid?"

"More reliable than most." Paxton described Ben's artistic talents and recollection of visual details.

"Well, I'm just glad I'm not the one has to put him on the stand," Mavis said.

"We need to make an arrest first. Then let the DA worry about that."

"And you're sure Mangham shot the three lawyers?"

"About as sure as I can be. When I questioned Williams, he said Mangham mentioned something about the killer taking souvenirs. The thing is, we never put that out. The only person outside the investigation who would've known that was the killer."

"Did Allen's killer take souvenirs?"

"Uh... well..."

She gazed at Paxton for a long time. "So, this 'Ice Queen' is a copycat who somehow knew about the trophies and wanted to make it look like Mangham did it."

"Maybe..."

"And how would she have heard about the locks of hair?"

Paxton clenched his teeth. "I intend to find out."

"You do that, Lieutenant. Meanwhile, you need to lock down Walsh's apartment in Smyrna and get some investigators over there."

Paxton stifled his anger at having this woman tell him how to do his job. "I'm already on it."

CHAPTER 28
CLAIRE DOWDY

Atlanta, Georgia
Monday, October 29

Meacham and White knocked on doors all morning, showing Ben Hogarth's sketches of the young woman, the Dark Avenger, and the Ice Queen to residents of Midtown. So far, no one recognized them. White suggested they take a lunch break.

It was noon, and the line at Popeye's Fried Chicken on Boulevard backed out onto the sidewalk. Meacham and White stood just inside the door, chatting about hunting and auto racing. Meacham glanced at the counter and saw a familiar face. He turned to White, and in a low voice said, "Don't look at the cash register. I need you to reach inside that envelope and take out the drawing of the young woman. Not the Ice Queen, the other one."

White did as he was told and looked at his partner.

"Now," said Meacham, "check out the girl taking orders over there."

"Oh shit!"

"Tell you what. I'm gonna slide down to the end of the counter, in case she tries to split. Work your way up to her without looking suspicious. You're just here for the chicken and biscuits. Okay?"

"Okay."

"When you get there, badge her and tell her we just want to talk to her out back."

Claire Dowdy knew immediately what the cops wanted. She thought about running but doing so would only make her problems worse. She turned to her shift leader and told him she needed a break. He gave her an annoyed look and took her place at the register without noticing either of the officers. The kitchen staff looked up as they passed but said nothing.

Meacham asked about the incident outside Allen's home. She started to prevaricate, then admitted two men had attacked her. She was rescued by a larger man in a hoodie. She never saw his face. She was so upset she immediately left the scene. It was the next day before she heard one of her assailants had died.

Meacham pulled two black-and-white photos from the envelope. They were mug shots of Derrick Lane and Mac Strong. "Are these the men who jumped you?"

She shrugged, as tears formed in the corners of her eyes. "I don't know. It was dark, and I didn't get a good look at either of them. All I wanted was to get away."

"If we put this guy in a lineup…" He tapped the picture of Lane. "Do you think you might identify him?"

"I just want to forget about him," she said.

"How about this man?" asked White, pulling out the sketch of the Dark Avenger. "Is he the one who rescued you?"

Claire studied it for several seconds. "That could be him."

"Okay," said Meacham. "We appreciate your help. We'll let you get back to work. Just give us your address and phone number, in case we have more questions."

As they watched her walk back inside, Meacham and White realized their lunches would have to wait. From Popeye's it was but a few blocks south and east to Randolph Street and the apartment of Derrick Lane.

Still bruised and walking with a limp, Lane answered the door. When shown the picture of Claire and confronted with her story, he hotly denied it. After changing his account three times, he finally admitted he and Strong had stopped and spoken to a woman that night.

They were coming home from Piedmont, as he'd said earlier, when they saw her walking north. Strong stopped and tried to talk to her. When she began to leave, he grabbed her arm. At that point, a large black man showed up and attacked both them with help from the woman. Lane and Strong were on the ground when the woman kicked Strong in the eye.

"You say it was a large black man who jumped you?"

"Yes"

"Did you get a good look at him?"

"No."

"Could this be him?"

Lane stared at the drawing. "I don't know. Could be him. All I know is he didn't have no cause to jump me and Mac like he did."

The two cops looked at each other and then back at Lane.

"You know what," said Meacham, "we like the young lady's story better."

White got up in Lane's face. "Tell you what, cocksucker. If I so much as see your ass out walking the streets at night, you're gonna take a long ride downtown. You understand?"

"C'mon Mark," said Meacham, placing a hand on his partner's shoulder. "Let's get outta here."

CHAPTER 29
STAN HADDEN

Atlanta, Georgia
Monday, October 29

Long stood on the porch of a two-story brick home in suburban Alpharetta and rang the doorbell. She'd travelled a long way from Midtown. Intuition told her the Ice Queen picture might dislodge something in Stan Hadden's memory. Too late, she remembered he'd asked her to call before coming to his house.

Thin, balding and middle-aged, Hadden was, according to Long's research, the principal of a middle school in Roswell. When he finally answered the door, panic swept his face.

"Officer," he panted, "is there any way we could meet somewhere else? My wife and daughter are home."

"Where did you have in mind?"

"There's a Dunkin Donuts on Main Street, not far from here."

He gave her directions and she agreed to meet him there, provided he didn't keep her waiting.

Ten minutes later, seated at a corner table and sipping a latte, Long watched Hadden climb out of a late-model Mercedes. He wore a baseball cap and Oakley sunglasses. She smiled. *He looks like he's here to score some drugs*, she thought.

She wondered how he afforded such a lifestyle. Then she remembered he was supporting not one, but two.

Out of breath and glancing about, he settled into the chair across from her. "I suppose you have more questions about Lou's murder. I assure you he was very much alive when I left and dead when I came back."

"You needn't worry, Mr. Hadden," she smiled. "You're not a suspect."

He exhaled slowly. "My wife and daughter know nothing about my... uhm... other life, and I'd rather keep it that way." He offered no explanation of how he'd managed to get out on Saturday night, and Long never asked, considering it none of her business.

Instead, she reached into an envelope and retrieved copies of Ben's and Sedgewick's drawings, including the Ice Queen, out of costume, with differing hair styles. "I was wondering if you might recognize this woman. We're not sure what her hair color is or how she wears it."

Hadden studied the picture carefully. "I'm afraid I can't help you." This seemed to distress him even more.

When Long showed him Ben's drawing of the woman in costume shooting Allen in his bedroom, Hadden's eyes widened. "Oh my God! It was her? I saw her at the party. I was wondering who she was. No one else knew her. At first, I thought she was a man dressed in drag, until I... uhm ... checked more closely. I mean, she had on so much makeup, and that blonde wig... oh, what a fright!"

"So, can you give me more details about her outfit? Start at the top and work your way down."

"Well, as you can see, she has this... hair, a sequined mask, and a full-length body stocking. *It left nothing to the imagination.*"

"Was she wearing anything on her hands?"

"Yes. She had white surgical gloves. I remember thinking *mixed metaphors*... Lady Gaga meets Nurse Jackie."

"What did she have on her feet?"

"White slippers of some kind. They came up over the body stocking."

Long had a sinking feeling. "Was any part of her body exposed?"

"By 'exposed,' you mean did I see actual flesh? All I saw were her eyes and mouth."

"And her face was covered with heavy makeup."

"Yes."

"Mr. Hadden, I appreciate your time. I assure you we'll do our best to keep this on the down low. If we make an arrest, however, it's possible you may need to testify."

Hadden blanched.

"We'll worry about that when, and if, the time comes. I'll promise I'll text you next time."

On her way back to the station, she called Paxton. They agreed that, under the circumstances, there was little point in questioning Allen's other guests. All anyone saw was the costume, which was, by now, in a landfill. A DNA match to samples from Allen's bedroom was also unlikely.

As they spoke, Long felt queasy. She wondered if there might've been something in her latte.

• • •

Later, as he returned from the men's room, Paxton ran into Deputy Chief Austin Murray. The two had joined the force in 1979 within months of each other, but their careers took different paths. Though they made detective at the same time, Paxton appeared destined for his next promotion ahead of Murray, thanks to a more impressive clearance rate.

Then came the Atlanta Child Murders. Paxton was vocal in his criticism of how the department handled the investigation. This made him the wrong kind of enemies for a man who hoped, someday, to make police chief.

When the *AJC* quoted an unnamed source as saying Wayne Williams wasn't the sole perpetrator, all eyes turned to Paxton. An internal investigation identified the real source. By then the damage was done. Paxton eventually made lieutenant, but that would be his rank for the rest of his career.

Meanwhile, Murray, the consummate politician, rose like a Martha White biscuit. His telegenic qualities made him a natural spokesman whenever there was a public announcement, such as a breakthrough in a major case.

"Oh, Paxton," he said as they passed. "I thought you'd like to know. We're closing the Midtown Murders investigation and identifying Ambrose Mangham as the killer. It'll be on the news at six. Good work on that." He said it loud enough for everyone down the hall to hear. "Also, there will be a posthumous commendation for Don Walsh."

Murray said nothing about the murder of Lou Allen. The press conference, if it mentioned it at all, would include some evasive statement that Allen's shooting was still under investigation. Murray could then make another TV appearance when Paxton caught Allen's killer. Watching the man stroll away, Paxton fought the urge to chase him down and kick his ass.

Instead, he returned to his office, sank into his chair, closed his eyes, and pinched the bridge of his nose. When he reopened them, the first thing he saw was the missing persons bulletin right where he'd laid it.

Again, he studied the face on the driver's license photo. According to her date of birth, Eleanor Heinz was forty-five years old. She looked sixty. The internet search listed her occupation as "consultant." Paxton wondered how many innocent lives her "consulting" had damaged.

A thought came to him. He reached for the phone and dialed.

"Hey, Lyman."

"Hey, Paxton. Man, I can't believe that shit about Walsh. I just seen him, what, fifteen minutes earlier."

"Yeah, maybe you can help me with something."

"What's that?" Gwynn sounded leery.

"The other day, when we were talking about Walsh, you mentioned his wife, in their divorce, claimed he molested their son."

"Yeah, man. That was some sick shit, too! Walsh denied it and even passed a lie detector. But they still wouldn't let him see his little boy."

"Did Walsh ever mention his wife's lawyer?"

"Nope"

"Do you remember his wife's name?"

"I think it was Sara. I'm not sure about the spelling."

"Thanks, Lyman."

Paxton called Long. "Beth, when you get back, I need you to pull up a divorce case, about a year ago, in Paulding County, Sara Walsh versus Donald W. Walsh. I want to know who represented Sara."

"I'm on it."

Forty minutes later she walked into his office. "It was eighteen months ago, Paxton. And guess who her lawyer was."

"Lou Allen."

"Yep. While I was looking, I checked into other cases of Allen's."

Paxton shook his head. The pieces were falling into place. "So, Walsh was a victim of Lou Allen and Eleanor Heinz. Shit like that could make a man wanna kill somebody."

Long stared back at him in disbelief. "But Walsh was already dead by the time Allen was shot, and the shooter, we believe, was this woman."

"If you wanted somebody dead, Sergeant, and you wanted a solid alibi, how would you arrange it?"

"I guess I'd put out a contract."

"Exactly."

"But where would Walsh get the name of a hired killer?" Long asked.

"Maybe he came across it while working in Narcotics."

"How could we find out?"

Paxton recalled his conversion the day before with Tom Williams. A smile crept across his face. "I think I know just the guy."

CHAPTER 30
ROLLO WITHERSPOON

Atlanta, Georgia
Monday, October 29

Darkness fell, and rush hour traffic on Ashby Street slowed to a crawl. Ducking into a corner grocery, Rollo Witherspoon reached into his pocket and fished out enough cash for an orange soda and a frozen burrito. He slid it into the tray beneath the bullet-proof glass. The clerk took it, counted it, and placed it in the cash register.

Rollo stepped out onto the sidewalk and pulled his moth-eaten jacket tighter against the evening chill. A burly man bumped into him then grabbed both his arms. Rollo nearly pissed his pants.

"Don't run, Rollo. I don't want to hurt you."

Beneath the watch cap and denim jacket he saw the face of Lyman Gwynn.

"Damn, Lyman, you scared the shit outta me."

"I don't want anybody to see us together. We just need a few minutes of your time."

"We?"

The answer came as a black Escalade rolled up. The tinted passenger side window came down with a whir, and Rollo was staring into the face of Paxton Davis. Behind the wheel sat a young white woman, another cop, no doubt.

This can't be good, Rollo thought.

"Hey, Rollo," Paxton smiled. "Been a long time."

"Uh, yeah. What brings you down here Lieutenant?"

"Why don't you and Lyman climb in the back? Get out of the cold. We'll just have a little chat."

Rollo got in, followed by Lyman. The door locks snapped, and the SUV pulled away. Paxton turned and studied Rollo's face.

"Rollo," he said, "I understand you been working with Don Walsh a long time."

"Uh… Yes sir"

"And you heard what happened to him?"

Rollo nodded. "Yes sir."

"We thought you might be able to help us clear up a few loose ends."

"Yes sir… I mean, I don't know nothing about that."

Paxton smiled. "I'm sure you don't, Rollo. We just wanna know what kinda work you did for Detective Walsh. For starters, what were you two discussing a couple of weeks ago, on a Saturday night, at Manuel's tavern."

Rollo stammered for a moment. "Mr. Walsh wanted to know about a white man buying guns, little throw-away pieces. He was looking for whoever killed them lawyers in Midtown."

"And you helped him find that out, right?"

Rollo nodded vigorously. "Yes sir. That's right."

"We appreciate that, Rollo, and I'm sure Detective Walsh did too."

Rollo gave him a solemn look, as though he sincerely missed Walsh.

"So, it was you who tipped Walsh to Hollywood Holmes. And it was Hollywood who gave up Ambrose Mangham for the Midtown Murders."

"I… I reckon."

"Rollo, did you also give Walsh any information leading to the bust of Maurice "Kingfish" Hamby?"

Rollo wasn't sure what to say.

"It's okay, Rollo," Gwynn said, in a soothing voice. He smiled and patted him on the shoulder with his broad, meaty hand. "Either you did, or you didn't. It ain't gonna come back on you."

Rollo took a deep breath. "I helped Mr. Walsh a little bit."

"How well did you know Kingfish?"

"I knowed him a long time. Grew up in the same neighborhood."

"Do you think Walsh may have been working with Kingfish?"

Rollo pretended to give this some thought. "Could be"

"Do you think they may have had a business disagreement, and that's what led Walsh to kill Kingfish and two of his crew members?"

"Could be"

Paxton nodded and thought for a moment. "As I recall, before it all went down, some of Kingfish's competition turned up dead. Old Kingfish always seemed to have an alibi. He was at church, he was at a party, folks saw him at a club, that sort of thing."

"Uh huh"

"Do you think Kingfish may have put a contract on those people?"

Rollo relaxed visibly and smiled. "Well, Lieutenant, there was this story. I don't know if it's true. I just heard it."

"Tell it."

"There was this white kid. I don't know his name. Kingfish called him 'Eminem.' He did a lot of dealing for Kingfish down south of town. Then he started banging this older white chick, real good looker from the way he told it."

Rollo glanced at Beth Long. She smiled, and he continued.

"Well, he was banging this woman, and something happened. Eminem turned up dead in a parking lot. He'd told Kingfish he was going to meet this woman."

"When was that?"

"Couple of months ago"

"Does this woman have a name?" asked Paxton.

Rollo furrowed his brow. "Not as I recall."

"Okay. Go on."

"Well, word was, this white chick started doing jobs for Kingfish."

"Jobs?"

"Yeah. Shooting people."

"Was she still working for Kingfish when Walsh raided his place and killed him?"

"Far as I know"

Paxton glanced at Long. She nodded.

"Rollo," he said, "you're an upstanding citizen, you know that?"

"Yeah. Well, if it's all the same to you Lieutenant, I'd appreciate it if you'd keep that to yourself."

Paxton smiled. "Sure thing, Rollo."

The Escalade pulled over and dropped Rollo at a vacant lot near the spot where it had picked him up.

• • •

The eleven o'clock news led with the APD announcement, broadcast earlier during prime time, that police had solved the Midtown Murders. The killer, newspaper writer Ambrose Mangham, had died in a shootout with Detective Don Walsh. The story lauded Walsh as a martyr and praised his skillful investigation of the case.

Paxton, already dressed for bed, stayed up to see Murray's statement and the press response. The camera turned to Sumatra Simms. She asked Murray why he hadn't mentioned the murder of Lou Allen, another attorney living in Midtown.

Murray pursed his lips. "That homicide is still under investigation."

"Isn't it true," she asked, "that Allen's murder occurred after the shooting of Ambrose Mangham?"

"Apparently," said Murray. "We don't know yet."

"So, what makes you so sure Mangham's the Midtown Murderer? Our sources tell us Allen's killer had the same MO as the killer of Mallory, Epstein and Lopez. Is it still possible, Chief Murray, that this is the work of a serial killer?"

In her follow-up on camera, Simms commented that Murray's statement reminded her of APD blaming all the missing and murdered children on Wayne Williams.

Paxton smiled. Girl, he thought, that was long before your time.

CHAPTER 31
M. BLOOM

Atlanta, Georgia
Tuesday, October 30

Paxton ran a gauntlet of local reporters outside his office hungering for a statement. His reply was a simple "no comment." He settled into his chair, called Mavis Wilson, and agreed to meet her at the home of the late Don Walsh. With help from Smyrna police, the APD padlocked the apartment. They notified the landlord it was a crime scene, off limits until further notice.

Closed since Saturday, the place had the musty odor of mildew and old socks. Walsh lived alone and, from the looks of things, hadn't cleaned in a while. .

A thorough search turned up an expensive laptop not issued by the department. Investigators found recent fingerprints matching Walsh's and latents from a different source. A stack of shoe boxes hidden behind a panel in the back of Walsh's closet yielded more than a hundred thousand dollars in cash.

Walsh had his cell at the time of his death, and the crime lab had already located Rollo Witherspoon's number under the name "Ardub." Another phone, a burner found in Walsh's bottom drawer, yielded a single contact, an "M Bloom."

Paxton shook his head. "Heard Walsh used to be a good cop. I guess he just crossed the line."

"Yeah," said Mavis. "He crossed that line and never looked back. Walsh was the kind of cop gives us all a bad name."

"Who the hell is M. Bloom?"

Mavis' eyes narrowed. "Maybe it's Molly Bloom." She described the James Joyce character who cheated on her husband with a younger man.

Paxton shrugged. From the way Mavis told the story, he wondered if she'd had similar experiences. He still had no name for the Ice Queen, but he was inching closer.

• • •

Back at the office, he ran a search on unsolved murders in counties south of Atlanta. He turned up a victim in Fayette County named Jeremy Coleman, killed with a small caliber round at close range, presumably a pistol. The case was still open and there were no suspects.

Among Coleman's priors were several minor drug busts, mostly marijuana. A call to Lyman Gwinn confirmed Coleman as a known confederate of Maurice Hamby.

The latents on the laptop and burner found in Walsh's apartment matched Hamby. What came next, Paxton knew, could transform his career, for better or worse. He called Tom Williams.

"Can you meet me at Cookout on Ponce?" he asked.

"Where the old Zesto's used to be?"

"Yep."

When Paxton arrived, Tom was in a booth tucking into a hamburger and Diet Coke, though it was only ten AM. A small notebook lay open in front of him. Paxton stopped at the counter and ordered a large milkshake.

"You sure that's on your diet?" asked Tom.

"I'm off my diet as of today."

"Okay."

"Tom, I never thanked you for helping us get Ambrose Mangham."

"You guys did all the work. I just asked nosy questions."

"Yeah. That's what you do best." Paxton took a quick sip then came to the point. "If I give you some information, will you promise me two things?"

"Like what?"

"That you'll keep my name out of it, for now at least, and you'll share it with some of your TV friends."

Tom gave him a wary look. "Okay."

"Sergeant Long and I spoke with Rollo Witherspoon last night. We don't have the Ice Queen's real name yet, but we think she's a housewife living somewhere south of Atlanta, probably Fayette County."

"That narrows it down."

"We believe she was screwing a teenage dealer named Jeremy Coleman. Lyman tells me he was one of Maurice Hamby's crew. We believe she and the young man had a... difference of opinion. One thing led to another, and she killed him. Hamby found out and pressed her into making hits for him."

"How does that connect to Lou Allen?"

"Hamby died in a shootout with Don Walsh and his partner a few months back when Walsh was still in Narcotics. Walsh was the lone survivor. IA thinks he planned it that way, so he could clean up some of Hamby's loose cash and dope. Among the things Walsh stole were a laptop and phone. The phone contained a contact we believe was the Ice Queen, using an alias."

Scribbling madly in his notebook, Tom asked. "And?'

"Turns out, Walsh went through a nasty divorce a while back. Guess who represented his wife?"

"Lou Allen."

"Bingo."

"And Allen coached the wife into accusing Walsh of molesting their..."

"...son."

"So, Walsh hires this Ice Queen to ice Allen while he's conveniently elsewhere."

"That's what we think." Paxton took a deep breath. "There's more. We think Allen had Eleanor Heinz, do her repressed memory magic on Walsh's son."

"And she's..."

"...the subject of a recent missing persons bulletin."

"Why are you telling me this?"

"I don't think the department is sufficiently... motivated, yet, to pursue this. They just closed the Midtown Murders, thanks to Walsh's *heroic sacrifices*. The last thing they want to announce is that Walsh hired a suburban housewife to kill Allen, especially when all we have are drawings by an autistic kid and rumors from a small-time drug dealer."

"You want me to light a fire under APD by floating a rumor that Walsh hired the Ice Queen to kill Allen."

"Something like that. You don't have to tell the whole story yet, just enough to make Austin Murray release the drawings. Maybe somebody'll recognize this woman and give us a call."

"Sounds pretty risky for both of us. You sure you want to do this?"

"Yeah." Paxton leaned across the table. His eyes bore into Tom's. "You see... I still wake up at night thinking about those kids got killed all those years ago. Wayne Williams didn't do all of them. There's at least one killer got away scot free. Now we'll never know who he was. I'm not gone let that happen again."

Tom nodded.

Paxton held up his right hand with thumb and forefinger a quarter inch apart. "Tom, I'm this close to telling Austin Murray and all his ass-kissers to go fuck themselves. Clarice already wants me to retire, and I'm not sure it's a bad idea."

Tom gazed out the window at the cars passing on Ponce and nodded slowly. "Okay. I may have enough time to get this on the noon broadcast."

Paxton left by the side door while Tom pulled out his phone and dialed Sumatra Simms.

. . .

Sumatra didn't come on until early afternoon. Relaxing at home in bath robe and slippers, she sipped coffee while watching her favorite soap opera... cable news. Her phone rang. She picked it up and frowned at the display before answering.

"So, have you come up with something else for me, Mr. 'No Comment'?"

"As a matter of fact, Sumatra, I have." He related the story Paxton had told him on condition she attribute them to him as a writer for the *AJC*. For all he knew, the paper had no interest in his story, but they might, once Sumatra mentioned it on her noon broadcast.

As she called the station, she spruced up her hair and changed into a conservative blouse and skirt. Within minutes she was on her way to APD headquarters. Her camera crew met her there.

Tom, meanwhile, called Mitch Danner, and, within minutes, was on the phone to the city editor at the *AJC*. He told the same story and agreed to co-write it with Danner, who had his own sources inside APD. Danner would call Austin Murray later, after Sumatra had ambushed him outside his office. Tom smiled at the thought of Sumatra playing "bad cop" to Mitch's "good."

• • •

Paxton decided not to return to work following his meeting with Tom. He called in and told the duty sergeant he wasn't feeling well. He was pulling into his driveway when his phone buzzed. The display read "Murray." He smiled and shoved it back in his pocket.

Clarice was out, and the house was empty. Paxton retrieved a bottled water from the refrigerator and turned on the radio. WSB broke in with an announcement that there was a lead in the Allen murder.

The house phone rang. It was Murray again. Paxton ignored it. He walked into his den and turned on the television in time to catch a replay of Sumatra attempting to question Murray in front of police headquarters.

• • •

The evening news led with a press conference on every channel. A chagrined Austin Murray announced that police were now looking for a "person of interest" in the murder of Lou Allen.

Allison Embry and her family had just settled in for supper. From the dinner table they had a clear view of the television in the den. As the announcer recounted Sumatra's attempt to interview Murray, up flashed Roy Sedgewick's composites of the Ice Queen.

Leslie was first to notice. "Mom, that looks like you."

Mug shots appeared on the screen. "Police believe the woman they're seeking may have had relations with eighteen-year-old Jeremy Coleman, whose body was found behind an abandoned Peachtree City warehouse two months ago."

"You been leading a double life, babe?" Rob joked.

Allison stifled a momentary panic. She forced a smile. "You never know."

"By the way," said Rob, "I've been called in tomorrow."

Allison recognized the old ploy. *Too bad*, she thought. *If only I still had that gun.*

. . .

Two miles away, Wendy Miller had just finished her supper and was sitting in her living room sipping a third glass of Chardonnay. Lon had retired early, as he often did before a long flight. Madison, seated at the dining room table, pretended to study for an upcoming test.

Wendy leaned toward the television and studied the police sketches. "Maddie, come here a minute."

Her daughter let out a long-suffering groan and closed her textbook. She walked into the living room where her mother sat transfixed.

"Doesn't that look a lot like Leslie Embry's mom?" asked Wendy. Had she bothered to look up she'd have noticed a curious change on her daughter's face.

. . .

Other Fayette residents saw the same broadcast. Few, even those who knew Allison, noted the resemblance. Carl Osborne was an exception. An aspiring photographer, he had a keen eye for detail.

He was leaving for work as delivery driver for Pizza Man. His mom, as usual, sat catatonic in front of her television. Carl stopped to give her a peck on the cheek.

"Don't be late," she said, not looking up.

He followed her gaze to the police sketch on the screen. It looked familiar, but he couldn't place the woman. Moments later, the thought banished to the back of his mind, he was out the door.

CHAPTER 32
HALLOWS EVE

Bartow County
Wednesday, October 31
Halloween morning dawned clear and cool over Red Top Mountain. A light breeze stirred the few remaining leaves, still vibrant in their autumn colors.

Ashley Case and her boyfriend Paul Rusk had camped at an unauthorized site and were hiking back to where she'd parked her car the night before. Paul was a senior and Ashley a sophomore at Kennesaw State University. Neither of them had classes on Wednesday, and they'd enjoyed what might be the last beautiful weather of the year.

As they neared the small parking lot, the trail wound past a scenic overlook that had become a makeshift landfill. Plastic garbage bags, many of them broken open by wildlife, dotted the hillside. Ashley frowned in disbelief. How could anyone dump trash in such a beautiful place?

A rank odor assaulted her nostrils. She turned and was about to pass by when she spotted a human foot peeping from beneath a pile of leaves and debris. She pulled out her cell and frantically dialed 911. Paul tried with his. Not until they reached the bottom of the mountain were either of them able to get a signal.

• • •

Paxton considered taking another sick day, thinking it might give Murray a chance to calm down. He decided instead to face whatever came. Murray might believe it was Paxton who tipped the media, but he'd never prove it.

Paxton had just poured his first cup of coffee when he looked up to see Murray crossing the office. The man was not happy. Paxton was about to offer a friendly greeting when his desk phone erupted. He smiled at Murray and picked it up.

"Davis"

"Lieutenant Davis, this is Deputy Ty Butler with the Bartow County Sheriff's Department."

"Yes."

"A couple of campers found a woman's body up on Red Top Mountain this morning. Looks like she's been there a few days. She's starting to bloat, and the animals have gotten to her, but we think she matches a missing person named Eleanor Heinz. I was told I needed to speak to you."

Standing in the doorway glowering, Murray caught the sudden change in Paxton's expression.

"Do you have a cause of death?" Paxton asked Butler.

"The crime scene techs aren't here yet, but it looks like she was shot once in the abdomen and once in each eye."

The deputy agreed to meet Paxton at the mountainside parking lot. Paxton hung up and explained to Murray.

"Fine. I'll ride with you," Murray said.

Paxton looked at the man then shrugged. "Sure." He called Beth Long and asked her to join them.

Long sat in back while Paxton drove and Murray rode shotgun. Murray stayed quiet, turning occasionally to scowl at Paxton. They were approaching the Cobb Cloverleaf when Paxton's phone rang. He pulled it out, gave the readout a curious look, and handed it back to Long.

"This is Sergeant Long," she answered, followed by a long pause. "Lieutenant Davis isn't available. May I ask what this is about?" Another pause. "Sure." She put the phone on speaker, placing it close enough for Paxton to hear.

"Yes," he said.

A young woman's voice came on, a teenager Paxton guessed.

"Is this Lieutenant Davis?" Her voice carried a Southern twang.

"It is."

"I'm calling about that picture they showed on TV last night."

"The picture?"

"The drawing of that woman, the one wanted for questioning in the murder of that lawyer."

Paxton almost ran off the road. "Who is this?"

"I'd rather not give my name."

Murray cut in, "Look, who is ..."

Paxton cut him off with a glare. "That'll be alright, Miss. Just tell me what you know."

"The woman you're looking for is Allison Embry. She lives in Peachtree City. I can give you her address."

Long typed it into her own phone as the young woman spoke. When Murray started to ask another question, the caller hung up.

Paxton was furious. "Thanks, Chief! Now we've lost her completely!"

"For all we know," said Murray, "it was just another prank call."

"Except for one little detail. Your announcement last night never mentioned anything about the Ice Queen living on the south side of town. Do you think it's just coincidence, *Chief,* that this Allison Embry lives in Peachtree City?" Paxton made a note to trace the call, though he knew it would be a waste of time.

Long listened quietly. Again, she felt nauseated. She had no idea what it could be. She hadn't been carsick since she was a little girl. When the car stopped, she jumped out, ran to some bushes, and lost her breakfast.

"Are you okay?" asked Paxton.

"Yeah. Just give me a few minutes," she said, wiping her mouth with a Kleenex.

"Take as long as you need."

Paxton and Murray hiked back to the crime scene while Long leaned against a tree and closed her eyes. They spoke to Case and Rusk, to Deputy Butler, and to two Bartow County crime scene techs, one of whom was busy taking pictures. Exhausted and weak, Long finally joined them. She stood well away from the corpse and upwind.

Paxton squatted for a closer look. Beneath the stench of decay was another odor, the unmistakable smell of bleach.

"We can't be sure this is Ms. Heinz until the medical examiner has a look at her," Butler said in his slow drawl.

"I understand," said Paxton. "Call me when you find out." He handed Butler his card, as did Murray and Long.

On the return trip, Paxton half turned to Long, seated behind Murray. "If you're feeling better when we get back to the station, I want you to find out everything you can about this Allison Embry, her family, if and where she works, where she goes to church, her sex life. I'd like to pay her a visit, and I want to be prepared when I do."

"Let me know when you're going down there," said Murray.

Paxton nodded and focused his attention on the swelling traffic. There was no way in hell he'd take Murray with him to interview Allison Embry or anyone else.

. . .

Long returned to the station without further incident. Though by now it was almost noon, she elected to skip lunch and rest at her desk. When she felt better, she began browsing government web sites for information on Allison Embry. Before long, she'd compiled a detailed portrait.

Meanwhile, Paxton was still stewing over Murray's ineptitude. Anxious to avoid further contact with him, he ducked out to a nearby sandwich shop. When he returned a half hour later, he began poring over crime scene reports and the coroner's statement on Allen's murder. He also reviewed his notes from their interview with Rollo Witherspoon.

Long knocked at his door. He looked up and said, "Talk to me."

She handed him a printout of a driver's license. "It seems Ms. Embry is the least likely contract killer imaginable. She has no priors. Her last traffic ticket was three years ago for running a stop sign. She lives in a Peachtree City neighborhood called 'Orchard Springs.' Her husband, Rob, is a Delta pilot, and their children, Kyle and Leslie, attend Starr's Mill High School. She stays at home and spends her spare moments exercising and doing volunteer work for her church… I hate her already."

"Were you able to trace our anonymous tipster?"

"She used a pay phone."

"Surprise, surprise," said Paxton. "Some nosy neighbor calls and gives us a suspect but won't identify herself. She's probably carrying a grudge and wants us to go jack up an innocent housewife. I do not need this shit!"

"I did find something interesting. Turns out our boy, Jeremy Coleman, also attended Starr's Mill before going away to juvie for possession with intent. He was, in fact, a classmate of Kyle Embry."

Paxton pursed his lips. "Probably a coincidence. Any connection between Coleman and Kyle?"

"Nothing I could find, but I did get this. Our investigators were able to trace the times and locations from which M. Bloom phoned Hamby and Walsh. One of them is the Peachtree City Public Library, less than a mile from the Embry home. The others were nearby malls and shopping centers."

"And Allison has a library card?"

"Yep."

Paxton shook his head. "That still doesn't give us anything. If we go down to Peachtree City and roust her with nothing more than this, Austin Murray will have my ass." He thought for a moment. "Bring me as many pictures of Ms. Embry as you can find and get me that kid... Sedgewick."

Five minutes later, Roy Sedgewick was in Paxton's office examining the photos of Allison, comparing them to the sketch of the Ice Queen. He shrugged. "I don't know. It looks like her. The facial structure's right."

Paxton turned to Long. "You think if we ran these by Ben Hogarth, he might recognize her?"

"It's a long shot. We need to handle him carefully." She stood silent for a long time, then said, "Maybe we need a different approach."

"Like?"

Sedgewick shifted his attention between Paxton and Long like a spectator at a ping pong match.

"Ask yourself," said Long, "what are the reasons no one would suspect Allison Embry of being a killer?"

Paxton thought for a moment. "No priors... no known connection to the victim..."

"Yeah, sure. But what are the three things we look for in a suspect?"

Sedgewick lit up like a school kid answering the teacher's question. "Means, motive and opportunity."

"Exactly!" said Long. "If Allison was Jeremy Coleman's mystery lover, then she certainly had opportunity. If they had a fight of some sort, that might have provided a motive. All she needed was a means." She waited while Paxton ruminated.

"All she needed was a gun," he said.

"What if we could tie Ms. Embry to a gun?"

"And how are we gonna do that? That gun's in a landfill by now."

Long spread her hands as she spoke. "I didn't say, 'tie her to *the* gun.' I said, 'tie her to *a* gun.' It won't prove she shot Coleman, Allen, or Heinz, but it'll prove she had the means. We're talking about a lot of shootings, and she's never been seen or caught. Our killer is familiar with small arms and knows how to use them."

"Where are you going with this?" asked Paxton.

"There aren't that many target ranges in Peachtree City," she said, "not so many we couldn't canvass them with Roy's sketches and see if anyone recognizes her. It'll at least get us going in the right direction."

Paxton smiled for the first time all day. "It's not like we have anything else to work with. Worst case, it's a waste of police resources, and I'll get fired." On his way out the door, he stopped. "While we're at it, let's bring pictures of Allen, Heinz, and Coleman in case there's some connection we're missing... And we can go by the library to see if anybody connects Roy's picture to Allison Embry."

Sedgewick asked if he could tag along, and Paxton agreed.

• • •

The trip to Peachtree City proved more productive than expected. The third firing range they visited was Baxley's Guns and Ammo on Highway 54 going toward Newnan. Its proprietor, Baxley Dutton, looked at Sedgewick's drawings and slowly nodded. "You know, that looks kinda like Mrs. Embry. She comes in here for target practice. She's one of the nicest and most courteous customers. Let me ask my helper... Hey, Hank."

An older man with a patchy grey beard sauntered over and gazed at the drawing. "Yep. That's Ms. Embry. I tell you she's one fine looking woman. Good shot too. I keep hoping she'll ask me for some lessons," he added with a wink, "but nope. She's a natural. Cool as an ice cube."

Paxton turned to Long and smiled. Neither of them had mentioned Allison's name.

"Could you tell me what kind of gun she uses?"

"Sure. She prefers a small pistol, a lady's gun, not real accurate at any distance, but she's a deadeye at close range. Like I said, she's a regular."

"Either of you notice anything unusual about her?"

Dutton thought for a moment. "You know, every time she comes in, it seems like she has a different gun."

• • •

At the library, two staff members also recognized the picture. But neither of them knew her name. One of them remembered she was always using the computer kiosks.

As they drove away, Paxton shook his head in frustration. "We still don't have a solid connection. She likes to shoot. A lot of people like to shoot. She uses the computer at the library. A lot of people do. We don't have a murder weapon. We don't have a witness who can put her anywhere near Jeremy Coleman, Lou Allen, or Eleanor Heinz. We ain't got shit so far!"

"Then what do we do next?" asked Long.

Paxton took a deep breath and thought. "We could pay her a visit. Tell her we're just tracking down possible leads and show her what we got. See how she reacts. Biggest risk is she freaks out and runs. That alone would make her a solid suspect."

"That's not likely," said Long. "She's got to be smart enough to know we don't have anything useful. Besides, she has a husband and kids. Kinda makes it hard for her to go anywhere."

"We just need to gauge her initial reaction," said Paxton, "We need to get up on her fast and brace her before she has a chance to think. Problem is, she'll see me coming a mile away and know I'm a cop." He chewed his lower lip. "Why would this woman get involved with shit like Jeremy Coleman and Kingfish Hamby? Look at these neighborhoods. It's not like she was broke."

Long shrugged. "Maybe she just got bored with her little Martha Stewart world."

Paxton chewed some more then turned to Sedgewick sitting in the back seat. The kid was twenty-five at most. With his fresh, boyish face, he looked like the farthest thing from a cop. "Ok," said Paxton. "Tell you what we're gonna do."

• • •

Distracted by the news from his doctor, Lon Miller almost missed the entrance to his neighborhood. The tightness in his chest returned for a moment, then subsided. He'd first noticed it two days earlier. Another pilot told him he didn't look well and suggested he might be running a fever.

Lon called Delta that morning and told them he was sick, describing flu-like symptoms. He didn't mention the doctor's appointment to Wendy or Madison, both of whom were still in bed when he left home. They thought he was out of town.

For fifteen years, Lon had flown commercial jets. Before that, he spent twenty years as a Navy fighter pilot. Flying was his life. It was all he ever wanted to do, and now it was over. A diagnosis of cardiac arrythmia was all Delta needed to force his retirement. From the doctor's office, Lon drove around for more than an hour, wondering what he'd tell his wife and daughter. He spent another hour contemplating on a bar stool at a Chili's out near I-85.

At the head of the cul-de-sac that had been his home for the past decade he stopped, wondering just where he'd gone wrong. In his driveway sat a new, white Lexus, right where he knew it would be. There was this one piece of business he needed to take care of.

• • •

Allison scanned the contents of her refrigerator wondering what to cook for supper. Rob was out of town again, supposedly. She'd been to the store the day before, but most of what she'd bought was gone. With Kyle living here, she could never make food last more than two meals. On cue, her offspring breezed in from school, grabbing snacks and retreating to their respective bedrooms, claiming they had homework.

There was a knock at the front door. Through the glass Allison saw a young woman, perhaps mid-thirties, and a man who couldn't be more than twenty-five, peddlers no doubt. She opened the door and was about to tell them she wasn't interested, when she found herself staring at a badge held by the woman at arm's length.

"Ms. Embry, I'm Sergeant Beth Long with Atlanta Police. We have a few questions. We hope you don't mind. We won't take much of your time."

Allison glanced at Sedgewick, who said nothing and showed no badge. Long inserted herself in the doorway before Allison could object.

When she offered them a seat, Long placed herself in the middle of the couch facing the picture window. Sedgewick took a wing-backed chair near the front door, leaving Allison the matching chair facing Long. From where she sat, Long had a clear view of the Escalade, parked across the street. Paxton sat inside unseen. In her pocketbook, Long's phone was on and dialed into Paxton's. He could hear every word they said.

"Ms. Embry, we're investigating the murders of Louis Allen and Eleanor Heinz." As Sedgewick pulled his sketches from an envelope and placed them on the coffee table, Long studied Allison's facial expressions. What they saw was a momentary look of panic, quickly stifled.

"I can't imagine," Allison said with a bemused smile, "what a murder in Atlanta has to do with me."

"You may have seen these drawings on television last night," said Long. "These are sketches of a woman seen by multiple witnesses at Mr. Allen's party last Saturday. We received a call this morning identifying her as you."

Allison took one look at the costumed, well-endowed Ice Queen and dissolved into laughter. "Oh my! Do you really think she looks like me? I'm flattered."

"Ms. Embry, can you tell us where you were Saturday night?"

Allison forced another smile. "I went shopping at Southlake Mall... by myself. I suppose if I'd known I needed an alibi I'd have arranged one."

"Do you have receipts?"

"I don't believe I bought anything."

"We just thought you might be able to help us, Ms. Embry." Long shifted forward as if about to leave. "There are a couple more pictures we'd like you to see."

From the envelope Sedgewick pulled a mug shot. "This is a picture of Maurice 'Kingfish' Hamby, recently deceased. He was a major drug dealer in the South Atlanta area. His connections extended down here to Fayette County. He was known to have hired contract killers on occasion."

Allison evinced a mild curiosity. "I can assure you my circle of friends doesn't include drug dealers or contract killers, living or dead."

"One of Mr. Hamby's dealers lived in this area," said Long. "He's also deceased."

As Sedgewick pulled the final photo, Long studied Allison more closely. A single bead of sweat formed high on her forehead. She forced herself to stare at Jeremy Coleman and shook her head. There was a slight quiver at the left corner of her lip. Sedgewick caught it as well.

Long gazed out the window and saw Paxton striding across the lawn. She turned to Sedgewick and motioned to the door with a nod of her head. He rose and opened it.

Paxton held his badge out so Allison could see it. He spoke in a deep bass that carried throughout the house. "Ms. Embry, or perhaps I should call you 'Ms. Bloom...' we know you and Jeremy Coleman were having an affair. We also suspect he was providing you with drugs. We have records of calls you made to Hamby and Detective Don Walsh from a burner. Now... you're about to make a choice that'll impact the rest of your life. You can tell us what happened, or you can just sit there and lie to us. You need to know this, though. If we leave here today without you, things will only get worse, much worse."

Allison's eyes narrowed at the mention of Don Walsh. The connection fell into place. Her *client* was the cop who died in the shootout Saturday night. There was no way the police would connect him to her.

She glowered at Paxton. "I have no idea what you're talking about, and I want you to leave my house right now."

Paxton nodded and gave her a sad look. "We'll leave Allison, but you might start looking for a good defense lawyer."

As the three strolled back to the SUV, Allison studied them through her picture window. She turned to see Kyle and Leslie standing in the kitchen doorway, speechless.

With great effort, she strove to convince them it was all a ridiculous mistake. Someone had seen the police sketches on television and thought they looked like her. She knew nothing about the murders, or the people involved. It was *so* preposterous!

It was Kyle who finally spoke. "Jeremy Coleman?" was all he said. He shook his head, turned, and walked away. Leslie stared at her mother for several seconds, dumbstruck, then followed her brother.

As they returned to their rooms, Allison shouted up the stairs, "It's all just a big mistake." She started to say something else and stopped.

She turned back to the window, a deep rage boiling inside. Wendy Miller, she thought. It had to be her who called the police. Why didn't I kill Rob and his white trash whore a long time ago?

Twenty minutes later, she was still pondering when she looked out to see two uniformed Peachtree City police walking across her lawn. This was too much. She grabbed the door handle and yanked it open before they could knock.

"Yes! What is it?'

This caught the officers by surprise. When they recovered, one asked, "Ms. Embry?"

"Yes."

"I'm afraid we have some tragic news. It's your husband. There's been a shooting."

. . .

Madison Miller made the slow uphill trek from the bus stop. Midway, she noticed cop cars parked along the street and neighbors standing in her yard. They turned in unison as she approached, looks of profound sadness on their faces. Before they could speak, a female officer intervened and took her aside.

"Madison?"

She nodded.

"I don't know how to tell you this. Something awful happened to your mom and dad."

Madison stared, first in shock and disbelief then in horror, as the woman explained. Both her parents were dead. She screamed and made a lunge toward the house, only to have the officer catch her.

The night before, Lon had told Wendy and Madison he had to fly out the next day. He lied. Returning home mid-afternoon, he discovered Wendy and Rob upstairs in a guest bedroom having sex. Before they could stop him, Lon pulled a gun and killed them both. He then turned it on himself.

As the policewoman spoke, an elderly neighbor approached. Madison ran to her and buried her face in the woman's bosom. The neighbor explained she was a friend of the family. Madison could stay with her while she contacted her grandmother in Fayetteville.

The officer nodded and said she'd come by later to take Madison's statement.

CHAPTER 33
MADISON MILLER

Peachtree City
Wednesday, October 31

Allison was frantic. Kyle and Leslie hid in their bedrooms and refused to speak to her. From Leslie's room came deep, racking sobs, from Kyle's the sound of objects hitting the wall. *Surely, they don't blame me*, Allison thought. *It's not my fault their dad was a cheating motherfucker who got exactly what he and that bitch, Wendy, deserved... Poor Lon... How did he find out about Wendy and Rob?*

Her eyes welled. Nowhere in her fantasies of murdering Rob had she thought about Kyle and Leslie or what the loss of their father would do to them. How could she be so self-centered? Asshole that he was, Rob was their dad, and now they would have to go on without him.

Allison was just moving on to the thought of poor Madison Miller, when the doorbell rang. She peeped through the lace curtain and tried to remember the name of the woman standing on her porch, casserole dish in hand. She opened the door, wiping her eyes, accepted the gift, and thanked her.

"How are you holding up, darling?" the woman asked.

"We're still in shock."

"Well, I just wanted to bring you this and tell you how sorry I am."

As the lady returned to her car, Allison recalled her name, Donna Frazier. They'd once served together on the women's auxiliary at church. It seemed so long ago, though it had been only three months.

Allison was about to close the door when Denise walked up with a dish of her own. She set it down on the top step and took Allison in her arms. Allison gave in and let the tears flow.

"Oh my God! How could I be such a selfish cunt! My children have lost their father, and now they won't even speak to me... Maybe they're right to blame me. I feel so guilty. I never wanted this."

Denise held her tight. "It's not your fault," she said. "You just need time away so you can begin rebuilding your life. We could go somewhere."

Allison gave her a horrified look. "I can't abandon my kids at a time like this!"

"I don't mean *right now*, silly" Denise smiled. "Give them some time to process. Maybe they could stay with your mom and step-dad over Christmas. We could fly down to the islands for a couple of weeks, relax, and get away from all this. You can call Leslie and Kyle while we're down there, and when you're ready, you can come back and get them. You'll find they're more resilient than you imagined."

Her mention of the islands got Allison thinking about her account in Antigua. She wiped snot from her nose and dried her eyes with a sleeve. "Maybe you're right," she said.

Footsteps bounded down the stairs. Kyle strode past wearing a track suit. He said nothing and looked at neither his mother nor her friend. The patio door slammed. Out back was a shed he and Rob had transformed into a small gym. Kyle began pounding the heavy punching bag.

"He just needs to blow off some steam," Denise said. "Why don't you go upstairs and lie down? I brought some soft drinks. I'll take care of your guests."

Kyle continued his rhythmic pounding, ignoring the fact that he wasn't wearing gloves. His raw knuckles began to bleed. His mind was empty but for a white-hot fury festering somewhere behind his eyes. Not until the next day would he notice the boxer's fracture on his right ring finger, the consequence of a sloppy punch.

Leslie sat on the floor beside her bed staring at her phone, wondering how she'd ever reply to all the condolences pouring in from friends. Her mind was blank. She hadn't worked up the courage yet to open her Instagram account.

• • •

Alone in the solitude of her grandmother's guest room, Madison Miller paced like a caged tiger. Like Kyle, she was angry. Unlike Kyle, her anger had a focus, *Allison Embry.*

Madison needed fresh air and time to think. What should she do next? She had to call Kyle… but what would she say to him? *Sorry my dad murdered your dad? Sorry your dad was fucking my mom?*

She picked up her phone. Cautiously she opened the door and listened. From an upstairs bedroom she heard her grandmother crying. She was almost to the back door when she suddenly stopped. The television was on in the den. It was the evening news, and a female reporter was describing a double-murder suicide in Peachtree City.

Behind the woman stood the home where Madison had lived most of her young life, the home where, only hours earlier, police discovered the bodies of her mother, her father, and Rob Embry. A caption identified the reporter as Sumatra Simms.

With the aid of Siri, Madison located the TV station's number and dialed. She stepped out to the patio where she could speak without her grandmother overhearing. With the sliding door open a half inch, she could still hear and see the television. It took all the persuasion Madison could muster to convince the operator to patch her through.

Sumatra stopped in mid-sentence. "Wait a minute," she said. "I'm told now that Madison Miller, daughter of Lon and Wendy Miller, is on the line. She wants to make a statement. Madison?"

As she spoke, there was a delay. Madison wondered whose voice she heard. She halted, then realized it was her own. "Yes ma'am." How small she sounded, like a little girl! She stopped and composed herself to avoid crying into the phone. Closing the sliding door softly, she continued. "My name's Madison Miller. I came home this afternoon to find that my parents and my boyfriend's father were inside my house. They were all dead." She stopped, wondering what to say next. *I can do this,* she told herself.

"Take your time, Madison," Sumatra said. "Our hearts go out to you tonight. We can only imagine how horrible this must be."

"My folks have gone through some tough times lately. They thought I didn't hear them downstairs arguing late at night. They thought I was in bed asleep."

"Madison, you're a very brave young woman. We want to thank you for having the courage to speak with us. Have you spoken to your boyfriend about this?"

The moment Madison replied, Sumatra regretted the question.

"Not yet. I don't know what to say to him," she said.

Her tone ignited. "It's all his mom's fault. If she weren't such a frigid bitch her husband wouldn't be looking for satisfaction somewhere else. He took advantage of my mom, and now they're both dead… And you know what?" she screamed. "That woman the police are looking for, the one who killed that lawyer in Midtown… that was Allison Embry, I guarantee you. Look at her and look at the police pictures. She's the same woman."

When she finally stopped, Madison heard a dial tone. On TV, Sumatra spoke. "We seem to have lost our connection." She shook her head. "Wow! What a brave young woman! I know all of our viewers will hold Madison in their thoughts and prayers tonight … Amanda?"

As the screen switched back to the anchor and the next story, Madison turned to see her grandmother staring at her through the glass.

• • •

Allison never saw the broadcast. She came downstairs to say goodbye to her remaining guests while Denise stayed behind to clean up. Denise made sure the TV was off.

"Thank you so much for being here today," said Allison. "I couldn't have made it without you."

Denise shrugged, "I can stay tonight, if you'd like."

Allison looked down and nodded. "I'd like that."

Denise placed her arms around her and gave her a long hug. When she pulled back Allison was staring into her eyes. She pulled her close and kissed her on the lips.

Kyle returned from the shed. Allison heard him in the shower, using up the last of the hot water. Leslie was still in her room, no doubt texting her friends.

That night, as Denise lay sleeping beside her, Allison replayed the past two days in her head. The police were onto her. Of that there was no doubt.

Ironically, Rob and Wendy's murder had been a Godsend. For that, Allison was blameless. Lon had taken care of things for her. For the time being, at least, Rob's death would provide all the cover she needed. With no more evidence than they currently had, the police wouldn't dare haul a grieving widow out of her home in front of television cameras, leaving her fatherless children alone.

Denise's idea about getting away to the islands sounded better and better. But how would they make that work?

Her mind raced. *The police will wait for the right moment. They'll show up with more questions, more evidence, eventually an arrest warrant. They'll never, ever quit. If I run, they'll just nab me. If I don't, they'll get me eventually... I can bide my time for now, though. I'll get a lawyer. Maybe he can do something to keep the cops away. I need to rid myself of this house and liquidate my assets. Tomorrow I'll file for Rob's life insurance.*

. . .

Miles away, sitting alone in the silence of her darkened apartment, Beth Long also missed the evening news. She took a deep breath and exhaled slowly. She had to do something. Staring at these four walls was not going to make her problem go away. She had to know.

Lately, she'd had trouble sleeping, despite her exhaustion. She began to wonder. She was a week late, nothing unusual. But then there was the nausea. Maybe it was nothing. *She had to know.*

She pulled out the early pregnancy test she'd picked up on her way home. She took another breath, sat on the toilet, urinated on the strip, and laid it on the side of the sink. She waited three minutes as instructed. Stunned, she watched the word PREGNANT slowly emerge. How could this happen? She'd been so careful. She took the pill every day.

Brandon had called earlier and asked if she wanted some company. She fobbed him off with the excuse of not feeling well. What would she tell him now? What did she expect him to do?

She'd never envisioned herself as someone's mom. For a moment she wondered if she should have this baby, then put the question out of her mind. Raised a devout Catholic, she would never contemplate an abortion.

How will this impact my work? she wondered. *How will I break it to Paxton?*

Before she made any decisions, she'd set up a gynecologist appointment to confirm the results. Meanwhile, brooding wouldn't help.

Her thoughts returned to Allison Embry, sitting in her posh Peachtree City home, with her smug smile, denying any knowledge of Jeffrey Coleman, Lou Allen, or Eleanor Heinz. How many other people had this woman gunned down?

Beth thought about the black-and-white glossy photo on the bookshelf above her flat screen TV, the image of her father, Police Sergeant Leonard Long, decked out in his dress uniform smiling into the camera. Her mother had taken that picture at a ceremony where he'd received a commendation for bravery in the line of duty.

Two weeks later, Beth and her mom saw him for the last time, wearing the same uniform, stretched out in an open casket. Leonard and his partner responded to a domestic violence call. An armed and drunk husband met them at the door. Clipped to the top of the photograph was his badge. Near its center was the hole left by a .22 caliber slug.

Beth kept that badge, against her mother's wishes. She was twenty-two years old at the time. The day after the funeral, she dropped out of Georgia State University and enrolled in the Atlanta Police Academy. She and her mother hadn't spoken since.

Paxton texted her to call him. He answered before she heard it ring.

"You couldn't sleep either?" she asked.

"Beth, there's been some… developments." He relayed the news about the murders in Peachtree City and Madison's statement on television.

It took Beth several minutes to process. "Oh my God! What do we do now?"

"Nothing… We do nothing. Madison's statement doesn't tell us anything we didn't already know, except that she's the one who called us this morning on the way to Red Top. Look, I wanna get Allison as bad as you do, but we gotta play this nice and slow. Right now, the whole world thinks she's just a grieving widow raising two teenagers by herself, the victim of an unspeakable tragedy. Next time we see her, you better believe she's gonna have a lawyer, and he's gonna be on the evening news talking about how we're harassing this poor woman in her darkest hour. You think Austin Murray's on the warpath now?"

"So, what do we do in the meantime?"

"We build a stronger case. We gotta have more to go on than the word of an autistic kid, a drug dealer, and a distraught teenage girl who just lost both parents."

"Every day we wait she gets further from our grasp, Paxton. What if she takes off? She can just tell everybody she and the kids need some time away."

"That's the risk we take. We'll keep an eye on her. If she bolts, we can stop her for questioning. But we won't be able to hold her with what we have now. We need physical evidence."

"Any luck on that?" asked Long.

"None so far. There's no transference on Allen's or Heinz's bodies, and there's too much random DNA in Allen's bedroom from all his orgies. Fayette County didn't find anything on Jeremy Coleman's body either. And we still haven't found Heinz's car."

"We've got a drawing that puts Allison in Allen's bedroom..."

"Puts the *Ice Queen* in Allen's bedroom. We can't prove Allison's the Ice Queen."

"... and she frequents the library where the calls to Hamby and Walsh originated."

"That ain't nothing but secondhand smoke. We couldn't even arrest Walsh right now, if the sonofabitch was still alive."

Paxton paused so long Beth thought he'd dropped the call.

"Paxton?"

"I'm just thinking." He took another minute. "If Walsh and Hamby paid Allison to kill people, there has to be a money trail."

Long brightened. "Do you think we could take a look at their bank accounts and hers?"

"Nope. But I know somebody who might, an old FBI friend. He owes me some favors. He might even do this off the books. Probably won't give us anything we could use directly, but it might help us rattle Ms. Embry. If we get lucky, we'll be able to freeze her accounts. That might keep her in town while we get more evidence."

"Sounds promising... I have some time off coming. Would it be okay if I spent some of it down in Peachtree City, perhaps do a little sight-seeing?"

"Nope. If she sees you, she'll be on the phone to her lawyer. Just take a few days and get some sleep."

Paxton hung up. Beth stared at the silent phone, forgetting her pregnancy for the moment. Recalling the sudden death of her father, she could easily imagine what Kyle and Leslie Embry were going through. Her heart ached for them. But Rob Embry's death in the bed of another woman changed nothing as far as Allison was concerned. She was still a cold-blooded killer of the worst kind. She murdered complete strangers and destroyed the lives of countless others, just so she could make a little extra spending money.

Whatever it takes, Allison, you're going away.

CHAPTER 34
THE HOMECOMING

Midtown
Wednesday, October 31

Marie's still at the office and the boys are at school. The afternoon sun peeps through the trees outside my newly repaired window. Shadows of bare trees sway across the floor.

I've worked all day on my feature for the Sunday *AJC*, gnawing on it like Bogie on an old bone. I begin with brief backgrounds on Lyle Mallory, Jacob Epstein and Felix Lopez, bringing them together as business partners of Ambrose Mangham in his ill-fated tax filing scheme. I relate, in terse language, the details of their deaths, culled from police accounts.

The story then pivots to Don Walsh and his handling of the homicide investigation. It outlines the sad history of Walsh's nasty divorce and his growing anger toward his ex-wife's attorney, Lou Allen. I describe the dubious techniques Allen and Eleanor Heinz used to establish a case for child abuse, techniques I compare to brainwash.

I end with Walsh shooting Mangham and an "unknown assailant" then killing Walsh. I avoid mentioning Shelby Lewis by name. These shootings alibi Walsh *and* Mangham in Allen's murder. Police are now searching for an unidentified female described by witnesses as a guest at Allen's costume party. I describe her from my memory of Ben Hogarth's sketch.

According to the news, Bartow police have now identified the female discovered by hikers on Red Top Mountain as Eleanor Heinz. There's no mention whether she was murdered with the same gun as Allen. Her car remains missing and the police have no idea how her body got to Red Top.

All this comes from off-the-record information provided by Paxton and interviews with neighbors. Oscar Arrington and Marina Kovacs, in particular. I'll contact them later today for more details. I'm hoping to hear more from Paxton.

I turn the radio to WSB. There's breaking news of a double murder-suicide in Peachtree City.

I'm contemplating calling Father John for his input, when Bogie signals me to let him out. I decide instead to take him for a walk. Along the way I run into Oscar returning from the grocery store. We stop. We chat. I fill him in on what I've discovered so far, careful not to give up anything. Oscar has little to add beyond what he's already told me about Mallory.

Returning home, I see William coming toward me. He's deep in conversation with a young brunette. I turn back hoping he hasn't seen me, not wanting to embarrass him.

Back at my office, I review my story and frown. It's incomplete. With no more information than I have on this Ice Queen, I'm at an impasse. What was her connection to Allen?

I hear William coming in the door. "Hey," he shouts, forgetting I'm only a few feet away.

"Hey," I shout back. "How was your day?"

"Great, but I have a lot of homework."

I can't resist. "Maybe you should have your classmate help you."

"Sure." He heads up to his bedroom.

An hour later the back-door slams, and Marie sings out, "We're home." Henry trudges up the stairs.

"What are you up to?" she asks.

"Writing a story for the Sunday edition"

She smirks and shakes her head, then brightens up. "You'll never believe this. I put a contract on that house in Smyrna. You'll love it. Three bedrooms and two baths. Small, but big enough for the three of us. Campbell Middle School is just across the street. It'll be convenient for Henry. Property values around there are going up. I can sell it in a couple of years and get something bigger."

"Okay. Grab yourself some wine. I'll get supper started."

"Why don't I cook tonight?" she asks.

I look away so she won't catch the expression on my face. My younger daughter has many talents. Cooking isn't one of them.

She gives me a hard stare. "Hey! Over the last couple of years, I've become a very good cook, I'll have you know..." Her look turns sour. "what with Bill being gone all the time... I'm cooking tonight."

I force a smile. "I can't wait."

As she heads for the kitchen, I set the table and pour two glasses of wine. Marie shouts to the boys to wash up. From upstairs I hear them talking.

"Mom's cooking," says Henry.

"Oh my god! No!" William protests.

"I heard that," Marie shouts.

The meal, chicken thighs smothered in cream of mushroom soup with spinach souffle', turns out pretty well. William and I dig into generous portions. Henry, as usual, has mac and cheese in lieu of spinach.

I turn on the local news. Sumatra Simms is describing the shooting in Peachtree City. I'm about to tune it out, when a brief camera shot shows the wife of one of the victims. She looks familiar. My mind flashes back to Ben's drawing of the Ice Queen.

Sumatra pauses and touches her earpiece. A young woman's voice comes on, a teenaged girl.

"Oh shit!" I exclaim.

Marie comes running. "What happened?"

I ignore her and dial Paxton.

"Are you watching this?"

"Yes"

"What do you think?"

"Tom, let me get back to you." He hangs up.

The young woman's voice abruptly ends. Sumatra touches her earpiece again. "We seem to have lost our connection."

The next story opens with another reporter standing on Ben and Max Hogarth's front porch. Beside her is Bonnie Baron. I almost choke on my chicken.

"Amanda, I'm speaking with Decatur artists' agent, Bonnie Baron."

The camera pulls back to reveal Max. Ben stands behind him, just inside the doorway, eyes averted.

"Ms. Baron has just landed a lucrative contract for young Ben Hogarth with publisher Millennium Graphics. It seems Ben, who suffers from moderate autism, is an accomplished artist with an eye for an exciting story. Ben, a neighbor of the late Lou Allen, has had no shortage of material in recent weeks. He may even be a material witness to Mr. Allen's murder.

"Watch out for the Ice Queen, Ben," I smile.

"Ms. Baron, how did you first find out about Ben?"

"I got a call from an old friend, a neighbor of Ben's."

I lift my wine glass in a mock toast. "Yeah. I'll be by to pick up my share of that commission, Bonnie."

Again, I reach for my phone. I get Sumatra's voicemail.

"Sumatra, this is Tom Williams. Please call me back as soon as you get this."

• • •

Carl Osborne returned from his pizza delivery shift just in time for the eleven o'clock news. To his mother's annoyance, he flipped through the local channels. Sadly, none of the stations replayed the segment.

He had caught Sumatra Simms's interview with Madison Miller earlier on his way to work. He was in his car by the time the missing memory fell into place.

"I have some homework," he told his mom. "I'll be up late."

CHAPTER 35
MADISON'S REVENGE

Atlanta, Georgia
Thursday, November 1

Sumatra had left her phone on charge overnight. She picked it up as she headed for the door and found twenty-two unanswered calls. One was a message from Tom Williams. She hit the call-back.

"Hey, Tom. Any more of your revelations?"

"No. I was just wondering if you'd heard anything else from Madison Miller."

"Nope. My manager won't let me go anywhere near her. He's afraid it'll blow up in our faces if the girl turns out to be wrong."

"*I'm* willing to take that chance. I was wondering if I could get Madison's phone number from you."

Sumatra hesitated. "I'll let you have it if you promise to call me back with whatever you get."

"Deal!"

• • •

Aching and exhausted, Carl Osborne spent all night on his "homework" project. Sickly pre-dawn light outlined the trees outside his window. *No point in trying to sleep now.* He padded down to the kitchen, made another cup of black coffee, took it back to his desk, and downed it with an Adderall.

He'd spent hours locating that one photograph among the images on his camera, but it was well worth the effort. He zoomed in and studied the facial contours. *Allison Embry, no doubt about it.*

In the photo, her hand rested on an outside doorknob. Carl allowed himself a moment to admire the composition and clarity. The timing was perfect. Staring back at him in his delivery truck, she wore a puzzled look.

Did she recognize him?

The number on the door was clearly visible, as was the Motel 6 sign in the background. Allison may have seen Carl inside the delivery van, but she wouldn't have noticed the Go Pro camera braced against the dash.

Carl had just delivered a large two-topping pizza to that same room. His one regret was he didn't catch the shock on Jeremy Coleman's face when he came to the door wearing nothing but a towel.

Jeremy was easily the dumbest of Carl's classmates at Starr's Mill. Ordering a pizza to his secret love nest only proved that.

Fucking stoner. Was he stupid enough to book the room in his own name? I'll find out. I'll also make a copy of the sales record when I get to work tonight... if I don't fall asleep in the meantime.

This was hot property. The question was what to do with it. He considered taking it straight to the police. But then he had a better idea. He closed his eyes and pictured little Maddie Miller in her see-through peasant blouse, denim cutoffs riding up in her crotch.

She'll owe me big for this.

He pondered the many ways she might repay him. The mere thought gave him an erection. If he was going to risk certain death at the hands of Kyle Embry, he was going to get laid first, a hand job at least.

• • •

Doris Clanton was fast running out of patience with her granddaughter. The girl was a handful in the best of times. These were *not* the best of times. After a night of grieving over the loss of Wendy, Doris awoke determined to focus her attention on Madison.

She suggested they go to the mall to buy Maddie some nice clothes. The things the girl wore these days made her look like a tramp. She needed something more suitable for the funeral on Saturday.

Doris parked her aging Camry near the J. C. Penney entrance. Madison hadn't uttered a word since they left the house. Instead, she gazed through the windshield as though staring into eternity.

"Madison, darling?"

No response.

Doris had had enough. "Madison, I'll be in Women's Wear when you're ready to join me."

She was halfway to the entrance when Madison yelled, "*Fine.* But I'm not wearing anything you buy at Penney's."

An hour later, still unable to agree on appropriate attire, they retreated to the food court. Doris excused herself and went to the restroom. Madison stirred the straw in her Pepsi, lost in thought. A voice from behind startled her.

"Madison?"

She turned to see Carl Osborne standing uncomfortably close. *What does this pimply freak want?* she wondered.

"Madison, I… uh… saw you and just wanted to say how sorry I am to hear about your parents."

She stood, picked up her purse, and was about to leave.

"You need to know that Allison Embry was fucking Jeremy Coleman, and I can prove it."

This stopped Madison in her tracks.

. . .

Allison stared at the glass in her hand.

Was I taking it out of the dishwasher or putting it in?

"Mom?"

Startled, Allison turned. She hardly recognized her daughter beneath the red, swollen eyes. Gone were the contacts Allison bought her three years ago, replaced by coke bottle glasses Allison had forgotten.

Leslie ran to her, threw her arms around her and buried her face in her chest. They held each other tight for several minutes before either spoke. Leslie made a vain attempt to clear her eyes. "I want you to know I love you. Dad was a jerk. I don't blame you for anything you did, and I don't believe all those horrible things people are saying about you."

"I love you too, baby," said Allison. "And I want you to know I'm here for you. We're going to get through this somehow, you and Kyle and me."

Leslie sniffed and nodded. "Mom, I'm worried about Kyle. He and Dad were so close. He's so angry, there's no telling what he'll do. The only time he comes out of his room is to go punch that stupid bag. You need to see his hand, Mom. It's all swollen and purple."

Allison followed Leslie upstairs and knocked on Kyle's door.

"Go away!" he screamed. "I don't want to talk to you." A shoe slammed the other side of the door.

"What are we going to do?" Leslie asked.

Allison thought for a moment. "I have an idea. Come on." They went back to the kitchen, where Allison retrieved a school directory for Starr's Mill. On the second page, scrawled in Kyle's hand, was the number of his football coach, Rich DuPont.

Fifteen minutes later, Kyle emerged from his room. Gingerly, he pulled his letter jacket over his injured right hand. Allison winced. He wouldn't look at her or Leslie. "I'm going to WellStar. Coach is meeting me there."

As he pulled out of the driveway, Allison turned to Leslie. "Let's go somewhere we can talk. How about the mall?"

On the way, Allison asked, casually, what *horrible things* Leslie had heard. With great effort she teased out the details.

Pulling into a parking space near the Penney's entrance, they spotted Madison Miller leaving with an elderly woman.

"Mom," asked Leslie. "Do you think Kyle and I could go back to school tomorrow? He can't just sit there in his room all day and mope. We need to get out of the house."

Allison stared at Madison, who was too far away to notice. "Sure, baby. I think that would be good for both of you."

She texted Denise. "Do you think you could come by later on?"

• • •

The afternoon turned crisp. Returning from their leisurely mother-daughter outing, Leslie went to her room to call her friends. Kyle's coach phoned to say they'd gone over to the school for a chat.

Denise arrived, and Allison suggested they go for a walk. A neighbor raking leaves looked away as they passed, as if he hadn't seen them. At the end of the block, Allison saw Donna Fraser staring from her picture window before turning away. Allison made a mental note to dump out the woman's casserole and leave the empty dish on her steps.

"Have you made funeral plans?" Denise asked.

Allison nodded. "I had Rob's body released to Sadler's funeral home. They'll cremate it, and we'll have a funeral there Saturday afternoon, family only. You're invited."

"Have you spoken with your mom and stepdad?"

"Yeah. They're flying in tomorrow night. They'll stay with us."

"What about Rob's family."

"His mom and dad are driving down from Canton and will meet us at the funeral home. He had a brother out in California, but they were never close. I'll give Rob's ashes to his parents. They can do with them as they choose."

Denise studied her friend's face. No emotion.

They walked on in silence for a few minutes before Allison spoke again. "You know... there are some things I need to tell you."

She explained that Rob came into a large sum of money. She had no idea how. "He moved it offshore. I'm afraid, with all these false accusations, it might get frozen. I've never been good with money. Rob always handled our finances. I was wondering if you might help me."

CHAPTER 36
DROPPING THE DIME

Atlanta, Georgia
Friday, November 2

Paxton's FBI friend called back sooner than expected. He'd traced Walsh's two hundred-thousand-dollar transfer to an offshore account. Sadly, that was all he had. The Commerce Bank of Antigua refused to divulge the depositor's name or freeze the account. That would require an official request from the FBI, which would take time.

"Oh! By the way," he said. "We found Shelby Lewis's car sitting empty in a Chattanooga parking lot. We're still looking for him.

I also spoke to Ambrose Mangham's tax fraud lawyer. He said Mangham expected his partners to bail him out after he took the fall. He claimed hiring commissioned salesmen and stealing Social Security numbers was Lopez's idea.

We think Mangham took a gun when he went to see Mallory, hoping to scare him. A fight broke out, and Mangham used it. He had to kill Epstein and Lopez so they wouldn't go to the cops. The serial killer angle was just an inspiration."

"Thanks," said Paxton, though by now none of this mattered. He'd seen people killed for less.

. . .

The afternoon bell rang, and Starr's Mill buzzed with rumors about Kyle Embry, Madison Miller, and Jeremy Coleman. The boys' primary concern was how their football team would do tonight without Kyle. The girls wondered what Kyle saw in Madison. *But they all knew.*

Madison had awakened in the middle of the night. She *had* to see Kyle. With great effort she convinced her grandmother to drive her to school. She promised her she'd get a ride home with a friend.

It was on Coach DuPont's advice that Kyle returned, not the pleadings of his sister or his mother. He wasn't talking to anybody. His classmates sensed this and gave him a wide berth. Crossing the parking lot, lost in thought, he almost ran into Madison, who'd rushed from her classroom to intercept him.

"We need to talk," she said. "You've got to stop your sister. You won't believe the things she's texting about my mom and me."

It was the first time he'd seen tears in Madison's eyes. He fought the urge to take her in his arms. He remembered her accusing his mother of murder.

"Why should I help you? I heard what you said on TV."

"Kyle, I'm so sorry. I was distraught over losing my parents. It's been horrible. You know what it's like. We're going through the same things."

He stared at his feet. He couldn't blame her. They *were* in similar positions. And Allison was hardly blameless. "I don't know, Maddie. But I don't think we should see each other anymore."

Madison's eyes widened. It was as though he'd punched her in the face. She doubled over and began to weep.

Flustered, he pulled her to him. In every direction, as far as he could see, students stopped in their tracks and stared. He'd give anything at that moment to disappear. "Hey, let's go somewhere we can be alone."

Fifteen minutes later, they pulled into an abandoned gas station outside Fayetteville. Now it was his turn for tears.

"Maddie, there's something I need to tell you. I don't know what's going on with my mom these days. This *friend* of hers..." He added air quotes with his fingers. "... has practically moved in. Now my mom's talking about selling the house and sending Leslie and me to live with our grandparents. It's like my whole world's ending. My football career's over, and now I won't be able to graduate with my class."

"That's bullshit!" Madison choked. "You'd think it was all our fault. People are looking at me like I have leprosy."

Her expression slowly changed. "Wait a minute! You say your mom's moving? Where's she going?"

"I don't know. I overheard her and Denise talking about going to Antigua, wherever that is. I think she's lost her mind."

There was only one reason Allison would leave the country. It had nothing to do with grief over the loss of her husband.

"Can you take me home?" she asked.

Madison turned away and allowed herself a bitter smile. Who should she call first... Carl Osborne, Atlanta police, or that reporter, the one who left a message on her cell?

Out of curiosity, she called Tom Williams. When he'd promised not to mention her name, she told him everything she knew about Carl Osborne's photographs of Allison outside the motel room and about Allison planning to skip town. He scribbled notes as she spoke.

"Have you talked to the police?"

"No. I was going to call them next."

"You'll want to call Lieutenant Paxton Davis directly. Do you have his number?"

She checked her call history. "Yes."

"I'd like to call you back when you're done."

"Sure."

This time, she made no attempt to hide her identity as she laid out for Paxton the details of her conversation with Kyle. She handed her phone to Carl Osborne, who introduced himself and told the story of photographing Allison at the Motel 6 with Jeremy Coleman.

Paxton stood behind his desk and made a silent fist pump. *This is it. Allison, your ass is going away.* Through the open doorway he motioned Long to join him.

"Young man," said Paxton, "I can't tell you how much I appreciate this. Where can I meet you?" He took Osborne's address and phone number and instructed him where to upload the picture. "Can you put Ms. Miller back on the line?

Madison, I know you want Allison to get what's coming to her. I need you and Mr. Osborne to do me a favor though. Please don't tell anybody about this until Sergeant Long and I can meet with you. Can you do that?"

There was a long silence.

"Madison?"

"I'm afraid I already spoke to someone, a newspaper writer."

Paxton groaned, "Dare I ask his name?"

CHAPTER 37
MOVING DAY

Peachtree City
Monday, December 22

Allison awoke, still exhausted from her trip to Tampa. Kyle had followed her in his Jeep. She signed it over to her mom for Kyle and Leslie's use. When she got back, she sold the Lexus and donated the Buick and golf cart to charity.

The past two months were a blur. Allison was still in shock. *We're going to Antigua!* When things blew over, she told herself, she could always come home. What she'd have done without Denise, she couldn't imagine.

Though she played no part in the deaths of Rob, Wendy or Lon, Allison couldn't shake the feeling she was somehow to blame. This was, after all, the outcome she'd planned months ago.

She hated winter and could think of no better time for a trip to the islands. She stared out the window at a sullen sky and forced herself to smile. *This'll be the first day of my new life.*

The movers arrived around nine and began emptying the house. They were gone by ten-thirty. Their supervisor gave Allison a strange look when she told him she wouldn't be around to supervise the unloading. She handed him the key to the rental unit and asked him to mail it to her mom.

She transferred a generous sum into a custodial account to help her parents care for Kyle and Leslie. Their disapproval of all this was palpable. She gave no details of her plans, only that she was taking a much-needed break.

The closing on the house, set for eleven, left her ample time to deposit the proceeds, transfer them to Denise for the new Antigua account, and make the seven PM Jet Blue. She gave meticulous attention to every detail, allowed for every contingency. Still, she had the nagging sensation something dreadful was about to happen. She signed over the cashier's check to Denise for all the funds in her account, including the proceeds of Rob's life insurance.

From there it was a short drive to Stockbridge. She found Denise waiting in her driveway, bags packed. She tossed them in the trunk, hopped in the passenger seat, and gave Allison a long kiss.

"I still can't believe we're doing this," she squealed.

"We're doing it girl."

"Thelma and Louise!" Denise cried.

Allison shuddered, remembering how the movie ended.

"Do you have the boarding passes?" Denise asked.

"Yep. We're running a little early," she said. "We can drop off the rental car, leave our bags at the curb, and relax with a couple of drinks before we leave."

They made it through security in less time than expected, given the pre-Christmas traffic. Neither of them noticed the three pairs of eyes following them. They were staring at an overhead monitor when Allison sensed a presence hovering nearby.

"Going on a little vacation, Allison?"

She whipped around to find a woman standing beside her, the police sergeant who had questioned her in her living room. She turned in panic, to find the black lieutenant standing beside Denise.

"Allison," asked Denise, "who are these people?"

"What we are, Ms. Weathers," said Paxton, "is the Atlanta police." He flashed his badge, as did Long. "And, standing behind you there, is an old friend, FBI Special Agent Walter Wadsworth. We'd like a little chat with you and Ms. Embry. We've reserved a couple of offices down the hall, where we can speak privately."

They escorted Allison and Denise to separate rooms behind unmarked doors. Allison sat alone, under the watchful eye of a female corporal. She fixed Allison in an expressionless stare.

When, at length, Paxton returned with Long and Wadsworth, he began by saying, "Ms. Embry, you don't need to say a word unless you choose to. We already have a sworn statement from Ms. Weathers implicating you in the murders of Jeremy Coleman, Eleanor Heinz, and Lou Allen."

Allison's leaned across the table, bringing her face close to Paxton's as she struggled to work some confidence into her voice. "Honestly? Do you think you can fool me with that bullshit?" She turned and glared at Long, who sat back and smiled.

"Allison," she said, "we got a call this morning from the East Point police. They found Eleanor Heinz's car at a chop shop. There wasn't much left, only the VIN and some DNA, which we sent to the lab. We'll tie that car to you, Allison. We've already tied Heinz to Walsh, and Walsh to you and your offshore account. Oh! And we have a photograph of you outside a motel room registered to Jeremy Coleman. You'll want to think very carefully before saying anything else."

Paxton leaned back, his face a mask of disgust. "Allison, we have the Antigua account number Hamby and Walsh used for your blood money. We can prove Hamby made his transfers just before several of his competitors disappeared, and Walsh just before Eleanor Heinz disappeared. Allison Embry, you are under arrest on multiple counts of first-degree murder."

As he worked his way through the Miranda warning, Allison sat in glum silence. Her one comfort was that when the authorities finally got to the Antigua account, they'd find it empty. She would beat this, and when she did, she and Denise would leave for the islands to enjoy all that money.

When Paxton finished, he asked, "Do you wish to make a statement?"

Allison shook her head and began to rock slowly, her arms wrapped tightly about her chest. Tears rolled down her cheek. In a soft voice she said, "I believe I'll call my attorney now."

• • •

Denise had put on a look of dismay so convincing that Paxton, Wadsworth, and Long decided to let her go. None of the evidence implicated her, nor did Allison. She watched as they escorted Allison away.

The door was just closing as she arrived, out of breath, and presented her boarding pass. Settling into her First-Class window seat, she looked out to see several pieces of luggage, loaded on a cart returning to the terminal. She recognized them as Allison's.

Denise had considered carefully before her anonymous call to Lon Miller, wondering how to tell him his wife was having an affair. She would miss Allison, she knew, but the woman was unravelling. Without Denise there to pick up the pieces, all that money would have sat in the Commerce Bank, until the Antiguan government or some corrupt official confiscated it.

With an enigmatic smile, she ran her hand along the side of her purse. Through the soft leather she felt the fake passport in its hidden compartment. It bore her picture and the alias she and Allison had used to set up the new account. It would never fool immigration, but it was good enough for Commerce Bank. The name read "Molly Bloom."

. . .

Afternoon traffic snarled I-75 in both directions as Paxton and Long inched their way back to the station. Triumphant but exhausted, neither spoke for a long time.

At length, he said, "Beth, there's something I need to tell you... I've already filed paperwork for my retirement... Before I go, I'm recommending you for detective."

Foundering in a sea of confused emotions, Long stared at the line of taillights in front of her and managed one word. "Thanks."

She regained her composure. "Paxton, there's something I need to tell you."

"Shoot."

"I'm pregnant," she said.

He pursed his lips. "Okay."

CHAPTER 38
CAREFREE HIGHWAY

Six months later
Somewhere in West Virginia

Hi. I'm William Wakefield, and I'm on a road trip with my granddad. I call him "Pops". He doesn't seem to mind.

A few months back, Pops helped solve a couple of big murders in Atlanta. One of the killers died and the other's sitting in jail awaiting trial. Pops wanted to interview her, like he did another killer a few years ago, but this one's lawyer won't let him anywhere near her.

So, Pops sold his house in Midtown, and he and I are hitting the road in a rented RV, something he's wanted to do for a long time. He somehow convinced my mom to let me go with him. She says this is just another of his late life crises. She isn't sure who's chaperoning whom.

Anyway, it sounded cool to me. My dream is to become a writer, just like Pops. Only, I plan to write about cool new technology, like the stuff my Uncle Sean's working on. He's a researcher at Emory University. From there I can move on to science fiction. I'm keeping this diary, starting today, and I've already taken dozens of photos with the digital camera my dad gave me for my birthday, a Fuji X-Pro 2. My mom had some things to say about that too.

We've been on the road for three hours. Pops picked me up at my other grandparents' home in Virginia. My little brother, Henry, and I stayed with them for a couple of weeks. Pops offered to take both of us, but Henry wanted to stay behind so he could spend more time with our dad.

PRONOUNCED PONCE

Henry felt guilty about not coming, but Pops said not to worry. He'll see him in a couple of months when we're all back in Atlanta. I'm just as glad Henry didn't come. He's okay, as little brothers go, but he can be annoying and whiny at times, especially on a long trip.

I miss being together as a family, with my mom and dad. I don't suppose there's anything I can do about that. Instead, I'm planning my own life.

Pops says we're setting out on a voyage of discovery. We're discovering America, which was mis-named, because Amerigo Vespucci didn't really discover it. Christopher Columbus did, and Ponce de Leon discovered North America.

A cold, wet nose on the back of my arm reminds me we have a third passenger on this voyage, Pops' dog Bogie, a German short-haired pointer. He's telling me he needs to stop so he can pee.

We're travelling on the interstate right now, but when we hit Chicago, we're going to follow Route 66 cross-country. It'll take a lot longer, but Pops says it's the only way to see the real America.

He keeps talking about what he calls "literary" journalists, writers like Tom Wolfe, Hunter Thompson, and Gay Talese. He's given me an old copy of a book called *Zen and the Art of Motorcycle Maintenance*, by Walter M. Pirsig. It's my summer reading assignment. It's about a man and his son crossing the country on a motorcycle. I'm just as happy we're in an RV.

Pops is teaching me how to write. I'm teaching him how to use social media. It seems like a pretty good trade.

He plans to publish a memoir of this trek called *Travels with Bogie*. I can't wait. He'll post daily updates on Facebook so all his friends can follow. He's so 2010.

From the RV's CD player comes the sound of Bob Seger singing "Running Against the Wind." It's from a library of travelling songs Pops selected. He says it's a classic. It's pretty good.

I finally got my driver's license three months ago. Pops says he'll let me drive some. When I do, I'll put on some real classics, like Cold Play and Nirvana.

As you can tell, I'm jacked about this. A few weeks from now, Pops will take me to the nearest airport and put me on a plane back to Atlanta. From there, he'll sail on to who knows where, an aging Ponce de Leon, still searching for his fountain of youth.

The End

NOTE FROM THE AUTHOR

Word-of-mouth is crucial for any author to succeed. If you enjoyed *Pronounced Ponce*, please leave a review online—anywhere you are able. Even if it's just a sentence or two. It would make all the difference and would be very much appreciated.

    Thanks!
    Ray

ABOUT THE AUTHOR

Ray Dan Parker's writing career began with *Unfinished Business*, a murder mystery set in 1968 in rural Florida. His second novel, *Fly Away – The Metamorphosis of Dina Savage*, takes place more recently in the Atlanta area. Pronounced Ponce is the third in the series.

He has spent four decades as a journalist, teacher and consultant. He is married and lives in suburban Atlanta, where he spends his free time reading, travelling, and enjoying outdoor activities.

Thank you so much for reading one of our **Crime Fiction** novels.
If you enjoyed the experience, please check out our recommended
title for your next great read!

Caught in a Web by Joseph Lewis

"This important, nail-biting crime thriller about MS-13 sets the
bar very high. One of the year's best thrillers."
–BEST THRILLERS

View other Black Rose Writing titles at
www.blackrosewriting.com/books and use promo code
PRINT to receive a **20% discount** when purchasing.